Our Lady of West 74th Street

HARRY STEVEN ACKLEY

To Dottie & Joe,
Enjoyed our evening together. Hope you like my story.

Our Lady of West 74th Street
Copyright © 2014 Harry Steven Ackley

All rights reserved. No part of this book may be reproduced in any form or by any electronic or mechanical means, including information storage and retrieval systems, without written permission from the author, except in the case of a reviewer, who may quote brief passages embodied in critical articles or in a review. For more information, email: harrystevenackley@gmail.com.

ISBN: 1502325918
ISBN-13: 978-1502325914

This is a work of fiction. Names, characters, places, and incidents either are the product of the author's imagination or are used fictitiously, and any resemblance to actual persons, living or dead, events, or locales is entirely coincidental.

For my parents, Harry and Lois,
who both passed away during the writing of this book

May their memory be eternal!

A Prelude
The First Icon

Thou art a vineyard newly blossomed
...young, beautiful, growing in Eden;
a fragrant poplar in Paradise.

From Shen Khar Venakhi
A medieval Georgian hymn to The Virgin Mary

Ephesus — 42 AD

A beautiful, warm day in early fall. A breeze blew in from the sea, rustling leaves in the trees. Three fishermen sat on a patch of grass in the shade, drinking wine, eating cheese and relishing their Sabbath afternoon.

Eli and Daniel were brothers whose family, decades ago, had moved from Palestine to Ephesus, where life was easier. The population was mostly Greek, and there was far less strife with the Romans. As long as they kept to their business, they were left alone.

John was a more recent arrival. He had come to Ephesus with his adopted mother, Mary, five years ago. Mary's true son, Yeshua, had been executed by the Romans nine years earlier for stirring political unrest. However, the real source of the irritation was religious. According to his followers, Yeshua had performed miracles and had taught that he himself was divine.

These were difficult teachings for the Judeans to accept. They branded Yeshua a criminal and besought the occupying Roman government to arrest and execute him, which they did. Yeshua's dying request was that his friend, John, take responsibility for his mother. After the execution, John took Mary into his care, and since that time always referred to her as "Mother."

Eli, the oldest of the three fishermen, gauged the afternoon sun. "We really should be going," he said. "I need a nap. And then I need time to work on the boat before it gets dark."

"You'll have time for your nap," said John. "You must stay and see her new outfit. She's been working on it for the entire week. She'll be hurt if you leave now. I'll go in and try and hurry her up."

With this, John rose and went inside the house, a small building made of stone. Inside were three rooms, one for Mary, one for John, and a large central room for preparing meals, dining, and hosting guests, of which there were many, especially children. Children were drawn to Mary like bees to a flower.

"Mother," he called. "Our friends will be leaving soon. We all want to see the new clothes you have made."

At this, a very elegant lady in her fifties emerged through a curtained doorway. She wore an indigo tunic and a dark red cloak. A separate piece of red cloth covered her head. Her complexion was olive, and, for her age, remarkably smooth. Her eyes were a deep chestnut brown. She looked at John steadily without expression. Finally, she smiled and laughed. "Well, what do you think?"

"You are the star of heaven, Mother."

"Oh please," she said, with a blush. "But I'm glad you like it. I can't believe I was given such fine cloth."

"You are the Mother of our Lord. You should have all the silk in India."

"Yes, well ... I'm just happy to have something new."

After Eli and Daniel had left, John suggested that he paint a portrait of Mary in her new clothes. Painting was something he had taken up since moving to Ephesus. It was a skill he had learned from neighbors who had come from Egypt. The Egyptians were renowned for their painting expertise.

"I have my paints all ready. I was working on a new picture earlier today and my paints are all out."

Mary looked cautiously at John. "Well, all right. But this is a private thing. You don't need it to show it to all your friends."

John simply smiled.

He found a smooth and heavy piece of oak in his supply of wood. Before beginning, he prayed that God would guide his hand.

John wasn't intending to paint a religious object — just a portrait of his dearly loved mother. However, as he began to work, the image before him took on a life of its own. He began to think of all the memories — memories so powerful that they fuzzied his thoughts of the here and now.

He remembered meeting Yeshua on the shoreline that day ... the feeling of absolute peace and assurance Yeshua gave to those around him. In a time when they all feared for where their next meal would come from, or when the Romans would ride through their little village, this man had no fear. *God would provide*, he told them.

And God did provide. In all the time he followed Yeshua, John had never known hunger; he had never known want. It was as if he were one of his Israelite ancestors following Moses. Just when things were darkest, God *would* always provide.

By sunset, John had completed the base colors of the portrait. He stopped to prepare and eat supper and, while doing so, let the paint dry by the fire. Afterward, he would apply the details.

"Let me see what you've started," asked Mary.

"Oh, no, no, no," answered John with a smile. "Not until it's done."

After the meal, John had Mary sit again. He would next complete the details ... the eyes and other facial features ... and the hands and hair ... and the folds of the cloth ... the shadows and light.

He worked by the light of an oil lamp and the dwindling fire. Before long, Mary was asleep. But he didn't need her to pose anymore, he had his vision. But, he too was getting tired and the light of the oil lamp was fading.

John's head sank to his chest as he began to drift off to sleep. He looked at the brush in his hand and suddenly he could see it as clearly as if he were holding it in the noon sun. He looked up and the entire room was lit. The walls were a brilliant yellow. The fire was rekindled and the oil lamp shone brightly — but the main light was coming from the seven radiant beings that were standing in a semicircle behind his blessed mother, who was still asleep.

The seven angels had come.

The one on the right spoke — the one with the jade eyes and copper-colored hair that swept back from his face in curls of fire.

"Finish the painting, John. We will give you light."

John then felt no fatigue at all. His mind was sober and quick. He worked through the night until the dawn came. When the sun began to shine through the windows, the angels faded into the morning light. *Strange beings,* John thought.

As the light grew, Mary awoke. Her eyes opened and she smiled at John. "They were here."

"Yes," answered John.

"I always know when they have visited me, even if it is in my sleep." Mary straightened herself a little.

"I had a very odd dream."

"Really? What was it?" asked John.

"I was in a great palace of some kind ... like I had never seen nor heard of before. There were beautiful clear glass windows and great wooden stairs. All the floors had richly colored carpets. And most of all, I remember the paintings on the walls."

"What were the paintings of?"

Mary smiled. "They were paintings of us ... of you and me and Yeshua and the others ... Peter and James. And there were many paintings of the angels.

"And then there were children. I remember the laughter of children playing. It was so real."

Mary stood and stretched. She looked out the window at the rising sun and said a brief morning prayer. Then she turned to John and said, "Speaking of paintings, let me see what you've done."

The painting showed Mary holding her infant son, cradling him in her left arm and pointing to him with her cupped right hand. Over her head, arrayed in a semicircle, were seven stars. In each of the stars the upper body and face of a winged angel leaned forward, looking down from heaven, as if they were peering out of windows.

Mary stared at the painting a long time.

"What is it, Mother?" asked John.

"I've seen this before. This painting was one of those in my dream."

Mary looked out the window again. The soft light of morning caught her face and she looked like the young mother from the cave, years ago.

"This is a very important thing," she said. "One day it will bring comfort and hope to many people. Make sure it is kept safe."

Part I
The House
on West 74th Street

*God chose what is foolish in the world to shame the wise;
God chose what is weak in the world to shame the strong.*

— *Saint Paul's First Letter to the Corinthians* —

— Chapter 1 —

Klaus Bronner's House — West 74th Street
Summer 1993

The beautiful hardwood floor was covered with small sections of sheetrock and bits of plaster. Klaus, a lean man in his early eighties with wavy silver hair, looked down at the mess and at his dust-covered shoes. He then looked up and examined the large hole he had just made.

He felt proud that, at his age, he was able to swing a sledge hammer so forcefully. In the open hole there was a thick horizontal stud, perfect for his purpose. He took great care to clean the wood with a damp cloth, wiping away the dust and residue that had settled over the last 110 years.

After the place was prepared, he went to the coffee table and picked up the icon. It was a wooden icon of the Holy Virgin and the Christ Child, surrounded by seven angels. He took a long look at it, kissed it, and then wrapped it, first in a piece or green silk, then in a small plastic sheet which he then taped around the edges. He placed the sealed icon on the stud, secured behind two partially driven nails, so it wouldn't slip when he repaired the wall. Lastly, he took out a letter he had written. But before placing the letter with the icon, he unfolded it and read it one last time...

To whom it concerns:

My name is Dr. Klaus Bronner. I have a PhD in Art History and, until my retirement, was a specialist in the preservation of ancient and antique paintings.

I was born in the countryside near Salzburg in the year 1911. My father was a dairy farmer and ran a small business. My family was Catholic.

My father sent me to the University of Munich, where I studied business and, my real passion, the history of the arts. When I was in my last year of studies, my father died. My younger brother Ernst was happy to take over my father's business ventures, allowing me to devote my full attention to the arts. In time, I had the honor to become graduate assistant to Professor Franz Dölger, an expert in Byzantine studies. This was also about the same time Adolf Hitler was coming to power.

By 1941, German forces had occupied Greece. Hitler had a keen interest in art, particularly religious art. A team was assembled to go to monasteries on the Athos peninsula in Greece to survey and catalog works of art for the purpose of bringing them back to Germany. Professor Dölger and I, as his assistant, were part of that team.

Though Athos is in Greece, there are certain monasteries that house mostly Slavs. St. Panteleimon is one of these. This also happened to be the monastery where we were most well-received and spent the most time.

The Slavic monks saw us as deliverers from the atheistic Joseph Stalin, whose army was roaming the east, burning churches and murdering Orthodox Christians. Little did they know that by looking to Hitler for protection, they were only running from one demon into the arms of another.

During my stay at St. Panteleimon, events would occur that would alter my life.

In addition to Dr. Dögler and myself, there were three other civilians on the team — all academics. The rest who accompanied us were German military. No women were allowed. That is the strict rule of all Athos monasteries. The tradition is that Athos is consecrated to the Mother of God and therefore off limits to all other females.

Our job consisted mainly of cataloging religious art. Unimportant pieces would remain. Anything remarkable was tagged and, at a later date, would be taken to Berlin. This first trip was mainly to find out what was there. Thankfully, for the sake of the monasteries, during the coming year, Hitler's energy and resources would be consumed by his invasion of the Soviet Union, and that first trip would also be the last.

During my work at St. Panteleimon I had the opportunity to visit the passages underneath the monastery. One day, while I happened to be by myself, I was struck by a beautiful mosaic that showed a man in a boat rowing the Blessed Mother. The place was illuminated by the light of many tapers. Being Catholic, I instinctively crossed myself and bowed.

At this, a young monk came forward from out of the shadows. He told me his name was Brother Jerome. He spoke to me in German. He asked me about my faith and I told him I was Catholic. He asked me if I truly believed in The Holy Trinity and The Creed. I told him that I did.

He went on to explain that, even though there was tension between our churches, he trusted me. As he spoke, other monks stepped forward into the light. I had no idea that I had been followed.

The mosaic, he said, depicted a story. After the ascension of the Lord, Our Lady lived with St. John the Divine in Ephesus, where he was her caretaker. On a journey to visit the Bishop Lazarus in France, they came

Our Lady of West 74th Street

upon Athos and that was how it became dedicated to the Blessed Mother.

I informed him that I was familiar with the tradition and that I was a well-versed in religious history.

Jerome looked around at the others. The monks closed ranks and crowded in. Jerome lowered his voice.

"What you probably don't know," he said "is that the Holy Mother made a second visit. And she has never left."

I reminded him of the assumption — that Mary was assumed into heaven at her death.

He smiled sheepishly and assured me that I was right. "I wanted to get your attention ... and to see how much you knew," he said.

"Well, now you have it," *I replied. I was growing impatient.*

"As you know, the tradition of icons is that they are not art. They are not based on an artist's imagination. Rather, they are transcribed, or copied, one from another, preserving the integrity and, we believe, the holiness, of the original.

"The original icons," he explained, "are believed to be based on first-hand encounters."

I could sense the monks were getting anxious.

"What is it you want to share with me?" *I asked.*

"We are afraid of Stalin and his army. He is destroying our holy places in the east. We think he may come here soon. That's why we are cooperating with you Germans. But there are some things we can entrust to no one." *Jerome looked again to his brothers.* "And yet we have to."

At this, one of the monks came forward and handed me an icon. I held it up to the flickering light. It was unusually heavy. When my eyes met with the face of The

Holy Mother, I froze. I couldn't hold a thought. It was as if the image itself were coming to life. Then I was suddenly overcome with a great sense of unworthiness. I could no longer bear to hold it or look at it. I became frightened, but not from any potential danger, rather I was in awe, like I had seen some phenomenon. I couldn't explain it. I had no words.

Jerome spoke. "This is the first icon. This, we believe, was made by someone who saw her ... who knew her, perhaps even one of the apostles. This is more precious than any other icon or relic we know."

"We must protect it from the Bolsheviks," another monk interrupted. "We want to you take it and keep it safe until this war is over."

I wasn't sure what to do. It was an odd request. I was apprehensive of the responsibility. However, I reluctantly agreed to take the icon.

As we returned to the main part of the monastery, Brother Jerome gave me one more bit of information. He said that the icon has the ability to produce faith. He said that, if a certain monk would begin to waver in his faith, the icon was brought out and that monk would be encouraged to venerate it — that this would bring great peace.

The icon has been in my possession ever since. I have been its protector. Shortly after my visit to Athos, I fled to the United States. I had always meant to return it, but I couldn't. The power of the icon changed me. I became in love with holiness as a result of having it. I also believe it has blessed me. I have enjoyed great prosperity during my life; surely, more than I ever deserved.

But more than that, I was also told to keep it — to keep it safe for a purpose that would be revealed in time. But I will say no more about that.

> *I know I am about to die. I have no one to entrust with the care of the icon. At this point, I don't know what to do, so I am sealing it my house. This house has been home to Our Lady for over 50 years. The angels will know what is best.*
>
> *Whoever finds this, may God protect you and Our Lady as He has protected me.*
>
> *Klaus Bronner*
> *July 13, 1993*

It was a rambling letter, but it said what it needed to say. Klaus started to refold the pages, but then stopped. Wearing a troubled expression, he walked over to the coffee table, sat down, and scribbled something on the first page. He then refolded the letter, put it in an envelope, and got up and placed it behind the icon. He crossed himself and proceeded to repair the wall.

— Chapter 2 —

West 74th Street — Five Weeks Later

Footsteps echoed through the old brownstone on West 74th Street as Kevin Peters and his sister Greta, both dressed fashionably casual, looking like escapees from an LL Bean catalog, made their way down the staircase.

Kevin and Greta were in their late 30s. Kevin was short, stout and muscular, with chiseled features and full head of slightly graying blond hair. Greta, a few years younger and also blond, had a bob haircut with frosted streaks. She was petite and tanned with stunning bright blue eyes — eyes that now took in the interior of the amazing house that she and her brother had just inherited.

"We're gonna make a fortune off this place, Kevin," said Greta.

"Yeah, finally the old guy did something worthwhile," he replied.

"The man is dead, Kevin. Show a little respect."

Kevin looked at his younger sister and shook his head. "He was a nut," he said.

The two siblings clomped down the stairs and went into the living room. The walls were bare and all the furniture was covered with sheets of heavy plastic. Kevin removed the sheet from one of the big old-fashioned parlor chairs and sat down.

He looked up at the high ceilings and then over at the great marble fireplace.

Then he looked at his sister who smiled at him and said, "Can you believe he lived here all alone for all those years? If this were my place, I'd be throwing parties. I'd be living like The Great Gatsby or something."

Kevin nodded but didn't speak. Greta then asked, "So he just went on an afternoon walk to the park, and died?"

"According to the timing of things, that's what it looks like," answered Kevin. "He died right in front of Bethesda Fountain."

Greta gave her brother a questioning look.

"It's the one with the big angel in the middle," said Kevin. "He once told me that he thought that fountain was a power center where angels gathered. That's the place where he keeled over. By the time someone got to him, he was gone."

"And where did you say he was buried?" asked Greta.

"He has a crypt in some Catholic cemetery up in Westchester — the Gate of Heaven. It's where Babe Ruth is buried," Kevin added with a short laugh.

"Why is that funny?"

"Because Klaus hated the Yankees. He was a big Brooklyn Dodgers fan. Then when Mets came along, he rooted for them."

Greta shrugged, "I guess I never understood the whole sports team allegiance thing."

The two sat in silence for a moment. Greta surveyed all the empty bookshelves lining the east wall and asked, "And you said he left all his books to the museum library?"

"Yes. The Thomas J. Watson Library at the Metropolitan Museum," answered Kevin. "He used to work for the museum. That library was important to him."

"And where did you say you moved the art?" asked Greta.

"It's with the rest of his collection in his warehouse on Long Island. There were too many valuable pieces to leave them hanging on the walls," answered Kevin with a slightly defensive tone. "If you're worried about my having clipped something, you're welcome to go out and take a look."

"No need to be touchy," Greta shot back. "I trust you. I just want to make sure nothing got missed."

"Believe me, nothing got missed." Kevin looked around the room. He seemed puzzled by something.

"What is it?" asked Greta. "Did you forget something?"

"It's nothing," said Kevin. "It's just kind of weird. A few days before Klaus died, he had this room repainted — just this room. I found the work order on his desk upstairs." Kevin then took a big sniff of the air. "You can still smell the paint. And then he put everything back — the artwork, the books. And then he died.

"This place just gets me nervous, Greta. The sooner we dump it the better. Uncle Klaus was a creepy dude."

"I agree that he was a little weird, Kev. But he was good to mom, even though they were never that close. He brought her over here from Europe and set her up. He helped her out after the divorce. He was a strange old loner, but I think he cared."

"Survivor's guilt," said Kevin, lost in his own thoughts.

"What?" asked Greta.

"Survivor's guilt. That's why he did all the charitable stuff — to ease his conscience. He was a Nazi, you know," offered Kevin as he shifted nervously in the chair.

"He wasn't a Nazi."

"How do you know he wasn't?" asked Kevin. "I think he just did it all out of guilt ... all the religiosity ... leaving all his money to charity. *La Maison Giroud!* Who knows what the hell he did during the war? Maybe he castrated Jews or something," Kevin said, raising his eyebrows.

"La Maison Giroud?" asked Greta. "What's that?"

"The Giroud House. It's some place in France — a school for teenage mothers and their children. He left them a huge amount of money. The lawyer was real tight-lipped about Uncle Klaus's finances, but I was able to pry a few tidbits from him," Kevin smiled.

"Well, what's wrong with him leaving his money to charity?"

Kevin just shrugged.

"He wasn't a Nazi," repeated Greta. "He had the misfortune of living in Germany in the 1930s. And so did our mother."

"Mom was just a kid. She didn't know what was going on."

"Uncle Klaus was a professor," Greta argued. "He didn't torture anybody. So he may have had some psychological baggage, so what?"

Kevin rolled his eyes. "Believe what you want."

"What happened between you and him, anyway? You've always had a chip on your shoulder when it came to Uncle Klaus."

"Nothing," snapped Kevin. "Let's just drop it, OK?"

"Fine," said Greta.

The two sat there for a couple of minutes, then Greta asked, "So how much did you say the place is worth?"

"The appraiser said two and a half mil," Kevin answered with a smile.

"Shit, Kev!"

Kevin's eyes continued to dart about the room. He fidgeted in his chair, shaking his leg nervously. The words echoing in his head, *You can never come into my house again. Never!*

"What is it?" asked Greta.

Kevin paused a moment then sat up straight, trying to look calm. "Let's just get out of here."

— Chapter 3 —

West 74th Street — Columbus Day, 1993

Trish Marquez, a tough-looking Hispanic real estate agent in her 50s, walked into the kitchen and announced, "And this is the kitchen. The people who inherited the place redid everything ... new appliances, new cupboards. The floor is new ... everything!"

Amy and Vince Cuthbert, a young couple in their late 20s, looked around with excited faces. Vince was a handsome man of medium build with styled blond hair, a thin goatee, and vacant, hazel-colored eyes — eyes which took in the room as if he already owned it. Amy was athletic, yet curvy, with straight, long, black hair, light brown skin, and exotic features. She looked as though she were part Asian and part Greek, or some other Mediterranean flavor.

"What's the story again on the guy who lived here?" asked Amy.

Reluctant to go through it again, Trish let out a bit of a sigh. "I don't really know all that much, other than what I've already told you. He was an eccentric old German fellow. He collected art. Apparently he came to the U.S. with a large collection worth an enormous amount of money. He sold a good share of it and bought this place. He did some investing. What can I tell you? The man was rich.

"Anyway, he was able to live here as a kind of recluse for over fifty years. The place has probably quadrupled in value during that time."

"At least," added Vince.

"Anyway," continued Trish, "he passed away last summer."

"He didn't die *here*, did he?" asked Amy.

"No. He was at the park when he died. He just keeled over. It was a stroke or something."

Trish let out another sigh, then tried to wrap things up. "He didn't have any children. His will left the house to his younger sister. However, she died a few years earlier, so his niece and nephew inherited the place. I think they did a nice job sprucing things up in the short amount of time they had."

"Yes, it's beautiful," Amy responded. "And big!"

"There are very few brownstones left that are single-family units — at least in Manhattan. There are some in Brooklyn. Not to be nosey, but if you take it, what are your plans for the place? Are you going to turn it into separate units?"

"No," Vince said sharply. "The plan is to live here ... to start a family."

Trish gave him a quizzical look, as if she'd never heard of such a thing.

Vince smiled at Trish charmingly and asked, "Have you heard of the Internet?"

She shook her head no.

Vince rolled his eyes at Amy and then told Trish, "Well, you will soon enough. I'm one of the key developers of some Internet software technology" — he stole another look at Amy — "and I was just part of a major sale of intellectual property. If we like the place, the money won't be an issue."

"I see." Trish tightened her expression a bit. "That must be nice.

— Chapter 4 —

West 74th Street — December 1993

Two months later, Amy Cuthbert looked out at the parked cars on West 74th street, all covered with snow. It was only 3 o'clock in the afternoon, but already the sky was dark and new flakes were beginning to fall. A big weather front was predicted to last through the night and into tomorrow.

Amy was glad to be indoors. Everything had been moved that morning, and now the work of setting up house was about to begin. A fire roared in the fireplace. Building a fire was the first thing Amy did after the movers left. The room was warm. It also felt safe, as if it were a great protection from the outside.

Before getting to work, Amy poured herself a glass of a dark red Malbec, and sat in the restored wingback chair she'd bought a few days before at an antique store on Long Island. She felt like a noblewoman from the 19th century, staring into the great hearth of her manor house. Time seemed suspended. She could very well have been in the 19th, or 13th, or even 1st century. The outside world was gone.

Because they'd paid cash for the place, the move went swiftly. Amy was glad they were going to be able to celebrate Christmas in the new house.

By the time Vince got home, the living room was somewhat arranged and the kitchen supplies had been put away.

"The place looks great, Honey! I'm surprised you got so much done."

"Yeah, I don't know. Everything just went quickly. I felt like Mary Poppins, ordering everything into place by magic."

Vince surveyed the room. "I like the antiques. That stuff we bought really fits the room." He looked up at the walls, "Wow, I didn't see all that art before."

"Well, you said get what I liked. I told the antique dealers what I wanted and it was all shipped. If there's something that drives you crazy, let me know."

"No. It all looks good." His eyes moved to a small picture sitting on the end of the mantle. It showed an older man with a gold circle around his head — a saint's halo — reading a book. The man had his fingers pressed against his lips and on his shoulder sat a miniature angel speaking into his ear. It was painted on a solid piece of wood.

"What's that?" asked Vince.

Amy looked to where he was pointing.

"I don't know. I saw it in one of the antique shops and it caught my eye. I'm pretty sure it's just a copy. I didn't spend that much. The shop owner wasn't sure either. He said it was a saint, but he wasn't sure which one. I thought it would go well with the room.

"To me, it's got a sort of "speak no evil" message to it ... the guy with his fingers to his lips ... the angel sitting on his shoulder. What do you think? Do you like it?"

Vince continued to stare at it. "It's a little weird. But if you like it, it's all right with me." He then leaned in and gave his wife a kiss.

Amy put her hands on the back of Vince's neck, pulled him toward her, and kissed him again. The two embraced and collapsed into the chair, Vince falling on top of Amy. Amy put her legs around his, and began rubbing her ankles up and down his calves.

"Let's do it," Amy whispered. She then lifted her sweater over her head and undid her bra, freeing her pale round breasts.

Vince moved his hands over her, then leaned in and began kissing one of her hard, pink nipples.

A log in the fireplace crumbled through the grate, diverting his attention. When he looked over, he saw the painting of the saint with his fingers over his mouth.

"Let's go upstairs," he suggested.

"It's cold up there," Amy protested. "I like it here by the fire."

"I feel like I'm being watched."

Amy looked up at the saint and giggled. "By *that*? I didn't know you believed in those things." She studied his face. "I can move it if you want."

"Let's just go upstairs," repeated Vince. "It feels weird doing it in the front room."

Amy laughed again, "Since when are you such a prude? ... Oh, all right."

Vince sat back on the floor and Amy stood up. All she had on was a pair of old jeans. As she moved toward the stairs, he studied how her lower back curved into her nice round butt.

Before heading up the staircase, Amy slipped out of her jeans and panties, smiled, and said, "Let's go make our own heat."

At 2 o'clock in the morning, as the two slept under a massive pile of blankets, a sharp slap echoed up from the first floor. Amy quickly sat up in bed, "What was that?"

Vince groaned and stirred a bit, then finally asked, "What?"

"That cracking noise. It came from downstairs."

"Go to sleep, Amy. Old houses make noises. Get used to it."

Amy remained still for a moment. It was quiet — absolutely quiet. She went back to sleep.

The morning was cold. Amy wrapped a blanket around herself and went to the window. The muted winter sunlight turned the fresh snow an unusual shade of white. She looked back at Vince lying in bed. He was out.

She put on her PJs, robe, and slippers and went downstairs. It was a Saturday and she planned to spend the entire day setting up house. There were still three other floors to take care of. However, the first order of the day was to start a new fire and get the place warmed up. Even though there was heating, it seemed that cold winter mornings were still to be reckoned with — the price of Victorian elegance.

Amy made coffee and then went into the living room. She noticed a flat piece of wood lying in the middle of the floor. It was the saint, face down. She picked it up and placed it back on the mantle. She concluded it must've been what made the sound she'd heard in the middle of the night.

After starting the fire, she sat in the wingback chair. The back of the house faced south and the morning sun was filtering through the kitchen doors and into the front room, reflecting off the opposite wall. She noticed a shiny, pear-shaped spot on the surface of the wall, about the size of a shoe print.

She went to examine the spot. It was oily to the touch. "Shoot," Amy remarked. "I hope it will clean up."

Later that day, Amy went back to wash the wall and the spot was gone. She attributed it to the change in light.

— Chapter 5 —

Emily Campbell's Office — December, the Present

There's something about snow that is like faith, thought Emily as she stared out the window into the twilight. *It's so ethereal as it falls, blanketing the ground in soft, bluish white. Viewed from a distance, it all makes sense. But when you pick it up with your fingers and examine it, it melts away into cold wetness. It causes your flesh to ache and your senses to dull. Yes, faith is a lot like snow — beautiful, white snow.*

And that was Emily's job. As a professor of cultural anthropology at Vassar College, her job was to plunge herself into the cold white snow and, using the heat from her brilliant intellect, melt away the shamanism and medievalism that dupes mankind, turning it into a cold, sobering, trickle of water.

Creating such metaphors was one Emily's favorite ways to entertain herself. She found it poetic. After all, that's how myths get started ... sitting around campfires inventing stories of Zeus, Noah, and Grendel's mother.

She turned from the window, walked to her desk, and picked up a framed photo of her own mother. In the picture, on a hot summer day many years ago, a red-haired woman with a blunt square nose (a nose that always reminded Emily of the tip of a square-toed shoe) stands behind two young girls. All are smiling. The woman's hands rest on the puffed sleeved shoulders of the girls' matching green, pink, and yellow summer dresses.

Emily put the picture down and looked back to the window. Twilight had given way to the light of a brilliant full moon. The snow had stopped falling and the ground was still and luminescent. She then noticed her reflection and how much she had grown to look like the woman in the picture — how she had inherited the same square nose.

Emily sat down and woke her computer screen. On the screen was the match.com profile of Henry471, a 43-year-old software engineer from White Plains. He was nice enough looking. He had a full head of hair. The profile said he was 5-foot-11. He liked cooking, backpacking, and going to Yankee games. He was divorced and had a dog. Just looking at him made Emily feel tired. She wasn't in the mood to meet anyone right now. *When the holidays are over,* she thought.

Emily shut down her computer and picked up a library book that she'd checked out a couple of weeks earlier. It was for the research she was doing for a book that she was working on with a couple of colleagues. She read the title: "*Habitibus Angelos*" ("The Habits of Angels").

The book was one she had found in the Thomas J. Watson Library at the Metropolitan Museum in New York. She had been down there looking into the history of angels in art.

"*Habitibus Angelos*" was a commentary by an anonymous writer on the habits of angels. It was in Latin and, judging from its condition, possibly written sometime during the Renaissance.

The title of the book Emily was working on was "Such Stuff as Dreams are Made On." The project was the vision of Dr. Martin Ellis, a senior member of the faculty. It was a collection of case studies on supernatural phenomenon. Each case featured a story about a reported supernatural occurrence that resulted in the perpetuation of a myth or legend. There were chapters on ghosts, UFOs, levitating swamis, even Bigfoot. There was a chapter on appearances of Christ and The Virgin Mary on trees, buildings, and other surfaces. And there was also a chapter on angels. The premise of the book was to look at the believer, as opposed to the phenomenon, and discover a common psychological profile — what types of people tend to buy into such things, and why.

Emily's responsibility was to write the introductory section of each chapter, giving historical background on each of the phenomena.

In addition to Dr. Ellis, the other contributor on the project was the Rev. Victoria Branham, an old friend and mentor of Emily's who taught at the Graduate Theological Union in Berkeley. She was editing the notes and bibliography and writing the preface. Even though she hadn't stood in a pulpit in well over a decade, Victoria liked retaining the title of Reverend. She once told Emily that it was her way of saying "up yours" to the religious establishment.

The two first met when Emily took a summer course at Princeton being taught by Victoria. Victoria's specialty was historical linguistics. She also had received a bit of notoriety when she published a book applying linguistic methods to the phenomenon of speaking in tongues. Having been raised by a Pentecostal mother, Victoria had always been intrigued by the practice. Such a willingness to take on unusual subjects led Emily to recommend her to Martin.

"*Habitibus Angelos*" looked like a promising source for the introduction to the chapter on angels. Something about it had caught Emily's eye when she found it in the library archives, perhaps the cover's unusual shade of green, or its design. It was embossed with a unique and intricate pattern, similar to medieval or Islamic scrollwork, but much more complex.

However, her Latin was rusty, and she'd procrastinated getting beyond its first few pages.

She let out a deep sigh and closed the book.

As she was leaving the office, Emily was stopped in the hall by none other than Martin Ellis. He was wearing a fur-lined parka and carrying an overstuffed leather bag and looked as though he was on his way out as well. In his late sixties, Martin was, as they liked to joke, the elder statesmen of the department.

He had been key in getting Emily her tenure a few years back. He was a plump man with a beard and a wild white fringe of hair around a shiny bald head, who, at this time of year, had to endure numerous references to Santa Claus.

Seeing Martin brought a smile to Emily's face. Martin had been on sabbatical that semester to finish the book and had only shown up at his office on occasion. As they approached each other, they exchanged their usual greetings.

"Doctor Campbell."

"Doctor Ellis."

"Good to see you, my dear. How have you been?"

"Everything is peachy."

"Good. Good. How's Heather?"

"Fine."

"What is she now, twelve?"

"Fourteen."

"Fourteen! My goodness, that's a yucky age."

"Indeed," agreed Emily.

"And how are the angels coming along?" asked Martin.

"I've found promising sources for the background section."

Martin squinted and gave Emily a long look.

"I'll have it done, Martin. I promise."

Changing the subject, she asked, "And how about you? Find any more ghosts to chase?"

Martin smiled. "As a matter of fact, I have a little field trip I'm taking this Saturday into the city. Perhaps you might be interested in coming along."

Martin set down his old leather bag, bent over, and dug through it. Emily looked down at him and shook her head.

"You know you don't need that anymore. We have pads and scanners these days."

"I'm the organic type," he said as he pawed through the bag. "Ah, here it is." He pulled out a file folder and leafed through its contents. He handed Emily a printout of a news article.

"It's a day care center on the Upper West Side," said Martin. "A couple of parents have complained that their children have reported seeing unusual things ... people who aren't there, objects moving around, singing."

"Singing?"

"Yeah, when the kids were singing nursery rhymes they heard choir voices singing along."

"Choir voices?"

"Read the article."

Emily looked at the piece of paper in her hands and read.

Parents Complain About West Side Day Care Facility

Two concerned parents have filed complaints with the city about Bright Beginnings, an Upper West Side day care facility.

The parents claim that their children have reported strange phenomenon such as phantom voices and apparitions, and that the center's director, Amy Cuthbert, has suggested that angels are responsible. The parents are alleging that Ms. Cuthbert is indoctrinating their children. In her defense, Ms. Cuthbert has downplayed the remark, saying that it was made casually, that she's not indoctrinating anyone. Said

Ms. Cuthbert, "If I said it was fairies or elves, no one would care."

The parents have countered that it's the intensity of their children's claims that concern them. Said Ms. Nancy Pettiford, "My daughter really believes there are angels now. I'm trying to raise my kids to be realists, to use reason and look to science for answers. When will we move beyond this kind of medievalism?"

New York law specifies that all non-religious, publicly licensed institutions that serve minors are not allowed to formally indoctrinate students, charges, or other clients. The city's Bureau of Child Care is scheduled to hold a hearing after the first of the year to determine the merit of the parents' claims. Until then, Ms. Cuthbert's day care center will remain open.

Emily handed the paper back to Martin. "This is stupid. The whole thing is stupid."

"I thought you were an atheist."

"That has nothing to do with it. What's the point of going after a woman running a day care center? These parents just want attention. If they don't like the place, then find another one."

"I see your point," Martin agreed. "Nevertheless, it's in our own backyard, so I thought I'd investigate. I called the woman,

Ms. Cuthbert, and she was very nice. I told her I was professor working on a book and I'd like to get her side of the story."

"Don't make her look like an idiot, Martin."

Martin organized the folder and put it back in his bag which he then picked up and slung around his shoulder. He frowned at Emily. "You're in an unusually charitable mood, defending the day care woman with such zeal."

"I just don't like witch hunts, no matter who the witch is."

"Right. We'll that's why you should come along — to keep me in check."

"I have Heather."

"Bring her along. We'll make it a day in the city with Uncle Marty. I'll buy dinner."

"I'll think about it."

"Right on." He grinned broadly and raised his eyebrows. "Where are you parked?"

"In the lot."

"Ah," he said. "I double-parked at the side of the building. I just stopped by to pick up a few things."

"It's good to see you, Martin. I promise I'll work on the book."

"Good to see you too, dear ... always a pleasure. Let me know about Saturday."

They exchanged a quick embrace and then Martin sauntered down the hall. With his bulging leather bag hung over his shoulder, he looked even more like Santa. When he got to the end of the hall he stopped and took a large red fuzzy object out of his pocket. It was one of those hunting hats with earflaps. Emily watched him put it on and then slip out the side door.

Before walking to her car, Emily lingered for a moment outside the front entrance of Blodgett Hall. The night was still and quiet. She stood and admired the expanse of fresh snow in front of the building. She began to think about her faith metaphor again.

Suddenly she was shaken from her thoughts by the sound of footsteps crunching toward her from the direction of the parking lot. A tall man came into the light. He smiled at her from beneath a bright green knit cap. He had a very handsome face, bordered by dark red curls of hair. It was a very warm and kind face. There was also something oddly familiar about him. They exchanged hellos and he went on his way.

— Chapter 6 —

Emily and Heather's House — Alfred Drive — Later that Evening

As Emily pulled into her driveway on Alfred drive, she could see Heather in the kitchen window, doing something at the sink.

Like Emily's ex, Heather was tall, blond, and blue-eyed, with a long, straight nose. She was only 14, but looked 18. Emily constantly worried about boys and other temptations, but so far most of their mother-daughter bickering had to do with lifestyle choices. For instance, about a year ago, Heather had decided to stop eating meat.

When Heather noticed her mom's car, she quickly disappeared from view.

It was Thursday — almost the weekend — and Emily hoped Heather didn't have any friends over. Emily didn't teach classes on Fridays, only worked on-call office hours, grading papers, and prep work, so Thursdays were like mini Fridays for her. She just wanted to eat dinner, drink some wine, and get lost in a mindless TV show.

Emily walked through the front door, went to the kitchen table, and plopped down her purse, computer bag, and a bottle of chardonnay. Heather was nowhere to be seen.

"Heather!" called Emily.

"Yeah?" replied a muffled voice from the back of the house.

"Just wanted to know where you were."

Emily cracked the wine, poured a glass, and went into the family room to watch TV.

As she surfed the channels, she landed on the Catholic channel. It was showing the Mass being celebrated at a church in the Midwest. She watched as the priest stood behind the altar and the congregation responded, *"May the Lord accept the sacrifice at your hands, for the praise and glory of his name, for our good, and the good of all his holy church."* The priest then prepared to consecrate the elements.

Emily wondered again about faith — how the priest managed to believe in what he did ... or if he really believed it at all. To her it was both sad and admirable, at the same time. She felt both pity and envy for the man.

"What are you watching?" Heather's voice interrupted.

Emily quickly changed the channel as if she'd been caught looking at porn.

"Nothing. I'm just flipping channels."

She landed on a commercial for a weight loss product showing a woman with ample cleavage jiggling down the beach.

"Did you eat?" asked Emily.

"Yeah, I ate when I got home from school."

"OK."

She changed the channel to a news program showing a group of protesters somewhere in Europe.

"Mom?"

"Yes."

"Katy asked if I could go into the city with her on Saturday. She has tickets to a matinee of 'The Nutcracker.'"

"Cool. Who's going with you? Katy's mom?"

The protesters had finished and now the news anchor — a classy looking black man in his late 50s — was back on.

"Uh, we wanted to go by ourselves."

"You're not riding the train by yourself."

"C'mon, mom. I'm in high school now. It's during the day."

"What did Katy's mom say? I can't believe Jenny's OK with it."

Irritation started springing up in Heather's voice. "She's fine with it. You're the only one who's paranoid."

Emily was starting to feel boxed. It was at times like these she missed having Terry around.

"I just got home. Let me think about it for a bit." She looked up at Heather, who stood there in shorts, socks, and a light blue hoodie, staring down at her with an angry expression. Emily looked at her long smooth legs and felt a bit of envy.

"Aren't you cold?"

"No," Heather shot back, and then stomped off.

The news was now showing the weather. Intermittent snow storms were predicted for the next few days.

Emily flipped back to the Catholic channel once more. Communion was being given to the faithful.

Her thoughts turned toward Heather. She reached for her phone and punched in a number. After a couple of rings, a woman's a voice answered, "Hi Em, what's up?"

"Hi Jenny. I'm calling to get the story about the matinee on Saturday. Are you really letting Katy go into the city on her own?"

"No. Did she tell you that?"

"Heather did," answered Emily.

"No. She asked. I told her I'd think about it, but then I said no."

"Good. I was a worried there for a second."

"I told her she'd need to have an adult along. Why, were they trying to play us off each other again?" asked Jenny.

"Looks that way," said Emily.

Our Lady of West 74th Street

"Too bad though. Katy got those tickets from her aunt. It's the Lincoln Center show — good seats, too. Shame to see 'em go to waste. I'll try to find somebody to take them."

"You can't go, huh?" asked Emily.

"No, I have to work. There are only two tickets. Someone would have to drop the girls off and then go do something for two hours, then pick them up. Katy and I were going to go together, but then I got commandeered."

Emily watched as the TV priest wiped the chalice after communion. He was an older man with a full white beard. It made her think of Martin and his *field trip*.

"Hey, I have an idea. I was asked to go into the city this weekend by a colleague on a sort of interview. I'll see if I can arrange the time so it's during the show."

"That would be great, Em. I know the girls really wanted to go."

"All right. I'll call around tonight and then get back to you in the morning."

"Cool."

Emily ended the call and then turned up the volume on the TV. The priest was concluding the Mass.

"Lord, may the sacrifice we have offered strengthen our faith and be seen in our love for one another."

— Chapter 7 —

The House on 74th Street — Saturday

Amy Cuthbert had aged over the past twenty-one years, to be sure, but she was still a beautiful woman. Her once black hair was now salted with gray and pulled back into a pony tail, but it was thick and healthy. She wore glasses, a light blue shirt, and a brown sweater. She still nicely filled out her pair of jeans.

Amy placed three cups of coffee on the kitchen table and sat down.

"I hope I got it right. You're cream and you're black, yes?"

"Yes, thank you," said Emily, taking the cup with the black coffee. "And thank you for showing us around your home. It's gorgeous."

"Yes, thank you," added Martin.

Amy smiled and let out a big breath. "I love Saturdays. It's so quiet around here. Don't get me wrong, the kids are great. I love what I do. But the older I get, the more I relish the quiet."

"Really?" said Martin. "I find I'm the opposite. Sitting around my office drives me nuts. It's like a tomb. Coming into the city is a treat. I love it — the honking horns, the yelling. It invigorates me."

"Hmm, we should trade places." Amy looked into her own cup of black coffee, reached for a spoonful of sugar and began to stir. "But that's not why you've come. You want to hear about all the *phenomena* that've been occurring." She gave them both a wry glance.

"Only what you feel like sharing," said Emily.

"We only know what we've read in the news," added Martin. "We want to hear your side of the story."

"It's funny. The first of the weirdnesses — that's what I call them — started happening about this same time of year, right after we first moved in. The very night we moved in, in fact." Amy stopped short.

"What is it?" asked Martin.

"That was over twenty years ago. It's just hard to believe it's been that long.

"Anyway, it's not like this place is haunted — anything but. My son Nick and I have always felt happy here ... comfortable and safe. We've had great parties through the years. Friends and family have stayed over. There's never been any rattling chains or footsteps or spooky sounds — none of that. It's just that odd things have happened from time to time.

"My husband Vince wasn't so complacent about it. Being an engineer, I guess he had to figure everything out. The problem is, and this is just my opinion, not everything is meant to be figured out.

"Vince wasn't a bad man. He just wasn't ever at peace. He couldn't accept what he didn't understand. And yet I think he knew, deep down inside, there were things he would never understand, and that drove him nuts. And even though he would never admit it, he was also superstitious.

"I'm sorry, I'm rambling."

Martin flipped open a large leather-bound notebook and took out a pen. "Not at all. Tell us about some of the things you've witnessed over the years, Ms. Cuthbert."

"Please call me Amy. Even the kids call me Amy."

"OK, Amy."

"When we first moved in, I put this icon up on the mantle in the living room. I later found out that it was an icon of St. John the Divine. Are you familiar with him?"

"Yes," said Martin as he scribbled.

"He was one of the twelve disciples," added Emily.

"That's right," affirmed Amy. "The big cathedral was named after him.

"Anyway, the icon would fall off the mantle during the night and land face down on the floor. It happened a few nights in a row. It would always be in the same place in the morning. Finally I moved it to another room and it stopped.

"It's on the wall right behind the two of you."

At this, both Martin and Emily swung around. In the narrow span of wall that separated the kitchen from the laundry area, was the icon. Martin stood up and examined it further.

"I know this piece!" he said. "This is in The Hermitage Museum in St. Petersburg. I've seen this before."

"I can assure you, it's not from Russia," said Amy. "I bought it in an antique shop out on Long Island."

"I mean it's a copy of the one in The Hermitage," said Martin. "It's called 'St. John the Divine in Silence,' by Nektary Kulyuksin. It's a very famous icon. It symbolizes the scene from St. John's Apocalypse where John hears the message of the seven thunders and the angel instructs him not to write down what he hears.

"Those kind of passages always frustrate me," said Martin, taking his seat. "I never cared much for censorship. In any event, it looks like a good, hand-painted copy. It was probably originally hanging in a church at some point."

"And now he just watches to make sure I don't burn the eggs," mused Amy.

"The other thing that happened was that a strange oil spot would show up on the wall on the days when the icon fell down," Amy explained, looking up at the icon. "That stopped too when I moved it. However, I have seen the spot from time to time through the years."

Amy's eyes moved from Emily to Martin. "So, do you think I'm crazy?" She took a sip of coffee.

"Not at all," said Emily. "We study these things for a living. Some people think that makes *us* crazy."

Amy continued, "The thing with the icon didn't freak me out. I kind of found it amusing. I can't say the same for Vince. Even though he didn't say anything, I could tell it made him uneasy.

"Vince was from a very superstitious family of old world Russians on his mother's side. I think it's one of the things that made him go into science and technology, where everything was explained by the laws of physics ... algorithms and formulas."

Martin took a big drink of coffee and then set his cup down, "This is very good coffee. So what else happened?"

Amy continued, "The next thing that happened was when I became pregnant with Nicolas.

"When we moved in, we decided we were going to wait a year or two to have kids. However, God had other plans. It was only a few months later that I found out I was pregnant.

"At the time, we weren't sure what to do. What made it even harder was that, when we had the ultrasound, the doctor said there was might be a birth defect — his legs didn't look right. I was a mess.

"One night Vince was upstairs working. I was out somewhere. He told me he heard a woman crying in the living room. Soft crying, he said.

"He said he went to the top of the stairs and looked down, and he saw the bottom half of her dress and her feet. When he began to come down the stairs, a sharp pain shot up his leg and he crumbled.

"He shouted, 'who are you?' at the woman. And she asked him to please stay where he was."

"Wow," said Emily. "Who was she?"

"It was at that point that I came in. There was this beautiful young woman, probably a teenager. She was dressed in a Middle Eastern robe, sort of like a burka, but without the veil ... just a scarf around her head ... and more flowing ... and red. I didn't know who she was. I was shocked. I couldn't think of anything to say. I didn't know if Vince was having an affair or what.

"She just looked at me. We stood there for about a minute then she came close and put her hand on my abdomen and said, 'He will be well.' Then she walked toward the door.

"I'll never forget that voice." Amy studied the two across the table. "*Now*, you think I'm crazy.

"Look, I wasn't religious. I wasn't looking for moving icons, or oil spots, or mysterious young girls to appear. I wasn't a conservative or anti-abortion or any of that. Vince and I were both big Clinton supporters. This is just what happened."

"Who do you think it was?" asked Martin.

"I don't know."

"The Virgin Mary?"

"I don't know." Amy took a sip of coffee. "Maybe.

"Anyway, Nick was born six months later, in the middle of September. He was perfect."

"And what was your husband's reaction?" asked Martin.

"Vince was killed before Nicolas was born — a car accident."

"I'm sorry," said both Martin and Emily together. They then waited for Amy to continue.

"After the thing with the young woman, Vince started going nuts. The next ultrasound showed Nick's leg to be completely normal. The doctors danced around the facts, blaming the equipment and blah, blah, blah. But we knew, we both knew. We had seen the girl.

"It was after that that Vince tracked down Mr. Peters."

"Who's that?" asked Emily.

"He's the nephew of the man who owned the house before us. Vince wanted to know more about its history."

They heard the front door open and close. A deep voice boomed from the front of the house, "Mom!"

"That's Nick," said Amy. "In here!" she shouted back.

A moment later a muscular young man about twenty years old, with olive skin and thick black hair, appeared in the kitchen doorway. His face strongly resembled Amy's. He was looking curiously at Martin.

"These are the college professors I told you about," said Amy.

"Ah," Nick said and lightened his expression. "I thought maybe you were interviewing a Santa for the kids."

Martin forced a chuckle. "Oh yes, it is that time of year. The Santa humor begins. No worries, I'm used to it."

"Well, thank God you're not with social services or something," Nick added.

"Oh no," responded Martin. "But we are interested in your mother's story. It's all very fascinating."

With Nick's arrival, Martin began to organize his things. "I'm afraid we got here a little late. The crowds are a mess this time of year, you know. Right now, Dr. Campbell needs to go gather her daughter from the theater. We're going to have to finish our discussion later, Amy."

"You do look at little like Santa," Amy smiled. "It's a funny thing. We can have Santa, but not angels."

"It's a weird world we live in," Emily agreed. "I'm sorry you're being harpooned for all this."

Amy walked the two to the front door. She put her hand on the door knob but, before opening the door, she paused and turned to Emily. "There's one other thing. On the night when the girl was here, when she left, I never heard the sound of the door. She walked past me, but then I never heard the door."

— Chapter 8 —

Kevin Peters' Office, Mid-town Manhattan — April 1994

Kevin Peters' midtown office was on the 12th floor of the Chrysler Building. As Vince walked down the beautiful art deco, marbled hallway, he questioned what the hell he was doing there. He finally arrived at Peters' office door. The door read: Kevin B. Peters — Financial Advisor.

Financial Advisor, thought Vince. *What a racket!*

Vince opened the door and was met by a petite brunette sitting behind a large reception desk. The office was well-appointed in shades of gray, brown, black, and rose. An Impressionist era painting hung on the wall in the waiting area. It looked expensive. Even though Vince was now a multi-millionaire, wealth made him nervous, especially the old money kind.

The girl offered a slightly flirtatious, well-practiced smile. "Good afternoon. Are you here to see Mr. Peters?"

"Yes," answered Vince, flirting back a little.

"And do you have an appointment?"

"I called. He told me to drop by."

Her smile softened a bit. "I see. Could I get your name?"

"Vince Cuthbert."

The girl called Peters' office, announced Vince's presence, then put down the phone.

"Mr. Peters will see you shortly. Please have a seat."

Vince walked toward where the painting was hanging.

The girl asked Vince if she could get him something to drink.

Vince turned around. The girl was now standing. She had a perfect body. Her dark gray dress revealed a generous amount of cleavage, but not enough to be sleazy.

"Sure ... a bottled water if you have it."

"OK." She turned and went behind the false wall behind her desk. Vince examined her backside — very athletic — a small waist, a perfect curve to the hips, and well-defined calves. He caught himself lusting, and tried to shake it off.

Ever since he and Amy had gotten married, it seemed like such thoughts came at him relentlessly. *The married man's curse,* he figured.

The girl returned and handed him the bottle. "Here you go."

"Thanks."

"My name's Dana. If you need anything else, let me know." She smiled again and went back to her desk.

To avoid staring at Dana, Vince turned his attention back to the painting. It was a picture of a pathway in the woods. The trees were in their autumn colors. The ground looked wet and muddy, with leaves stuck here and there.

In contrast to the reception area, Kevin Peters' office was full of natural light. Vince admired the view of Midtown Manhattan.

After a cursory hello, Kevin Peters seemed distracted. He sat behind an antique wooden desk with papers strewn across the top. His sleeves were rolled up, his tie loosened. He finally leaned back in his chair, looked at Vince, and asked, "So you and your wife are living in my uncle's house? How do you like it?"

"It's gorgeous. We feel fortunate to be there. It's hard to believe we live in a place like that."

Peters studied Vince a little more closely. "I have to say, when I saw you, I was surprised how young you were. I understand you paid cash for the place. If you don't mind my asking, how did you come by so much money?"

"Oh, not at all. I'm a software geek." Vince smiled.

Peters continued to stare, waiting for more.

"Have you heard of the Internet?"

Peters raised his eyebrows a bit. "Yes. Al Gore. The Information Superhighway."

"I went to NYU. I got interested in graphics software ... computer animation, that sort of thing. After I graduated, I worked with a team of people to develop media transfer protocols across networks. With the coming privatization of the Internet, certain investors became very interested in what we were doing. We ended up being asked to configure our software to work across the Internet. The team — there were five of us — sold the intellectual rights to it for around 20 million, four million to each of us. That's about all I'm allowed to say."

"Really? Wow! You computer guys are like the oil barons of your day. Good for you. I assume you already have a good financial advisor." Peters smiled for the first time.

"Yeah," Vince nodded.

"I should hope so," said Peters as he turned his attention to his computer screen. "Well, I hope the house brings you and your wife years of happiness. So, what can I tell you?"

Vince hesitated a bit. "Well, my wife and I were interested in knowing more about the history of the house — your uncle in particular. We only know what the real estate agent told us. It was really just kind of a snapshot."

"Well, to be honest, I didn't know my uncle that well. My sister and I were born and raised in California. I came back east to go to graduate school and stayed with him for part of the summer before my first semester started. I didn't see him much after that. He was a very private man.

"He and my mother were each from a different time and place. He was from the old world; she'd come to America when she was really still a girl, she married an American, moved to California, and tried to be as un-German as possible."

"But she still named her daughter Gretchen," Vince said.

Kevin looked a little perturbed.

"I found both your names in the records," said Vince. "I came to you see you, because you're in town."

"I see," said Kevin. "Gretchen was my Austrian grandmother's name. I never met any of my mother's family except for Klaus. They were all killed during the war.

"My sister has gone by the name Greta since childhood. My mother thought it sounded less German. It was also the name of one of mom's favorite actresses — Greta Garbo.

"Greta decided to finish law school a couple of years ago, after she split up with her husband. She's due to graduate from Stanford this summer.

"I'm sorry I'm not much help. Why are you so interested?"

"I dunno. Weird things have been happening. I guess I'm a little superstitious."

Peters' expression became more serious. "Weird things? Like what?"

"When we first moved in, my wife had this painting that kept falling over. It would fall into the same spot on the living room floor every night. Finally we moved it into the kitchen, and it stopped.

"Then, the other night, this woman came into the house and gave my wife this strange blessing for our unborn child."

"Your wife's pregnant?"

"Yes. I think this girl must've found out somehow. Maybe she's with some religious group. I don't know. She was dressed in a Middle Eastern robe of some kind. Then I had the thought that she might have known your uncle, that she might have a key. We never had the place rekeyed."

Peters' eyes widened. "A girl? Was it a girl or a woman?"

"I dunno. I guess a teenager."

"Hmm." Peters absently studied the papers on his desk.

"What?" asked Vince.

"Nothing. Sorry, I don't know the girl."

Peters got out of his chair and looked out the window. "If you don't mind my asking, what's your religion, Vince? Are you a Buddhist or a Jew? Do you believe in God? Heaven? Hell?"

"Nothing. I'm agnostic."

"That means you don't know. That's convenient." He paused.

"In the time I did spend with my uncle, one of the things he loved to do was share his ideas on religion with me. He especially loved to talk about the spiritual world. He would tell me about spiritual beings — not just angels, but cherubs and seraphs — things like that. He believed in a whole hierarchy of heavenly creatures, each with their own set of powers and purpose. And each with their own set of physical attributes.

"For instance, he maintained that angels were all the exact same height ... six foot something inches tall. He said that only angels had that exact height and that was how they recognized each other when they took human form ... he had all kinds of information like that. Maybe he was crazy, I don't know.

"You haven't seen any exceptionally tall men showing up uninvited, have you?"

Vince smiled, "Now you're just messing with me." He shuffled in his chair and then checked his watch. "Well, I guess that's it then."

"I'm afraid so."

Vince stood up and moved toward the door.

"There is one thing," Peters said.

"When my uncle died, my sister and I took possession of his entire estate ... all except for his personal library. He donated that to the Metropolitan Museum. In addition to the house and his money, we also inherited his art collection. There was one piece missing from the collection. A piece of religious art: a painting of the Virgin Mary and the Christ Child. It was quite dear to my uncle and he was quite protective of it. I think he may have hidden it somewhere. You haven't seen anything like that, have you?"

"No."

Peters grabbed one of his business cards from his desk and handed it to Vince. "If you do ever run across it, please give a call. It has great sentimental value to me."

"Sure," Vince responded.

Peters watched keenly as Vince left the room. When the door was fully shut, Peters picked up the telephone. His hand reached down and, shaking, he began to punch in numbers. The phone rang once and Peters face went white. "I have some information for you."

— Chapter 9 —

New York City — December, the Present

Martin tried to hail a cab as Emily madly dialed her phone. She waited, listened for the ring, and then got voicemail. "Dammit, she's not answering either."

"The girlfriend has her phone off too?" asked Martin.

"Yes, the show should have ended ten minutes ago."

"Well, just relax. We'll get a cab soon."

"This weather sucks, Martin. It's gonna take us forever to get to the theater."

"I'm sure they'll call you soon. They probably both turned their phones off during the show. Did you send them texts?"

"Of course."

Just then a bus stopped about twenty feet away.

"Do you want to try the bus? It's not that far." asked Martin.

"Sure."

The bus was about two-thirds full. Martin and Emily found two seats facing each other, near the back. Martin sat next to a young mother with her two children; Emily sat next to a tall man with dark olive skin, long curly black hair, and bright blue eyes. He was extremely handsome, but in an almost unnatural way. His face was smooth like a child's. He reminded Emily of a Renaissance painting.

Our Lady of West 74th Street

The sky outside was getting dark.

"Relax," repeated Martin. "They're probably out getting something to eat and enjoying their little bit of independence."

"So what did you think of Ms. Cuthbert?"

"She seemed very nice," said Emily. "I think what these parents are doing is absolutely stupid."

"Perhaps you're right."

The bus pulled to a stop at Broadway and West 72nd Street, and a tall, oily-looking young man in a pea coat got on. As he walked down the center aisle, he stared at Emily. She wondered if she knew him — perhaps he was a former student.

He was handsome, but in a cold, chiseled way, like a male model in an ad for cologne. As he moved closer, his gaze shifted to the right, to the man seated next to Emily. He looked angrily at the man with the blue eyes, and then turned and went down into the stair well at the back exit of the bus.

"Back door!" he said. The door opened, and he was gone.

"Wrong bus, I guess," said blue eyes.

"He was a little spooky," said Emily.

"Indeed," he agreed.

She studied the man. She looked at his hands. His skin was extremely smooth. His form was perfect. She wondered if he was gay.

The bus was now at West 68th Street and the sky outside was completely dark. Emily tried both numbers again and still no answer. It was now thirty minutes past when the ballet was to let out.

"Dammit, Martin. Where the hell are they?"

"I'm sure they're fine."

"You're not a parent. You don't get it."

Emily looked out the window. Lights were blinking everywhere; the cars were moving at a crawl. Despite the cold and snow, the streets were packed. It was Saturday night and all the Christmas crowds were out. She thought about all the negative possibilities that could befall the two girls.

"Shit!"

Just then her phone beeped. She picked it up and looked at the screen. *getting coffee @starbucks broadway n 63rd. where r u?*

Emily quickly typed in, *on the bus. cudn't get a cab. b there soon.*

She stuck the phone back in her purse.

"Was that Heather?"

"Yes."

"There. You see. Everything's fine."

When the bus stopped at West 66th Street, blue eyes got up. Because of his height, he had to duck a little bit to avoid the hand rail. As he began to make his way to the exit, he said to Emily, "I don't have kids, but if I did, I'd be worried too." And then he smiled.

"Thanks," Emily smiled back, thinking to herself, *if only...*

She looked at Martin who was scowling. To change the subject she asked, "So what did *you* think of Amy? Are you going to use her story in your book?"

"I don't know. Between you and me, she sort of blows the stereotype."

"You mean she's not like the whackjobs chasing UFOs in the Arizona desert?"

"Something like that, yes."

"Well, I hope you choose *not* to exploit her. She seemed like a nice person."

The bus stopped at West 63rd Street and the two got off. Starbucks was located just a half-block from the bus stop. As Emily and Martin approached the corner, they could see the two girls through the window. They were chatting and laughing.

Emily went up and tapped on the glass. Rather than being met with expressions of excited welcome, the girls' faces turned serious. Heather lifted her cup, pointed to it, and mouthed some words to Emily who shook her head and pointed at her watchless wrist. Heather typed something into her phone and a moment later, Emily heard her phone beep from inside her purse. She took it out and looked. The screen showed the words *almost finished*. Emily then did the same and typed *hurry up!*

Emily turned back around to Martin who asked her, "So, where do you want to eat?"

"Oh God, Martin, are you sure you want to hang out with two hormonal teenage girls for another two hours?"

"Sure. We can have a good old fashioned palaver — F2F."

Emily gave Martin a confused look.

"Face to face, my dear. C'mon, you gotta get up to speed. How about we go to Ed's Chowder House? It's only a block up. Then we can get a cab to Grand Central."

"Let's ask the girls. They'll probably want pizza or something. Plus, Heather is a vegetarian now. So I don't know if she'll be up for Ed's Chowder House."

A few minutes later, Heather and her friend Katy emerged through the crowd in front of Starbucks. It had just begun to snow again and the two looked as though they were dressed for a winter magazine shoot ... long wool coats, hats and scarves, their blonde and brunette hair being blown up by the air from the subway. It made Emily miss being young.

To Emily's surprise, both girls were all for getting chowder with Martin. Heather explained that she was a pesco-vegetarian and that fish was OK.

* * * * *

"So what was it you guys were doing today?" asked Heather between spoonfuls of soup.

Emily answered, "We were interviewing a woman about some experiences she's had in her house — paranormal events."

"Really?" said Katy. "That's cool. What kind of stuff?"

Martin cleared his throat. "Among other things, the woman maintains she had a visit from the Virgin Mary."

"She didn't say that, Martin. She just said a young woman ... a girl, about the same age as you two." Emily pointed her spoon at the girls.

"Really?" asked Heather. "I didn't know the Virgin Mary was that young."

"Oh, yes," Martin spoke up, "According to tradition, she was only 13 or 14 when Jesus was conceived."

"Wow," said the girls in chorus.

"And also according to tradition, Joseph was an older man, a widower, probably about my age."

"Ew!" echoed the girls. Martin rolled his eyes and scowled at their response.

"But," inserted Emily, "Also according to tradition, Mary was a virgin all her life, so the old man never had sex with her." She chuckled and turned her attention back to her soup.

Martin smiled and shook his head, "Well, as you say, it's all just tradition. No one's ever proved a thing." He took a healthy sip from his glass of white wine and surveyed the restaurant. His eyes rested upon the exposed legs of a very elegant lady in her early 40s at a nearby table.

"Why are you guys always so down on religion?" asked Heather. "What if there really are things we can't explain?"

"But that's the whole point, my dear," said Martin with a new excitement in his voice. "I agree. There are things we can't explain. That's why people come up with these stories, to explain things they can't understand."

"But what if they aren't just stories? What if they're real?"

"To be real, there has to be proof," responded Martin.

"But isn't that what faith is? Believing, even if there isn't proof?" asked Heather.

"Faith is a convention of the mind ... a coping mechanism. That's all."

"Well, I don't agree," said Heather. "But even if it is a convention of the mind, it's something that comes naturally. People have believed in God or gods as long as humans have been here. Why do you feel it's your job to pick it apart?"

"That's pretty good, Heather," said her mother. "Wow. I didn't know you thought about this stuff that much."

"Oh yeah," said Katy. "Some of the kids at school call her the guru, 'cause she's always talking about the meaning of life and shit." Katy caught herself. "Sorry."

"It's OK," said Martin with a smile. "'Meaning of life and shit' is a very appropriate way of putting it."

The four fell to eating their soup. Emily's eyes stayed on her daughter for a while. She was reminded of another teenage girl from years ago, and how similar they were. She thought about how interesting family genes were.

On the train ride home Martin and Emily sat together in one car and the girls in another. The ride from New York to Poughkeepsie was an hour and a half. Emily sat next to the window and watched as lights whizzed by. She thought Martin was asleep until he piped up, "She's a smart girl, that daughter of yours."

"Yes," said Emily softly.

"She takes after mom."

"Yes, she does."

* * * * *

At the bar at TGI Fridays on East 42nd Street, the oily-looking young man from the bus was drinking beer while watching the TV with interest. On the big flat screen, a very frazzled-looking man in a suit was answering a reporter's questions about the claims against Amy Cuthbert's day care center.

"Will the center be shut down?" asked the reporter.

"At this point, no," answered the man in the suit. "If parents want to remove their children from the center, they're entitled to do so. But until there's proof of any law being broken, it will remain open."

At the corner of the bar, near the front door, an attractive young woman in tight-fitting office attire was having a martini and stealing looks at the man.

He caught the women's stare and pointed at the TV. "What do you think of that?"

The woman looked up at the screen. "I don't know. It doesn't really affect me."

"So you're indifferent?"

"I suppose."

"Good." He took a sip of his beer. "Indifference is good."

He nodded at the TV. "But not everyone is so indifferent. You watch. Someone's gonna end up going after her, and someone's gonna get hurt. Just hope it's not any of those kids." He took a long drink and finished his beer. "They should just shut her down."

The woman gave him a cautious smile then turned away.

A few stools away sat the other man from the bus, the blue-eyed fellow who has sat next to Emily. He was sipping a glass of red wine and watching the same TV screen as the oily one. He set down his glass and turned and said, "Due process, my friend ... due process. Isn't that still the law around here?"

This startled the oily one, as if the man had been invisible until then.

"And you are?" he asked.

"Raphael," he responded.

At the mention of the name, the oily one looked surprised.

"And you? What's your name?" asked Raphael.

"Onock."

"Onock," repeated Raphael. "That's an ugly name. It sounds like some creature from a human science-fiction movie."

Raphael shot Onock a penetrating look, then said, "You are being watched."

Onock nodded back over his shoulder at the TV screen, "As is she ... the day care woman."

"No harm will come to her. But if you are the one who tries, I pity you."

Onock sniggered. "Pity? Are you allowed to pity the likes of me?"

"You don't have the slightest idea what you're being asked to do." Raphael smiled and nodded towards the door. "Looks like the one you were attempting to sway has left you."

Onock did a quick about face to see that the girl by the door was gone. When he turned back around, Raphael was gone as well.

Part II
The Habits of Angels

These Angelic substances,
Since they first gathered joy from God's face,
Have never turned their eyes away

— *Dante Alighieri, The Divine Comedy* —

Harry Steven Ackley

— Chapter 10 —

St. Panteleimon Monastery — Mt. Athos, Greece — Great Lent 1941

Brother Jerome woke with a start. He looked at the small wind-up clock he kept in his cell and began to panic. It was precisely midnight. He had forgotten to set the alarm.

During Great Lent it fell to the younger monks to keep the tradition of censing certain icons at each hour of prayer. Afterward, they would keep vigil before the icon until the next monk came. On this night at midnight, it was Brother Jerome's turn to cense the icon of Our Lady of Faith. He was late. The monk who had been at the shrine since Compline would be wondering where he was.

As he hurried to go, Jerome already felt embarrassed and angry at himself for being so negligent. As he rushed down the main corridor of the monastery, the moonlight spilled through the windows against the white walls. Jerome passed with his great black cassock billowing behind, making him look like a giant cloud of ink.

When he came down the stairs to the basement where the icon was, the air was unusually warm. He could also smell incense. *The brother before him did not wait,* thought Jerome. *And well he shouldn't have,* he continued to berate himself.

Yet, as Jerome turned the corner to where the shrine was, it wasn't a monk that was standing before The Lady. It was an angel. The monk who had served at Compline, Brother Philip, was lying asleep on the floor.

All Jerome could see were the backs of his giant wings and the top of his head, covered with fire-red hair. The being radiated heat and light against the walls. His tall, lean body rocked back and forth as he swung the censor. Smoked wafted up above.

Jerome's eyes followed the trail of smoke. Looking up, he no longer saw the ceiling of the basement, but rather a huge chandelier hanging from a high barrel vault. Beyond the chandelier the vault was covered with icons of the angels. To his right and left he saw great windows covered with beautiful rose-colored glass. Even though it was midnight, light was streaming through them.

Taking all this in, Jerome felt himself grow weak. He felt his mind beginning to fade as if he were falling asleep and there was nothing to be done. He went to his knees and then to his hands. He looked down to see a beautiful carpet covering a floor of white marble. He fell to the carpet.

A moment later he felt a cool wind blow over him. He opened his eyes, he saw the stone floor of the monastery. He looked up to see the shrine. The icon of The Lady was in her rightful place, lit by the dim light of a few tapers. Everything was normal. However, Brother Philip was still asleep on the floor a few feet away. And the scent of incense still hung heavy in the air.

Jerome got to his feet and turned to see a tall figure dressed in a green robe standing in the shadows near the wall. His still expression was fixed on Jerome.

Jerome couldn't speak. He looked back at Philip to see if he were awake yet.

"He is asleep," said the figure. "I will awaken him when I go."

The angel stepped into the light of the tapers. Jerome studied his face and thought, *he is like an icon himself ... passionless, serene ... holy.*

As he got closer, Jerome noticed the smoothness of the angel's skin and the texture of his hair. He was like no one he'd ever seen before.

"I am Cassiel. I am the seventh angel.

"I have seen the wars raging on either side of St. Panteleimon, coming from Germany and Russia. I fear for the safety of the icon. You must find a way to protect it, Jerome."

"What should I do?" asked Jerome timidly.

"It must leave the monastery. There is a group of men coming from the west. You speak their language. Look for the one who is spiritual. Explain its importance and give it to him. Send it away from Athos. I will help the man see to its safe journey."

Jerome bowed to Cassiel.

"It's not meant to be hidden away," said Cassiel. "It's been here too long."

Just then Jerome heard a groan on the floor behind him. He turned to see Philip slowly propping himself up onto his elbows.

When he turned back around, the angel was gone.

— Chapter 11 —

Emily and Heather's House — The Present

The next morning, Emily awoke full of energy. Per arrangement, Heather had spent the night at Katy's and wouldn't be home till late afternoon. Emily decided today was the day she would dig into "*Habitibus Angelos.*"

Emily made coffee, sat at her dining room table, and opened the book.

She'd already read through the introductory chapters, which consisted of a long preamble that compared a faithful versus a faithless society.

When a society loses faith in the loving God, men will begin to discount and disbelieve the miraculous. They will be enamored with their own intellects, forgetting that they themselves are fashioned in the image of God. As disbelief grows, loving acts will be despised, miracles will become rare, and the angels will become invisible. The Mother of God will then hide her face in sadness. As the prophet writes: "Woe to those who are wise in their own eyes and clever in their own sight!"

When faith returns, the signs will reverse: The Mother of God will then show herself, the angels will become visible again, miracles will follow, and mankind will love and believe. As God lifted up Abraham, Moses, and David, God will bring these things to pass when the time is ready.

The next section of the book described different heavenly entities that exist: principalities, powers, thrones, dominions, cherubim, seraphim, and angels. However, special attention was given to angels, who are the only beings who serve as intermediaries between God and man.

For Emily, this is where things got interesting. The text maintained that angels take three forms. They can become invisible; they can take human form; and when they are in the act of praising God, they become glorified winged beings of light.

"When they take human form they are all exactly the same height."

Emily converted the Latin units and it came out to 6 feet, 5.314 inches.

"All exactly the same," the text reiterated. *"And there's not one human who has that height. Not one."*

Emily looked out the window. "What were these people on?" She said aloud.

She continued to read.

"And they cannot produce beards. They are male in appearance, but with no beards."

What she found especially interesting was that angels do not have nipples. *"When humans are formed, they have the potential of being male or female. Nipples are a reminder of this. Because angels are only male, they lack such marks."*

The book went on to describe how Angels tend to dress in the clothes of the day in order to blend in, quoting an old Pauline text, *do not neglect to show hospitality to strangers, for thereby some have entertained angels unawares.*

Other attributes included:

Angels frequent the lives of those who the Lord would use to fulfill his plan so as to protect them from adversities that might prevent them from doing so. And although angels do not cause violence or catastrophe, they sometimes use it, in order to protect the righteous.

Because of their interaction with humans, unlike other heavenly creatures that exist outside of time, Angels are constrained by the confines of human time. They are immortal but they cannot know the future. Events unfold before them in the same way they do with man. There are rare exceptions to this, but they are, indeed, exceptions.

Angels cannot physically manipulate. They only influence and protect and, when taking human form, speak, but only in accordance with God's will.

It is the nature of Angels to adore the Mother of God. When her presence is near, Angels will appear, as animals are drawn to water and plants are drawn to light.

Because they are not omnipresent, Angels often work in pairs. When doing so, one angel will serve as the primary, the other his second. When in such relationships, they are still able to communicate with each other wherever they are, effectively allowing them to be in two places at once.

By 4 o'clock that afternoon Emily had made her way through much of the book. Her kitchen table was scattered with notes. Looking at the mess, she recalled how, only a couple days earlier, she had chided Martin for not being more digital. *Oh well,* she thought, *I suppose pen and paper are the academic's way of running home to mama.*

Emily's phone rang. It was Terry's ringtone — "Money," by the Beatles.

The best things in life are free
But you can give them to the birds and bees
Give me money, that's what I want
That's what I want, yeah, that's what I want

Terry had moved to Rochester a few years ago, right after the divorce, to take a job with a law firm. A year ago he was made partner. He made almost three times the money Emily did, but, other than child support and a small chunk of alimony,

Emily and Heather saw none of it. What's more, he was always weaseling out of spending time with Heather, always working on a big case, or off on some trip with his latest girlfriend.

Emily picked up the phone. "Hi, Terry, what's up?"

A thin but firm voice on the other end spoke up, "I want to talk about Christmas plans."

"OK."

"I know I was going to take Heather over Christmas, but something's come up."

"What?"

"A big client has asked a few of us to come up to Canada for a working vacation. It's a very lucrative deal and we really have to go."

I'll bet. Emily thought. *Terry and a couple of young associates — the kind with the nice butts — up at some cabin in the Canadian woods, drinking hot rum and pretending to work. Shit! What an asshole.*

"So, when *do* you plan on seeing your daughter?"

"I'll be back for New Year's. How about if she comes up then?"

Emily knew there was no point in arguing or reading him the riot act. All it would do is stress her out. She'd accepted a while ago that she was a single parent and all that went with it. She only hoped that when her daughter got older, she would understand what a turd her dad was. Besides, she had no plans for Christmas anyway. It would be nice having Heather home.

"Let me talk to Heather about it."

"Fine."

Emily then thought about something she'd been wanting to say — something that she was reminded of the night before.

"Hey, before you hang up."

"Yeah?"

"Except for a couple of lunches, you haven't really spent any time with Heather since last summer."

Terry's voice tightened, "I know. Look, I've been really busy —"

"I'm not criticizing you."

The phone was silent.

"I'm not criticizing you, Terry. It's just that Heather's changing."

"I'm listening."

"She's acting remarkably a lot like Sarah ... her attitude ... her thoughts ... the way she looks at things ... even her facial expressions."

More silence.

"I know we swore we'd never do this, but I think we should tell her."

Emily waited. She was expecting a tirade, perhaps even some sort of lawyer saber rattling. Instead the phone was silent.

"Terry?"

There was a long very audible sigh on the other end. The words that came next caught Emily completely off guard: "I just hope she doesn't hate us."

For the first time in quite a while, Emily felt some tenderness for the man. Perhaps he really did care.

"She's not like that, Terry. She's not like you and me. She's like her mom."

There was another long pause. Then finally Terry said, "OK, but just remember, *you're* her mother."

"I'll talk to you later and let you know how it goes ... and about New Year's."

"OK."

The phone went silent.

Emily turned to the big pile of papers. As she stared at them, a shadow moved across the table. Emily looked out the window to see a new silver Honda CRV pull up. It was Katy and Jenny dropping off Heather. She watched as her daughter got out of the car and turned toward the house. Her skin was rosy and she was smiling. She looked like she'd had a good day.

Heather came into the dining room and set her backpack down on one of the chairs. She was wearing her maroon Vassar hoodie under an oversized denim jacket. Emily always liked to see this. She liked the fact that Heather wasn't completely turned off by the idea of going to the school where her mom taught. If she decided to go there, it would be a full ride, tuition free. Something Emily was always selling — but not too hard.

Heather looked at all the papers. "Hey, Mom. Whatcha doin'?"

"I'm working on research for Martin's book."

"*Martin's* book? I thought it was a team effort."

Emily smiled. "It is, officially. But Martin's the one driving the train. The section I was just working on has to do with angels. I was going through an old book in Latin."

"I see. More religion."

"Yes."

"For someone who eschews religion, your time sure is absorbed by it a lot ... paranormal events ... Latin manuscripts."

"*Eschew?* Where'd you learned that word?"

"The Poughkeepsie public school system." Heather smiled.

"Well, it's good to see my tax dollars at work."

"I'm gonna take a shower." Heather started to turn and go.

"Wait a second." Emily hesitated. "I just had a talk with your dad."

Heather's face became steely. "Yeah?"

"He wants to have you come up for New Year's instead of Christmas. He said he has to work."

Heather winced. Tears began forming in her eyes, but she turned before they could go anywhere. "Fine," she said shortly and began to climb the stairs.

"Heather."

"I don't want to talk about it," shouted the pained voice.

A moment later, the door slammed.

Emily let out a long sigh. "Fucking Terry," she said to herself. "Why do I always get stuck cleaning up his shit?"

She then sat down at the table, flipped her laptop around and typed in the words: *St. Hilda Abbey Vermont.*

— Chapter 12 —

St. Hilda Abbey in Northern Vermont — The Present

At the beginning of every Advent, Sister Sarah Ruth Donohue would pray a novena for Heather. As part of the short prayer she would add her own petitions, asking that God guide her sister Emily and give her wisdom and the spirit of truth.

It was nighttime at the Abbey and, after Vespers, Sister Sarah went out into the colonnade around the Abbey's inner courtyard. It was a starlit night with an almost full moon. The light shone brilliantly off the white snow covering the courtyard.

In one of the corners of the courtyard was a shrine to the Blessed Virgin. Sarah approached the statue, crossed herself and knelt.

O Most Blessed Mother, heart of love, heart of mercy, hear my prayer. I implore your intercession with Jesus your Son. Receive with understanding and compassion the petitions I place before you, especially for my sister Emily and her daughter, my child Heather. Give them peace. Surround them with your heavenly angels to protect them.

When she finished the prayer, she crossed herself again and stood.

As she walked back to the chapel, she saw a very tall man standing in the middle of the courtyard. She noticed there were no footprints in the snow anywhere around him. Suddenly there was the sound of a loud crack, like a sail catching wind. His entire outline became that of a giant winged angel. He lifted his face toward the night sky and wind began to blow through his hair. His face became illuminated and he began to sing. He sang a music that Sarah had never heard.

Sarah walked toward him but began to feel weak. She fell onto her knees in the snow. When she looked up he was standing before her as he had he had appeared before — as a man.

"Your sister and child are safe. You shall see them soon."

And then he was gone.

Sarah still felt very weak, but was filled with joy, hanging on the words, *you shall see them soon.* She was going to see Heather.

— Chapter 13 —

On Monday morning, Emily was driving down Spackenkill Road on the way to Heather's school. Her old VW GTI was a noisy thing, but it was good on gas and its heater worked. At a stoplight, Emily turned and looked over at Heather on the passenger side. The outline of her head was illuminated by the sun reflecting off the snow along the roadside. Single strands of blond hair danced above the curve of the top of her head.

"Light."

"What?"

"The light, Mom. It's green." Heather nodded at the stoplight.

"Oh. Sorry." She hit the gas and car moved forward.

Emily spoke up. "I've been thinking, Heather. I know you and your dad were planning on going skiing over Christmas."

"Yeah?"

"Well, I was thinking, how about if we go instead?"

"But you don't ski."

"I know. But maybe you could take a friend. Maybe Katy or Roxanne or someone. You know Martin's family has that cabin in Vermont? Remember we stayed there once? I called him last night and asked if it was available, just to check. If it's not, maybe we could find a hotel somewhere."

"But it's Christmas. Katy's gonna be with her family. And Roxanne doesn't ski."

"Well, maybe Katy could come up the day after. Or maybe somebody else. You have a lot of friends."

"I'll think about it."

"OK."

As they got near Heather's school, as was their arrangement, Emily pulled over to the curb a half a block away. As Heather began getting out of the car, Emily said, "I'm sorry your father flaked out again, but I'd really like to do something special with you over Christmas."

"It's not your fault, Mom. I'll talk to my friends and see."

"OK. I love you."

"Me too, Mom. Bye."

The door shut and Heather joined a small group of down-coated, Ugg-booted girls trudging along the slushy sidewalk and staring into their cell phones.

How do they keep from bumping into each other? wondered Emily.

* * * * *

Even though Emily was now a full professor and had been teaching at Vassar for almost ten years, she never quite got used to being addressed as Dr. Campbell. Every Monday when she went through the doors of Blodgett Hall, she felt like she was donning a mask. *If these kids only knew that I'm just as human as they are,* she would think. *I lust and I masturbate and I spend money that I don't have on stupid stuff. And, despite my academic pedigree, I really don't know anything about anything.*

"Good morning, Dr. Campbell," said a nerdy East Indian boy who was walking along with a gawky girl in an overcoat and a fur hat that made her look like a reject from the Red Army.

"Good morning, Raj," answered Emily. She then chastised herself for having such a bad attitude towards the students. *I hate Mondays,* she thought.

Emily's first class was a lecture course on symbolism — the last lecture of the semester before finals. It was a class of about fifty students, mostly underclassmen, where she did most of the talking. For the class curriculum she borrowed heavily from the 20th century grand poobah of myth, Joseph Campbell. Even though they shared the same last name, there was no relation. Nevertheless, there were times in her career when she had played off of it, letting people think there was. The class was a survey of themes which appeared over and over again, with uncanny similarity, throughout the world's religions, from animistic tribal religions, to the great five religions of Hinduism, Buddhism, Judaism, Christianity, and Islam. She would emphasize how the stories we tell all try to address the same human questions and meet the same human needs.

This particular lecture was about powers that are supposedly intrinsic to physical symbols themselves. In this part of the course, the students were to consider things such as talismans, relics, and certain religious art. It was interesting in that it departed from the philosophical into the realm of physics. Could an object itself contain power? Does the power come from what it represents or does the material itself contain the power? What did the ancients believe? What happens if the object is destroyed or ends up in the wrongs hands?

These kinds of lectures were sometimes unpredictable, because there were no right answers. It was a true open discussion, and it was never certain which direction it would take.

There was a short slideshow at the beginning in which Emily showed pictures of everything from horseshoes and four-leaf clovers to animal parts used in Santería rituals. Also voodoo dolls and the shriveled fingers of saints displayed in glass reliquaries.

Emily spoke of the Kachina in the American Southwest, and the belief that their masks were imbued with special power. She read a story from the New Testament where a cloth St.

Peter used to wipe his face was brought to the infirmed and resulted in their physical healing.

"So what do you think? Can things themselves possess supernatural power?"

As was the case with most morning lectures, there was dead silence. Emily decided to take a different direction.

"What do these objects and the events surrounding them have in common? Anything?"

One hand went up.

"Yes." Emily had to think for a moment. Even at this point in the semester she was still a little fuzzy on some of the names. "It's Tara, correct?"

"Yes," said Tara, a plump blonde with her hair tied back. "Well, other than the obvious, they provide comfort to the believers. I mean, in the absence of teachers or holy writings, the lore that surrounds these objects, gives them — the believers — some kind of faith."

"True. That's good."

Emily then decided to push a bit more, hoping one of the students would say something really stupid that she could jump on. "But what about the objects themselves? It is possible that there really could be some sort of magic that emanates from an inanimate object?"

A male voice answered from the back, "Why not?"

Some heads turned around and Emily craned her neck to see who had spoken. Between the turned heads she could see a face she recognized. It was the face of the young man she'd seen a few days before as she was leaving the building — the man with the green knit cap. He smiled at her and gave a small wave of the hand.

"And you are?"

"Ron Cassiel, Professor."

"I see." His name was vaguely familiar but she was sure she would have remembered meeting him before. "And are you enrolled in this class?"

"No. I'm just sitting in. Professor Wells recommended your lecture."

Dr. Wells was the department chair.

"Did he now?" She smiled back. "So what are your thoughts on this subject, Mr. Cassiel?"

"I was thinking about the physics of what you're describing — like quantum physics. You know, going back to the idea that subatomic particles are just charges of energy ... all matter is really made of ether, when you think about it. Everything is ultimately ethereal. So why couldn't an object have spiritual power? If God can breathe his spirit into a being, he can breathe his spirit into anything, can't he?"

In that class, at that time of day, Emily wasn't used to those types of responses. She searched for an academic's retort but couldn't find a good one. Finally, she answered, "Yes, I suppose he can."

Normally, Emily would have felt a little chagrined for not having challenged the question. But instead she felt relieved — almost happy that the young man had moved the conversation away from the mundane.

She added, "And even though the ancients didn't have the advantage of quantum physics, I'm sure they wouldn't argue, Mr. Cassiel." As the name rolled off her tongue, she suddenly remembered where she'd heard it ... *Cassiel ... the watching angel.*

Emily sensed that Cassiel had more to say. "Is there something else?"

"Well, I just had a thought."

Emily studied the blank faces around the room and grinned. "Imagine that." At this, many of the students rolled their eyes and shuffled in their seats. "That's fine, Mr. Cassiel. We encourage thoughts around here. Please continue."

Cassiel put his hands together in the shape for prayer, then inclined them towards Emily, as if he were giving her a Hindu greeting. "Well, if God breathes his spirit into his creatures, is it possible for us then to breathe something of ourselves into what we create? And, in the case of saints, would then not that holiness be transferred to the creation?"

Emily waited.

Cassiel took his hands apart and rested them on his knees. "For some reason I was thinking of Michelangelo and how he said that God had put the statues into the marble and that it was simply his job to carve them out. Regardless of whether you believe in the supernatural, the effect of such reverence is evident. Don't you think?"

Emily looked up at the clock at the back of the room. She still had twenty minutes to go. She hoped that Cassiel's input would cause a few more hands to go up. "I see your point. Anyone else?" At this a few hands did go up. She nodded at Cassiel in gratitude.

After class, as Emily gathered her materials, Cassiel came forward. "Sorry, if my comment was an intrusion."

Emily looked up at him. "Not at all. We needed some nudging in this class. Monday morning, you know. Everyone is half asleep ... including myself, sometimes.

"So what connection do you have with Dr. Wells?"

"None really. I was actually looking for you. Dr. Wells only informed me that you had a lecture this morning. He said I might be able to catch you afterward. I took the liberty of listening in."

Normally this kind of presumption bothered Emily, but the fellow was so charming, she let it go. "Well, you found me. Here I am."

"I tried catching you last Thursday, during your office hours, but I just missed you. I saw you on the steps as you were leaving, but you looked tired and I was reluctant to bother you."

Emily frowned a bit. "Yes, I remember. What is it I can do for you, Mr. Cassiel?"

"I heard about the project you're working on with Professor Ellis. I was curious whether you needed any help, as in like an intern or something."

"I see. Well, you'd really have to talk to Dr. Ellis. He's in charge of the project. I'm just helping with research. It's funny, I've never seen you around before. Are you a grad student?"

"Well, I am a student, but not in the Anthropology department. My interest is more scientific ... physics. As I indicated by my questions, I think there's a profound connection between science and the supernatural. I thought perhaps you could use someone with such a perspective."

Emily studied him for a moment. He had a handsome face that was strangely like a child's. He had red hair like hers, only his was an odd hue — almost like metal. "Well, as I said," she smiled, "you'll have to talk to Dr. Ellis."

"OK," said Cassiel.

Emily had an appointment at 11 a.m. This gave her an hour to kill. She went to the student union to drop off some flyers for a class she was offering next semester, and ended up in the cafeteria, having coffee. Other than the muted clatter of pans being washed in the kitchen, the place was unusually quiet. It was the week before finals. The students there were hunkered down over laptops. Many empty tables were strewn with cups, trays, and other trash. One weary-looking kid in a black T-shirt with a plastic apron and rubber gloves was slowly picking up trash and throwing it into a large garbage can on wheels.

After getting her coffee, as she was looking for a place to sit, she spied Ron Cassiel in a corner of the room. He smiled at her and motioned for her to come over.

Why not, she thought. *He's probably close to twenty years younger, but he'll at least be easy on the eyes.*

"So we meet again," said Cassiel, rising to greet her.

"Yes," answered Emily with a cautious smile. "When you introduced yourself, I couldn't help but take notice of your last name. I recognize it from the Kabbalah, am I right?"

"Very good. Yes, it appears there," answered Cassiel, as they both sat.

"The watching angel," added Emily.

Cassiel smiled. "Yes. He also appears in the German movie, 'Wings of Desire.' Ever see it?"

Cassiel recited:

"Als das Kind Kind war,
wußte es nicht, daß es Kind war,
alles war ihm beseelt,
und alle Seelen waren eins"

Then in English:

When the child was a child,
it didn't know that it was a child,
everything was soulful,
and all souls were one

Emily raised her eyebrows. "Very good. I'm impressed. You know your foreign films."

"It's one of my favorites."

"Yes, I've seen it. It's very good," said Emily. "Then there was that terrible American remake with Nicolas Cage. 'City of Angels.'"

"Yes," agreed Cassiel. "... except for the beach scene. The beach scene was somewhat accurate."

"Accurate?" asked Emily.

"I mean believable," said Cassiel.

"So, tell me again exactly, what interest does a book about supernatural phenomenon have to a scientist, Mr. Cassiel?"

"Please, just call me Ron."

"Ok ... Ron."

"I think the separation between science and faith is problematic. What today is thought of as science is only logical methodology. Whatever can be proven. Whatever can be tested. Whatever can be deduced. But that's only part of what science is.

"True science, and perhaps science isn't even the right word, is the acknowledgement and appreciation of the whole, not just the parts that can be explained.

"We can understand what forms the clouds and causes the snow to fall. We can understand the geometry of the snow crystal. But we can also give glory to God for its beauty. Why does one have to negate the other?"

Emily looked out the window at the snow on the ground. She recalled her thoughts from a few days earlier ... *Faith is like snow.*

"Likewise," continued Cassiel, "When one encounters a seemingly unexplainable phenomenon, I believe it's fair to consider the physics behind it ... divine healing, the uncorrupted body of a saint, an appearance of the Blessed Mother. We shouldn't be afraid to put scalpel and microscope to such things."

"I see." Emily was starting to have regrets about sitting down with the guy. Cute or not, he was turning out to be a little weird. "So what do you want, Mr. Cassiel? Are you here to influence what I write?"

Cassiel smiled and cast his eyes down to his full cup of coffee. "No. I wouldn't presume."

The two of them sat in silence for a minute. Emily finished her coffee, wiped her lips with her napkin which she then wadded into a ball and stuffed in her cup.

Cassiel turned and looked out the window. As the light changed on his face, he became different in appearance. Emily remembered his earlier reference to Michelangelo. He became like one of those statues that had held the same expression for centuries. She then remembered the man on the bus from Saturday evening; how he similarly reminded her of an old painting. Cassiel then turned back to her and again his face changed, as if coming back into focus. He then spoke slowly, like a grandfather imparting wisdom to a child. "I think faith and science both originate from the same place — it is the part of humans that is of God, that reaches back to Him."

Sensing that the sermon was now over, Emily got up. "This has been a really interesting conversation, Ron, but I'm afraid I've run out of time. I have an appointment with a student at 11 o'clock."

"Of course. I really appreciate you taking the time to speak with me. Let me walk you back."

As they approached the front of Blodgett Hall, Emily asked, "So, I'm curious. What is your religion?"

Cassiel let out a soft warm laugh. "Some other time. You have a meeting to get to. We would need a few more cups of coffee to discuss that one." He nodded toward the building.

"OK," said Emily "Well, the next time you're in the neighborhood, you know where to find me." She then turned and went to the door. When she reached the door she looked back around. Ron Cassiel was nowhere to be seen.

Emily got back to her office and found the red light on her telephone blinking. She punched in the required numbers and played her messages.

"Hi. Professor Campbell? This is Amy Cuthbert. The woman you met last Saturday. I'm sorry to call you at your work. It was the number on the card you gave me. After you and

Professor Ellis left, I got to thinking. There are some other things that have happened that I think you might be interested in. I called Professor Ellis, but he said that he was sick and asked me to call you."

Sick, thought Emily. *Oh dear!*

After the message ended, another came on.

"Hello Dear. It's Marty. Got your message about the cabin. As fate would have it, there's room ... that is if you don't mind sharing it with my sister and her family. I usually take the upstairs and Marie the down. I'm afraid I'm not feeling well. Dunno what it is ... dizzy ... weak. I'm thinking it may be the onset of the flu. Anyway, it doesn't look like I'll be going to Vermont for the holidays, so the upstairs is yours.

"I do have a return favor. I got a call from our Mrs. Cuthbert. She says she has some more information she'd like to share. I told her about my predicament and asked her to call you. Would you be willing to make another trip to town and take some notes for me? No rush. Whenever is convenient. Give me a call when you get a chance. I'll just be lying around. Cheers."

Her 11 o'clock didn't show, and suddenly Emily found herself with another hour and forty-five minutes on her hands. Her next class, a senior-level seminar on the Greeks, began at 1 o'clock. She thought about Amy Cuthbert. She felt bad for the woman, but it wasn't her business. It was really Martin's project. She had just gone along for the ride on Saturday as an excuse to escort Heather into the city.

That being said, she didn't want to leave the woman hanging. She decided to get it over with and picked up the phone.

— Chapter 14 —

Times Square — April 1994

The dark one who enjoys calling himself Hellmann sat at a small table outside a burger joint on Times Square. He looked much as one would expect a devil to look when taking human form — dark, slicked-back hair and a pallid face that bore an expression of indifference. He was dressed in the style of the times with a leather jacket, tight-fitting jeans, and a pair of black ankle boots. He watched as a crew worked on the New Amsterdam Theatre across the street. The place had been bought by the Disney Corporation, which had plans to turn it into a venue for family entertainment. Its renovation would mark the turning point of the transformation of Times Square, from a center for porn theaters, addicts, and prostitutes, to a tourist destination for families, school groups, and foreign visitors.

He took a long drag on his cigarette and noticed the length of the ash at the end. He disposed of the ash by pointing the cigarette toward the ground and tapping the end of the filter.

Onock cautiously approached Hellmann from the sidewalk. He too was dressed in the fashion of the day, with worn-out jeans, a T-shirt and a black jacket. Without looking at Onock, Hellmann motioned with his hand for him to sit down, which he did. Together, the two of them looked like members of a punk band.

Onock spoke first. "Too bad about all this clean-up going on. This place won't be much fun anymore." He then sniggered nervously.

"All things change," said Hellmann. "It had a good run while it lasted." He then turned and asked, "What happened at the house?"

"I couldn't get in ... couldn't even go up the front steps. It's still there."

Hellmann adjusted himself in his seat, sitting up straight and folding his hands together. "I thought that would be the case. Old Bronner was a pretty smart fellow."

"What about the nephew, Peters?" asked Onock. "Is there anything more we can get out of him? Perhaps if we —"

"He's of no further use," Hellmann cut him off. "He has his riches and will soon be on his way. Perhaps in the future we will need him again, but for now he's out of the picture. There is the niece in California ... going to law school. But she's useless, too. I think we're better off focusing on the new owners, particularly Vince, the husband. He's nervous and vulnerable. He has spiritual awareness, but he doesn't trust it. And he's young. His wife is pregnant and has become sexually remote. We need to find some way to get to him."

Hellmann thought for a moment, then a smile came to his lips. "Let's get Mr. Peters to perform one last task for us." Hellmann took a long drag on his cigarette and exhaled slowly. "I believe you're familiar with the lovely young secretary, Miss Stewart?"

The two shared nods and smiles. Hellmann then took a final puff and pitched the cigarette to the sidewalk. He got up and moved off across the street toward the construction.

— Chapter 15 —

April 1994

About a week after having met with Kevin Peters, Vince Cuthbert got a strange call at work. It was Peters' secretary, Dana.

"Hello, Mr. Cuthbert?"

"Yes."

"This is Dana Stewart. I'm Kevin Peters' secretary. We met a week ago."

"Hi." Vince remembered the cute brunette and his heart beat a little faster.

"Mr. Peters wanted me to let you know that, when he and his sister removed his uncle's effects from the house on West 74th Street, that he mistakenly took some fixtures that were part of the property. He apologizes and would like to get them back to you."

Vince could only think of the girl's firm round breasts. "Fixtures? What do you mean?"

"Wall pedestals, corbels ... things like that. They're quite nice and were custom-made for the house."

"I see. Well, OK. Sure. Where are they?"

"They're in a storage unit on Long Island, near Hempstead."

The thought of going out to Hempstead for a few pieces of carved wood seemed a little ridiculous to Vince. But the thought of seeing Dana again was enticing.

He then remembered Amy, his pregnant wife at home, and he hated himself for thinking such a thing. Before meeting Amy he'd had quite a few flings. Old habits do seem to die hard.

"Look, Dana. I'm pretty busy. Perhaps there'll be a weekend when my wife and I can come out and pick them up. We like to frequent some of the antique stores out that way. Maybe we can make a day of it."

There was a pause on the other end.

"Dana?"

"Yes. I'm here. The problem is that Mr. Peters is leaving the country on Thursday and he'll be changing the security code. Today's Tuesday, so there really are only a couple of days."

The wheels in Vince's head started to turn. It was still early. Unlike what he'd told Dana, things were actually fairly slow this week. Amy wouldn't be expecting him home until around 8 o'clock.

"The only time I could possibly do it then would be this afternoon."

"That works for me," Dana piped up. "I'm closing up my boss's office, but the movers are done and the cleaners aren't coming till tomorrow."

"Where did Peters move to so suddenly?"

"I'm not supposed to say. Out of the country. Something very lucrative came up overseas."

The two made arrangements to meet on the ground floor of the Chrysler building. Peters had conveniently left Dana the use of his car as well.

When Vince got there, he found Dana standing by the elevator. She was wearing jeans and a pink sweatshirt with a crop top neckline and cutoff sleeves. She smiled when she saw him. "Are you ready?"

Vince moved closer, reminding himself that this was strictly business. Yet he found his heart pounding again and his face beaming back at the girl like he was some horny high school kid. "This all seems a little weird to me. I still don't understand why this all has to happen so fast. Is Peters on the run or something?"

Dana gave a chuckle. "That's funny. No, it's nothing like that. The move has been planned for a while. It's just that, the other day, he was out in Hempstead with the movers and he realized he'd forgotten about the things ... the fixtures."

"OK." Vince smiled. He realized he was probably never going to get the full story. Peters was an odd one. But he was here now. He might as well go for a ride with Dana.

As the two of them rode the elevator down to the garage, Vince took in all the fine appointments ... wood paneling, mother of pearl buttons. He then looked up to see that the ceiling was a mirror. He could see right down into Dana's cleavage.

"Something interesting up there?" asked Dana.

Vince abruptly looked down.

"It's OK." She smiled.

Peters had left Dana with a black BMW M5 sedan — a nice ride for a guy in a three-piece suit, but a little big for a petite girl in her early twenties. Even though the seat was all the way forward and all the way up, she looked like a child playing in her parents' car. Vince stared at the backs of Dana's hands on the steering wheel. Her skin was smooth and tan. She wore a couple of simple plastic bracelets on each wrist.

"On the way back, I'll drive." offered Vince.

"Fine with me," said Dana.

They drove through the sprawl of Long Island for about forty-five minutes. It was the last week of April and a windy day. Rain was threatening. By the time they reached the storage units, rain was falling.

The place was a concrete building near the water that was built like a bunker. It had been sectioned into units. When they got out of the car the weather suddenly hit hard, the wind ripping into them and a stinging rain peppering their faces.

"I didn't think it would be this cold," shouted Vince over the wind.

"Me neither," responded Dana. "But it's OK. This place is sturdy. Plus there are a couple of space heaters inside."

Dana opened the door, which required both a key and a security code, and the two went inside. It was a large unit, about 25 feet wide and 50 feet long, with a very high, angled ceiling. Once the door was shut, all was quiet, except for the faint sound of the wind outside. The side where the ceiling was highest was lined with a large wooden rack that held dozens of paintings covered by movers' blankets.

In the center of the floor were several statues — mostly nudes, some in erotic poses. There was one of a young woman with large breasts being embraced from behind by a rather fiendish-looking man. It made Vince recall the story of Apollo and Daphne, when Daphne turned into a tree to escape Apollo's clutches, only this woman lacked such powers.

"This unit used to belong to Mr. Peters' uncle. Many of the pieces in here were his. When he died, Mr. Peters decided to store his own collection in here as well."

Dana went over to the rack of paintings and whisked away a couple of the blankets. The paintings at the front of the rack were decidedly erotic. Dana turned around and smiled at Vince. "This is Mr. Peters' porn collection — so to speak. Go ahead and have a look. I'm gonna turn on those heaters."

As Dana went about firing up a couple of large electric floor heaters, Vince took a look at the paintings, flipping through them in the rack like a stack of old vinyl records. The first one that met his eyes was of a man and woman. It seemed to be a recent work. Very realistic, in the style of Alberto Vargas. The woman was on top, straddling the man. Her arms were raised over her head. She had her fingers laced together and looked like she was stretching after having just awoken from a nap.

Vince could hear the heaters buzz as they came to life.

He flipped through more of the paintings. Most were heterosexual couples. Some were groups. As Vince stared at them, he saw the reflection of the orange light from heaters begin to glow on their surfaces. He felt the warmth on his back.

There was one of a bunch of naked girls playfully teasing a man who was wearing a blindfold, whose erect penis protruded out in front of him — a sexually charged version of blind-man's bluff. Dana came up quietly behind Vince. She looked over his shoulder at the painting. "It looks like they're having fun."

Vince quickly let the paintings fall back into the rack. He turned around. "It's quite a collection."

Dana had a large brown folder under her arm. "Here, check these out."

Vince took the folder and opened it. It contained photos of Dana. The first few were of her by herself ... in a pair of men's silk pajamas ... her taking the pajamas off ... lying in bed naked with her legs playfully up in the air. Then there were pictures of her with another woman ... embracing, kissing, then giving each other oral sex.

"It was for a magazine shoot." Dana smiled at Vince. "That's actually how Mr. Peters and I met. He had a stake in the magazine." Dana walked closer to the heaters. Vince noticed that she had spread out the blankets on the floor in front of them. She stood there, warming her hands. Quickly, she moved near the door and flipped the light switch. The room went black except for the light from the space heaters.

Dana's shapely silhouette was outlined by the orange light as she warmed her hands again, this time slipping off her bracelets and putting them in her pockets.

She continued, "The photos were never published. The other girl pulled out ... said she was gonna sue. Peters felt sorry for me and ended up giving me a job."

The light from the heaters reflected off the walls. Vince's eyes adjusted and he could see Dana more clearly. She turned around and put her back to the heat and then removed her sweatshirt. She had only a bra underneath. The top halves of her breasts were perfectly round and, from the light, her skin was a soft peach color.

"Why are you doing this?" asked Vince.

"Mr. Peters likes you. He told me to take care of you." She then quickly removed her pants and moved toward him.

Vince looked over at the statue that reminded him of Daphne and Apollo. He thought for a moment that it would be good if *he* could turn into a tree. He said weakly, "I shouldn't..."

Dana giggled and looked into his eyes, "You're *way* past 'I shouldn't,' mister." She then proceeded to undo his belt buckle.

As he felt Dana's small warm hands reach down into his underwear, Vince looked back at the statue. The heater light made it seem as if the fiendish man were now laughing at him.

After loading the trunk of the car with the few wooden pieces that they had ostensibly come for, Dana went back into the building to turn off the lights and lock up while Vince got into the car and started the engine.

Inside the unit, Dana walked toward the back and asked quietly, "Did you get what you needed?"

From a shadow formed between two large crates, emerged a third shadow. It was Onock, holding a camera, "Oh yes."

Dana handed him the key and told him to lock up when he left.

* * * * *

As Vince drove back toward Manhattan through the dark streets of Long Island, he stared into space as Dana napped. The sex had been tremendous. Dana was an amazing lover and a beautiful woman. But now his thoughts turned to Amy. He couldn't believe what he had just done. What's more, it was well past 8, and she would be wondering where he was.

He reasoned that it was a one-time thing. His libido got the best of him and he'd screwed up. Dana had no real interest in him anyway. He'd make up a story and that would be that. But still, the guilt persisted. He really loved Amy. Life had been good to them both. They were rich and were going be parents. Why did he risk all that?

God! What was I thinking? He scolded himself again.

He looked over at Dana and wondered what the real motive was for all this. It certainly wasn't about corbels and pedestals. What did Peters *really* want? It was something about the house, but he wasn't sure what. He then remembered the icon that he'd asked about.

With his attention on Dana, Vince didn't see the light change. He didn't see the truck coming. One moment he was looking at Dana's youthful, sleeping face. The next, everything was a ball of flame, boiling flesh, and twisted metal.

As the car burned in the intersection, at a distance, looking though the flames, stood Hellmann. On the opposite side of the wreck, Cassiel stared back at him.

— Chapter 16 —

December — The Present

The Saturday following Emily's meeting with Cassiel was sunny and almost warm. Light gleamed off the cars and windows as Emily and Heather walked up Amsterdam Avenue from the subway. Some of the snow had melted and the pavement was wet and slushy. The shop windows displayed their full array of Christmas decor. Many New Yorkers were out shopping, toting large, brightly colored bags.

The plan was to meet again with Amy Cuthbert, to follow-up on whatever new bits of information she had. To Emily's surprise, Heather had asked to come along. She wanted to meet Amy and hear all about what was going on in the house on West 74th Street. When Emily asked Amy if it was OK, she responded that she'd love to meet Emily's daughter.

As they turned onto West 74th, Emily said, "Perhaps we can do a little Christmas shopping when we get done."

"Sounds like a plan," responded Heather.

Emily's phone conversation with Amy had been brief. When Martin had alerted Amy about his illness, he also told her that he would ask Emily to go in his place. When Emily spoke to her, Amy sounded relieved that Emily was coming alone with Heather, which was understandable, since Martin could be a bit of a crust.

When they got to the house, Amy's son Nick answered the door. He looked much more relaxed than he had the previous weekend. He smiled and said, "Oh good, you're here. I'll let Mother know. Come in, come in."

As they entered the house, they were met with the sounds of children. In the front room there were six or seven children making paintings at a little table. They were doing something Emily remembered from Sunday school when she was a child. Using potato halves that had had their ends carved into different shapes to make stamps. There were stars, snowmen, Christmas trees, and angels. The paint-covered children were giggling away in high production mode.

"I thought you were closed on Saturday?" asked Emily.

"During the weeks before Christmas, we stay open on Saturday. It's our Christmas shopping special," Nick explained.

An aproned Amy emerged from the kitchen and added, "It helps bring in a few extra bucks." She then looked at Heather. Her eyes widened and she smiled. "You must be Heather." She wiped her hands on her apron and shook Heather's hand. "I'm Amy."

"It's nice to meet you," Heather said with a smile.

"Come in, come into the kitchen. Nick will watch the children."

At this, Nick went into the front room and sat down. He started chatting with the kids. "OK, how about we use these to make scenes now?"

"What do you mean?" asked an African American boy with a smear of green on his cheek.

"Well, Jerry," said Nick as he reached for a new sheet of paper, "Instead of doing random patterns, let's put the snowman in front of a house."

The three women went to the kitchen, where Amy asked her guests to sit. She put out a plate of cookies and asked if anyone wanted anything to drink. Heather and Emily sat, hesitating.

"I'm gonna have some eggnog and a couple of those peanut butters. If you two want to sit there like ascetics, I won't stop you. I can also make some coffee or tea if you'd like."

"I'll have some eggnog," Heather chirped.

"That's my girl," said Amy.

Emily said that, if it wasn't too much trouble, some tea would be great. Amy promptly filled the kettle and set it on the stove. She then poured two ample glasses of eggnog and went to the table. As she set the glasses down, she remarked, "I wouldn't mind a shot of brandy in mine, but considering all the attention I'm getting, I suppose it might fuel the fire. They'll be saying I'm a chronic alcoholic next. *The religious fanatic puts brandy in her eggnog — the sky is falling.*" She sat down, grabbed a cookie, and grinned.

"And how is that going?" ventured Emily. "I read in the news that things were in limbo."

Amy took a bite of her cookie, savored it a bit, and washed it down with some eggnog. "Eggnog is one of the best things about Christmas," she said as she licked her lips.

She looked at Emily, "To tell you the truth, Emily. I'm about ready to throw in the towel. I'm getting pressure from both sides. They both want me to be some kind of test case. I'm weary of it.

"The hearing, or whatever it is, will be in early January. And whatever they decide, I'm calling it quits."

"Really?" asked Emily.

Amy paused for a moment, looking from Emily to Heather. "The only reason I started the center was to keep this house.

"We used most of the proceeds from the tech sale to buy this place in '93. Vince had just become a principal in a new company, making something in the mid six figures, so money wasn't going to be an issue. But that was a long time ago. Over time, life has eaten away at it. In recent years, I've lived off the equity, renting rooms — then finally, the day care center."

The tea kettle began to whistle. Amy got up and removed it from the stove. While she fixed the tea, Emily asked, "this is none of my business, but I don't understand ... you were a software engineer too, right? Why didn't you go back to work?"

"No, I don't mind you asking. I've often asked myself the same question.

"I've done some freelance work over the years, but it's nothing that's made me rich. The thing about technology is that it's a continual learning curve." She nodded towards the front room, "Nick's a lot more up to speed on things these days than I am."

Amy returned to the table and set down Emily's tea, but remained standing. "Do you take anything?"

Emily shook her head no.

Amy stared out the back window, thinking, then continued, "At first it was because of the pregnancy and then having a baby to take care of. I was alone. I was grieving over Vince. I had people stay with me to help. Things eventually became better. I thought about getting back into the workforce ... perhaps even falling in love again." She cast a thoughtful look toward Heather, "How about you, do you have a boyfriend?"

Heather blushed. "Not right now." She then took a bite of her cookie and big drink of eggnog so as not have to say more.

Amy looked at Emily, then said, "The real reason I've stayed close to home all these years, is because I felt I couldn't leave."

"Excuse me?" asked Emily.

"There's something about this place," said Amy. "I mean, sure, I'll go out of the house sometimes ... to the store, to a restaurant. But the thought of having to be away all day, every day, makes me feel cold ... unprotected ... I can't explain it."

She then turned around, went to a cupboard, and retrieved a bottle of brandy. She poured a generous slosh into her half glass of eggnog and looked at Emily. "To hell with it," she smiled. "Want some?"

Emily hesitated, then nodded and Amy poured a slosh into Emily's tea. She looked at Heather, "Sorry, my dear, but you're gonna have to wait a few years. Don't tell the authorities, OK?"

"Your secret's safe with me." Heather smiled.

"Good girl," said Amy. She then sat down and advised Emily that she might want to take notes.

"After you left, I received a very strange phone call. It came to my house phone, which I hardly ever use anymore. It was the subject matter of that call that prompted me to call Professor Ellis.

"The man said he was an old associate of Kevin Peters. Kevin Peters was the nephew of the man who used to own the house before we did — an old German guy. I think his name was Klaus something. Anyway, the night Vince died, he was driving Peters' car, along with Peters' secretary who was also killed. After the accident, Peters vanished. So I never learned what Vince was doing in that car with that woman out on Long Island. Vince was a very insecure man. You can fill in the blanks.

"They looked for Peters for years, but never found him. His friends and business associates said he'd talked about moving overseas. He had a younger sister on the West Coast. She knew nothing. The family of the woman who died knew nothing. It was all a mystery.

"Then, after over 20 years, out of the blue, I get this call. The guy identified himself as Howard Onock — weird name. Anyway, he said that he'd read about my situation with the city and had some information about the house — that he knew Peters and his uncle and this wasn't the first time such things had occurred in the house.

"Wow," injected Heather. "That must've freaked you out."

"Yes," Amy raised her eyebrows. "Indeed it did."

"He also told me that back in the day, Peters wanted Vince to search for something in *this* house."

"Wow," said Emily.

Amy took a long drink of eggnog. "But that's just the beginning.

"This Onock guy continues and tells me that, because of all this attention I've been getting, there's renewed interest in the object and that I should be on my guard."

"And what is the object?" asked Heather with keen interest.

Amy leaned toward Heather and lowered her voice, "The guy wouldn't tell me. He said it was better if I didn't know ... to protect me. He would only say that it was something hidden here by Peters' uncle. He said that he was still in contact with Peters and that Peters himself would probably be getting in touch with me."

Emily began to wonder whether Martin was right about Amy in the first place. Perhaps she would be a good candidate for his book. She looked down at her note pad and saw that she hadn't written a thing.

"What made you decide to tell *us* all this?" asked Emily.

"Because I want there to be a record. In case something happens. You can think I'm crazy, if you'd like. But I want the story known."

"I don't think you're crazy," said Heather, emphatically.

Amy finished off her eggnog and continued, "Throughout the years I've lived here there have been certain experiences I've had, like the one I told you about before with the girl, but I've never found any mysterious objects. And I've seen every square inch of this place."

"What other experiences?" asked Emily.

"I've seen the girl again, but only twice more," answered Amy. "The second time was when I brought Nick home from the hospital.

"I kept his crib in my bedroom. One day when I was taking a shower, I started hearing singing ... beautiful singing. My bathroom window faces out to the house next door. I assumed it was the neighbor, but when I turned off the shower, I realized that it was coming from inside the house ... from my bedroom.

"I started to freak out. *Someone's after the baby,* I thought. I got out of the shower and, still wet and naked, I ran into the bedroom. And there she was.

"She was wearing the same clothes as before. She smiled at me and said, 'He is beautiful.'

"Realizing I was naked, I quickly grabbed a blanket off the bed. I took my eyes off her for only a second. When I looked back up, she was gone." Amy's eyes went from Emily to Heather and back to Emily, trying to gauge their reaction.

"The last time I saw her was shortly after we opened the day care center. There was this one girl named Olivia. She was a precocious little thing ... good natured, but always testing the rules. One day Olivia decided to play hide and seek without our knowing it. It was late in the afternoon during clean-up time and we couldn't find her. We checked every bathroom and every closet. Let me tell you, we were scared. Every horror story imaginable was running through my head. I started thinking, *what am I going to tell this girl's parents?*

"Finally in my panic, I prayed. I don't remember what exactly ... something simple ... primal. Then I heard someone calling, 'Olivia ... Olivia!' But it wasn't any of the staff. Then I heard a little girl's laugh. It was coming from the kitchen ... right here. I ran out and saw the young lady again ... standing with Olivia ... her hands on the child's shoulders ... the both of them laughing. Olivia runs to me. I looked up and the sun was beaming through the back window and the lady was fading into the light."

"Where was she?" asked Heather.

"She was right there, in front of the back doors."

"I meant Olivia," said Heather. "Where was she hiding?"

"Oh," Amy laughed. "She was in the pantry, behind a bunch of aprons. I'm big into collecting aprons and that's where I hang them. We all have our quirks."

"Is there anything else?" asked Emily, who was now taking notes like a shrink.

Amy waited a minute, then responded, "Are you sure you want to hear more? I think there's probably enough crazy there for Dr. Ellis's book, don't you?"

"That's up to you," said Emily. Then, after a pause, she added, "In the article Martin showed me, you had mentioned something about angels too."

Amy stood up and took a deep breath. Emily was afraid she was going to tell them it was time to go, but instead Amy excused herself and said she had to go ask Nick something. After she'd left the kitchen, Heather turned to her mom, "I hope you and Marty aren't setting her up for something. I think she's nice and I believe her."

"I'm just doing what Martin asked ... gathering information. You're the one who wanted to come along and hear about all this. I agree, she's a nice woman but, really, Heather ... *the Virgin Mary?*"

"Well, I think she saw something. What? Do you think she'd make all this up just to get sued and ridiculed by the media?"

Emily finished off her tea. "Like I said, I'm just gathering information."

Amy returned to the kitchen and shut the door behind her. "Good. Nick said he'd handle things as long as we need. It's a small group this afternoon, anyway. Just four kids left.

"And since he's covering that, I'm gonna have just a taste more."

Amy took the brandy off the counter and poured about three fingers worth into her eggnog. She looked at Emily, "you want?"

Emily hesitated, then nodded, "maybe about half that much." Amy poured three fingers into her empty cup.

Amy continued, "The thing about the angels was really said quite innocently. One day I was singing with the kids. It was actually during Christmas time a year ago. We were singing Deck the Halls. The kids love the *fa-la-la-la-la* part. When the song ended we heard this echo, 'Fa-la-la-la-la, La-la-la-la.'

"We all heard it. The kids thought it was cool. What bothered me was that, in all the times I'd played music or sung in this house, I'd never heard that kind of echo. It was these pure voices — they sounded like some old school English boys choir."

Emily and Heather both nodded.

"Beautiful voices!" added Amy.

"Anyway, that's happened a few times. Always with the kids. I told them it was angels. It just came to mind. But I think I'm right."

Amy took a sip of her brandy. "One of the day care parents actually gave me this brandy. It's very good.

"I have one other little gem for your notebook. Then I think that should do.

"Recently, there has been another unexplained visitor — a very pleasant young man. Very calm, but warning of changes that are coming. And telling me to be cautious.

"He was very tall, probably close to seven feet. And with very smooth skin ... he had a kind of baby face really." Amy sniggered a bit.

At this, the hairs on the back of Emily's neck began to rise. *When they take human form they are all exactly the same height. And they cannot produce beards. They're male in appearance, but with no beards.* She set her pen down and took a sip of brandy.

"He had red curly hair with bright green eyes," added Amy.

A mental picture of Ron Cassiel popped into Emily's mind. She quickly dismissed it.

"Weren't you afraid when a strange man showed up in your house?" asked Heather.

Amy looked to Heather, "He wasn't in the house, dear. He met me one morning out front, near the top of the steps. And I wasn't afraid. I had the feeling that he was there to protect the place.

"He told me to be faithful, be diligent, and watch. He said, 'The time for the Mother of God to be known is at hand.' Then he just disappeared."

Amy took a long drink of brandy and set down the glass. "That's it."

"Wow," said Heather. "I wonder what it means."

Emily sat there leaning over the table, with her chin cradled in one hand, as if waiting for the story to continue. When she realized that wasn't going to happen, she reached for her cup and drained the small amount that was left.

As the three made their way through the front room, Emily noticed that there was only one child left — Jerry, the boy with the green smudge on his cheek. He was helping Nick organize the furniture and put away art supplies. Emily and Heather said their good-byes to Nick and followed Amy to the front door. When the door opened, a blast of cold air hit them.

"Oh shoot, we forgot our coats." said Emily. "I'll go get them."

Emily went back into the front room to retrieve her and Heather's coats. With the kitchen door left open, the afternoon sun was filtering down the hallway and into the room, covering everything with light. As Emily turned to leave, she saw a bright shiny spot on the wall. As she moved closer, she saw that it was pear-shaped, and even closer, she could see faint lines in the shape, but couldn't really make them out.

Just then a small voice spoke up behind her. "You see it."

She turned around to see the boy. She smiled and asked, "I see what?"

"You see the shape," he said. "You see The Lady."

* * * * *

After Emily and Heather left, Nick turned to his mother and asked, "Why do you tell people that story about us being in such dire straits ... having to rent rooms and borrow against the house?"

Amy's eyes widened, "You were listening? You eavesdropped?"

"Yes," answered Nick. "Someone has to watch these people. I wanted to know what kind of information they were digging for."

"We'll I appreciate your concern, but I think I can manage just fine on my own."

Nick shook his head, turned, and said, "C'mon Jerry. Let's finish cleaning up."

"People are more open and honest when they don't know," said Amy. "They're kinder and act more naturally."

Nick stopped and looked at his mother.

"You see, Nicky, I am looking out for myself. I know it's wrong to lie like that. But I just don't like going into it — explaining about the millionaire philanthropist who runs the day care center. I've gone to great lengths to keep my foundation entirely separate from the person of Amy Cuthbert. I want to keep it that way. It's no one's business."

— Chapter 17 —

The Ellis Family Cabin — Vermont — December, the Present

Emily and Heather arrived at the cabin in the late afternoon of Christmas day. Katy and her mom Jenny were due around noon the next day. The plan was to stay until the 29th, then head back home. Heather would leave for Rochester on the morning of New Year's Eve and stay with Terry until the third.

At the time of their arrival, Martin's sister, Marie Robinson, and her two older children, Krista and Chad, were already there. The father, Doug, had to stay in the city for work.

Marie was quite a bit younger than her brother — probably in her mid-fifties. She was small and athletic, with short dark hair, with just a light peppering of gray. And she turned out to be an excellent skier.

Krista and Chad were both in their twenties. Chad was a sophomore in college and Krista worked as a waitress in the theater district in Manhattan. As per the arrangement between Martin and Marie, the Robinsons took the downstairs bedrooms; Emily, Jenny and the girls had the upstairs.

The second floor had two bedrooms. Emily and Jenny took one room; the two girls the other. The walls of each room were paneled from floor to ceiling, with beautiful, honey-colored knotty pine. On either side of each room was a twin bed covered with a patchwork quilt. All was very traditional New England — a great place to spend Christmas.

On the afternoon of Christmas day, Emily and Heather had the place to themselves. The Robinsons all went skiing. Emily told Heather that it would be OK if she went too, but Heather declined, telling her mom that it didn't feel right to leave her by herself on Christmas. She added that she'd just as soon wait until Katy got there to go skiing. This made Emily smile.

After the Robinsons left, Emily gave Heather her Christmas presents, which included pajamas, a couple of gift cards to her favorite retailers, and a frying pan, two sauce pans and a wok, all of which they already had at the house, but which had been used to cook meat. Heather had been complaining for months that she needed a separate set of cook pans that hadn't been tainted by animal blood.

Emily's first present from Heather was a pair of fleece socks (a yearly tradition).

"Sorry for the lack of originality, Mom."

"What do you mean?" smiled Emily. "They're great. I love them."

Her second present was a framed picture of the two of them taken in San Francisco's Chinatown. They'd taken a trip there together about six months after the divorce. Heather was eleven in the picture. It was the time of Chinese New Year and behind them was an explosion of color — lanterns, banners, and people in all kinds of festive regalia.

Heather never knew it, but the trip had a dual purpose. Emily's friend and former mentor Victoria had set up an interview for her at UC Berkeley. At the time, Emily thought a big move might do her good. However, the offer never came.

"That's from when we went to visit your friend Vicky in Berkeley. You always said you liked that picture of us. I had it printed on glossy paper at Office Depot then put it in a frame."

Emily stared at her daughter for a long moment. The news she planned to share with her would change everything. She didn't want that to happen, but she knew it had to. She knew everything would change soon enough anyway. Heather was becoming a woman. However, today was Christmas. It could wait.

Heather furrowed her brow and asked, "What?"

"Nothing," answered Emily. "Thank you. Thank you so much. And Merry Christmas. I love you, Heather."

"I love you too, Mom."

* * * * *

By the last night of their stay, the girls' room was strewn with clothes, luggage, cups, and junk food containers. They would be leaving in the morning, and all would need to get cleaned and packed. But for tonight, there would be one last time for staying up late, gossiping, and doing whatever.

The girls had returned from the slopes an hour earlier. Katy sat on one of the beds with her back against the wall. She had just taken a shower and her dark wet hair spilled over her shoulders like tendrils. She was wearing only an oversized light blue T-shirt and panties. Her legs were propped up, and Heather noticed that her olive complexion was still a light brown.

"You're lucky you don't get all pasty white in the winter." observed Heather.

"It's that Italian blood. My mom's a Regusci — a bunch of wild Sicilians."

"Yeah?"

"Yeah. I'm one of those hot Italian babes — I like to drink, and argue, and have hot sex."

Heather rolled her eyes and grinned. "OK, if you say so. I think I'll take my shower now."

"This place is awesome, Heather," said Katy. "It's too bad we have to leave tomorrow."

As Heather got up to go to the bathroom. There was a knock at the bedroom door.

"Yeah?" asked Heather.

"Honey, it's me," came her mother's voice through the door. "All of us adults are going to go into town for a couple of hours — we're gonna have one last drink at the pub before we leave tomorrow. Will you guys be OK?"

Heather went to the door and opened it. Her mom was standing there all dressed up. Heather smiled back, assured her mother that they would be fine, and then shut the door.

"Woo-hoo! Party!" hissed Katy as she twirled her fist in the air.

Heather gave a smirk, "Yeah, right. *Big* party. Leftover pizza and watching dumb videos."

"*Actually,*" said Katy, "I was thinking we could make ourselves some hot toddies and fire up Uncle Marty's hot tub."

Heather looked at Katy, who was sitting cross-legged now. She could tell Katy wanted to be a little mischievous on her last night at the cabin. "What is a hot toddy, anyway?" she asked.

Katy perked up, "it's tea, with honey and lemon, and whiskey. We have all the ingredients. I checked the kitchen."

The description of the hot toddies reminded Heather of their visit to New York a few days earlier and Amy Cuthbert pouring brandy into her mother's tea. She remembered Amy saying that she was "gonna have to wait a few years."

"C'mon, Heather. Nobody's here. We got at least two whole hours."

Heather shrugged, "OK, whatever."

Heather decided to forego the shower. Katy slipped on a pair of PJ bottoms and the two went down to the kitchen. Before long the kettle was singing and the girls were mixing their drinks, which were about half tea and half whiskey. They clinked cups and said "cheers."

The whiskey stung as it went down Heather's throat. "Damn!" she said, putting her cup down on the counter. "This is strong, Katy."

Katy smiled and took another sip.

The two walked to the living room and snuggled into the couch. A fire crackled in the fireplace.

"They made a fire before they left," said Heather. "That's nice." She took another drink. This time it didn't burn as much. She began to feel warm inside.

"I've never had whiskey before," said Heather. "Only my mom's wine."

Katy looked into the fire and pulled her legs up onto the couch. "My dad drinks it sometimes. He has a decanter full of it for guests. I've tried it. It's nasty when you drink it straight."

"How did you find out about hot toddies?" asked Heather.

"The Internet," answered Katy. The two girls laughed at this.

"So, your mom was all snazzed up. You think she might be doing a little man-hunting down at the pub?" said Katy, while giving Heather a big nudge with her shoulder.

"I don't know," answered Heather with a smile. "I know she looks at online dating sites; I've caught her a couple of times. It's funny how she kind of straightens up when I come in, and switches over to looking at Yahoo or something."

The two laughed again.

"Well, I think it's good," said Katy. "Your mom should date. How long have your parents been divorced?"

Heather quietly thought, then answered, "It's going on four years now."

They both stared into the flames for a long moment then Katy spoke up. "So what about the hot tub?"

"I don't know," said Heather. "I don't know how it works."

"C'mon, Heather. It's not rocket science. Krista was out there late this afternoon. I'm sure it's still nice and hot. Let's go."

Katy took her drink, got up and went to the linen closet in the downstairs hall, where she grabbed a couple of towels.

"What about our swimming suits?" said Heather.

"We're alone. The backside of the cabin faces the hills. No one can see us."

Without further discussion, Katy opened the sliding door and went out on the back porch. Heather got up and followed.

The night was cold and clear, the sky awash with stars. Snow clung to the wooden railing along the back of the porch, and beyond that were bluish-white drifts illuminated by light from the house, and beyond that, the darkness of the hillside.

Katy put her cup and the towels down next to the hot tub, then lifted off the big plastic cover, setting it against the railing. Steam billowed off the water. She found the panel with the buttons, pushed one, and the jets started.

"Like I said, not rocket science."

Katy removed her T-shirt, and her large breasts fell free. She quickly stepped out of her PJ bottoms and panties. Heather studied her friend's body for a moment. She was 15, but already had the hour-glass figure of a woman. Heather was taller, but had yet to fill out. It made her self-conscious.

Katy slowly stepped down into the water and let out a long sigh. "This feels awesome, Heather."

Heather turned her back to Katy and undressed, carefully placing her clothes on one of the wooden Adirondack chairs. She then quickly got in the tub. The hot water felt great, and being naked made it all the better, with the jet bubbles comforting her tired joints and freely probing her body. Finally, she came to rest on the bench along the inside of the tub. She took her cup and had another drink. She began to relax. The whiskey was as soothing as the roiling, hot water.

The two were sitting in the water with their eyes half-closed, basking in the starlight and steam, when the sliding door opened.

The girls turned their heads around in an instant. Chad Robinson was standing there. He was wearing slippers, a pair of jeans, and an unbuttoned flannel shirt over an old New York Mets T-shirt. His wavy light brown hair was disheveled. He looked like he'd just gotten up from a nap.

"What are you two doing out here?" he asked.

"Nothing," snapped Heather. "We thought you went into town with our moms and your sister."

"Naw," said Chad. "They went out for drinks. I'm only 19. No point in going out for drinks when you can't get served. I was asleep. I heard the hot-tub motor go on."

Chad's eyes narrowed, then he smiled. "Besides, I got something I like better than booze."

He walked out to the porch and shut the door behind him. He held up a joint.

"Don't come over here, Chad," said Heather.

"Why?" he asked. "Because you're naked?"

"We thought we were alone," said Katy.

"It's OK," he said. "I'm just gonna sit over here and smoke a bit."

He sat in a chair about ten feet away from the tub, propped his feet on the railing, and lit the joint. He took a big hit, held it, and then exhaled with a hiss. "Besides," he said. "It's dark, I can't see anything anyway."

After taking another hit, he looked over at the two in the water and extended the joint. "You want some?" he asked.

The two girls responded simultaneously, with different answers. Heather, an emphatic "No!"; Katy, "Sure."

"What?" said Heather.

"It's our last night," Katy said. "One little toke won't kill me." She looked up at Chad, who was now standing, and said, "Heather doesn't smoke."

Chad got closer and peered down at the girls. He leaned over and extended the joint to Katy. "I'm trying not to get too close."

To take the joint, Katy had to rise out of the water. In doing so, she exposed her breasts. Chad was staring at Katy with the intensity of a lion. She took a long hit and then handed the joint back.

"That water looks real good," said Chad.

Katy moved back to her seat and exhaled. She looked up at him and then flicked water on his leg. "There's room for three," she said.

"No!" shouted Heather. "No way. I can't believe you, Katy. Chad, if you try to get into this water, I swear to God I will scream."

At this, Chad reached down into the hot tub. He dipped his hands in the water and, smiling, extinguished the joint with the tips of his fingers.

"Settle down," he said. "You two are a little young for my taste anyway." He walked back into the cabin.

"What the hell were you thinking?" asked Heather.

Katy replied defensively, "I just wanted to have some fun." Then she snapped, "You're such a fucking prude, Heather!"

* * * * *

The next morning was cold and gray. After a quick breakfast, the two girls were up in their room, quietly packing their bags. The Robinsons were staying for a few extra days and had already taken off for the slopes. Finally, Heather broke the silence.

"I can't believe you're still pissed at me."

Katy didn't answer immediately. She pawed through her bag, pretending to check that she had everything. Finally she looked up at Heather. "I'm tired of being a little girl, Heather. When are you gonna grow up? When are you gonna learn to have some fun?"

Heather zipped her bag and hoisted it onto her shoulder. Then she walked out of the room.

Downstairs, Heather whisked past her mother and out the front door.

When she got to the car, she flung her bag in the backseat, then climbed into the front and waited. About ten minutes later, Emily came out and opened the door. "Are you OK?"

"I'm fine. Can we just go?"

"Don't you want to say goodbye to Katy and her mom?"

"I already said goodbye."

Emily gave her daughter a concerned look. She was about to say something else, paused, and then said, "OK, well, give me a few minutes, and let me check everything once more."

"Fine."

Just after that, Katy and Jenny made their way out to their car. They were parked nearer the road, so they had to walk past Heather. Without looking at Heather, Katy went straight to the car and got in. Jenny waved at Heather and smiled. Heather responded with a small wave, and watched as Jenny got in the car and started it. The engine zoomed to life with ease.

Finally, Emily came out and got in. She had to try a couple of times before the old VW finally turned over. Then they had to sit a few minutes for it to warm up.

"When are you gonna get a new car?" asked Heather.

"When I can afford it," answered Emily. Heather gave an annoyed hiss.

"What's up with you, anyway? Did you and Katy have a fight?"

"I don't want to talk about it."

"Well, don't take it out on me."
"Can we just go?"

    The two cars followed each other from the cabin out to the highway. Jenny and Katy were in the lead and Emily and Heather drove behind. When they got to the main highway, there was a stop sign before two onramps, one heading north and one heading south. After stopping, Jenny's car turned right, heading south and back to New York. Emily watched as the small SUV headed up the onramp.

    Heather grew impatient and snapped at her mom, "What are you waiting for?"

    Emily hit the gas and turned left, heading north.

"What are you doing, Mom? New York is south!"

"We're taking a detour."

"What? Why? I'm tired. I just want to go home."

"Be quiet and listen," shot back Emily. "Just listen."

— Chapter 18 —

The road north was empty. Everyone was heading south, back to the city — back to civilization. Emily and Heather rode in silence for about five minutes. Finally, Heather asked, "Well?"

Emily took a deep breath and cleared her throat. "How well do you remember Grandma Donohue?"

Heather was a bit thrown by the question, but seemed to calm a bit. "She died when I was a kid. Plus I hardly ever saw her. I don't remember her much at all ... just her face really. And that's probably more from her pictures than anything. She looked like you."

Emily rolled her eyes and pursed her lips. "I know, I know."

"What's this about anyway? Where are we going?"

"What I'm about to tell you is going to be very difficult. I didn't just plan this ski trip to make up for your dad flaking out. I had an ulterior motive."

"OK," Heather responded, then waited in silence.

"My mother, your grandmother, was a bit of a nut. She'd been raised a strict Irish Catholic. Growing up, her life was filled with rules and guilt trips. She was also very proud — always trying to prove that she was better than everyone. She would never ask for help and never admit she was wrong. 'The great working class hero' — 'Neither a borrower nor a lender be.' She was cold and judgmental. To put it bluntly, she was a self-centered bitch.

"That's part of the reason she married your grandfather. He was a successful business man. He traveled the world —"

"Mom, I've heard this stuff before," interrupted Heather. "I know you and grandma couldn't stand each other. I know she squandered Grandpa's fortune. Does this have anything to do with why we're headed the wrong direction on the highway?"

Emily took another breath and exhaled. She studied the road ahead. St. Hilda's was another hundred miles. A hundred miles in the wrong direction. A hundred miles into the hills of northern Vermont in late December. *Why am I doing this?* she thought. And as soon as she had the thought, the words came back, *faith is like snow*. And then she had another thought.

"Heather, do you know that picture I have on my desk at work, of me with your grandmother?"

"Do you mean the one of you with your friend when you were little? Yeah?"

"Do you remember the name of my friend? I think I've told you more than once?"

"Sarah."

"Yes, Sarah. Well, that much is true. Her name is Sarah. Did you ever notice that, in the picture, Sarah and I are wearing the exact same dresses?"

"I didn't really pay much attention to the dresses, Mom. Where are you going with all this?" Heather's voice grew tighter.

"Matching dresses are usually something one buys or makes for their daughters." answered Emily. She let the last sentence sink in.

Heather paused a moment and then turned in her seat towards Emily. "What!? You're saying she's your sister? You had a sister? What!? Is she dead? Did grandma kill her or something? Is that what this is about? Why didn't you ever tell me?"

"Calm down, Heather. Please calm down. This is hard enough as it is."

"My God, Mom. I can't believe this."

Emily continued to drive. Light snow began to fall on the windshield. There was a truck up ahead. She slowed down.

"Well?" demanded Heather.

"I'm waiting for you to calm down," said Emily in her best classroom voice. She hadn't had her daughter's full attention this way for a long time. Suddenly she felt in control. *I can do this*, she thought. *It's right, that I am doing this.*

"I'm calm. I'm upset, but I'm calm," said Heather as she turned back in her seat and faced the road. She then folded her arms to indicate she was waiting.

"OK. Good." Emily continued. "Yes. Sarah is my sister.

"The reason I started out by reminding you about your grandmother is because she's the reason Sarah isn't around. She didn't kill her — although maybe she wanted to — but she sent her away. They had a very big fight and Grandma Donohue sent her away to a school in Europe.

"Sarah had gotten pregnant her senior year in high school. Grandma Donohue sent her to a school in France for unwed mothers called *La Maison Giroud*, where she was to have the baby and then put it up for adoption. There was just enough Catholic left in the old girl that she wouldn't allow Sarah to have an abortion. And she was so proud that she didn't want any of her friends to know. So she made up a story about how Sarah needed to go to this special school because she had a learning disability — which was stupid, because Sarah is brilliant. One reason for her going to France is because she was practically fluent. She'd taken French in school and completed a summer immersion program in Montreal.

"I remember mother bringing home a bunch of brochures one day. She'd gotten them from some priest. She told Sarah to choose one. Besides being in France, *La Maison Giroud* also had a new performing arts center —"

"Mom!"

"What?"

"You're digressing."

"I'm digressing ... yes." Emily paused for a moment. "Well, the thing is, once Sarah had the baby, she refused to give it up. While she was over in France, she was strongly influenced by the religious community there and her conscience got the best of her. She decided she wanted to keep the child and raise her on her own. She was barely 18. She begged mom to be able to keep the baby. But your grandmother only thought of herself — and the shame it would bring. I felt so sad for Sarah."

Emily stopped talking for a moment. There was a passing lane. She went around the truck. Then drove in silence for a few minutes.

"Mom, why didn't you ever tell me any of this? Grandma's been dead a long time. Why didn't you say anything?"

"Because I promised Sarah I wouldn't."

"But why? This doesn't make sense."

Emily took a big breath. *This was it.* This was the moment she'd been dreading and yet wanting for 14 years. "I intervened for Sarah. I was an adult. I could do what I wanted. At the time Sarah got pregnant, your dad and I had just gotten married. We were newlyweds. We'd just gotten our first apartment. We were both going to graduate school together. He was going to get his law degree, and I my Ph.D.

"I told her I would take the baby."

After a long silence, tears began rolling down Heather's cheeks.

"What?" she asked, in a whisper. "What?" she mouthed the word again. The profile of her wet face, ripped by shock, was framed by the steamed up windows of the Volkswagen.

"I'm so sorry. I love you, Heather," said Emily, her own face streaming with tears. "I've always loved you. It was wrong not to tell you sooner."

"This is a nightmare," blubbered Heather.

"No, it's not a nightmare. I love you. Your dad loves you. It was just a mistake not to tell you. We were kids in our twenties. We had decided that we weren't going to have children. We were just going to focus on our careers. Then Sarah got pregnant. We were told not to tell you — by counselors, by grandma, and later by Sarah. It was a confusing time. Then life got in the way."

"What do you mean, 'Life got in the way'?" demanded Heather. "This is my fucking life! WHAT ABOUT MY FUCKING LIFE!"

"I'm sorry," said Emily, who then waited a bit more.

"What I meant was, you were our child then. There was pre-school, then grade school. When were we supposed to tell you?"

"Before now!" cried Heather.

"I'm sorry."

"QUIT SAYING YOU'RE SORRY!"

Emily almost said she was sorry again, but stopped. She saw an exit in the distance that seemed to hold promise. There was a gas-food-lodging sign.

"How about we pull over and stop ... sit down. If you want to turn around and go back to New York, we can."

Emily took the exit and headed down the off ramp.

"Where were we going anyway?" asked Heather.

"We were going to see Sarah."

The two drove up to what was little more than an aggrandized gas station, with a food place off to the side. They both ordered coffees — Emily black and Heather with cream — and sat and waited. Finally Emily spoke.

"Sarah is a nun. She's at an Abbey in northern Vermont, near the Canadian border."

Again she let her words hang. Finally, Heather shook her head and let out a snort of laughter.

"This isn't some sort of weird cruel joke is it? To see how I would react? Like on some reality show or something?"

"I'm afraid not."

"She's a NUN?"

"Yes ... at Saint Hilda of Whitby Abbey."

Heather absently stirred her coffee for a minute and then took a long drink as if it contained something stronger. She looked very hard and long back at Emily. Then Heather seemed to relax. She took a deep breath.

"So what's she like?" asked Heather. "Have you seen her? Have you kept in touch?"

"I've seen her a few times," answered Emily. "Once when your grandma died, and once when your dad and I split up. And then a couple of other times when you were off with your dad. But we've written ... we've written a lot."

"What does she look like?" asked Heather.

"Like you," smiled Emily. "She looks like you."

— Chapter 19 —

St. Hilda Abbey is located about ten miles off Interstate 91 — about five miles, as the crow flies, from the Canadian border. To get there, Emily had to turn west at the town of Newport and then circle back to the southeast.

A short, tree-lined road led up a gentle slope to the Abbey. It was just after 1 o'clock when they arrived. Looking up at the bell tower of the chapel, Emily remarked, "Sarah asked that we come after sext — that's the noon hour of prayer." Emily caught an incredulous look from Heather. She then added with a wry smile, "I've learned a few things over the years.

"It's also Christmastide," she added.

"What's that?" asked Heather.

"Back in the good ol' days, Christmas wasn't just celebrated for one day. It was a twelve-day feast. That's where we get the song, "The Twelve days of Christmas," or Shakespeare's play, "Twelfth Night," which was written to entertain the royal court on the celebration of the twelfth night of Christmas. By my reckoning, today is the fifth day of Christmas. There're still seven days to go.

"We had to wait until the end of Advent to visit. Advent is a fasting season when the nuns are devoted to prayer. During Christmas they're allowed to loosen up a bit ... have visitors ... drink wine."

"How come you know all this but you've never told me before?"

"I didn't think you cared about such things."

"Well, I do care."

They parked the car in a small, round lot, about fifty yards down the hill from the Abbey. The two then walked up a foot path to the main entrance. The snow had stopped and low sunlight was just breaking through on the western horizon.

"I'm scared," said Heather. "I just want it to be yesterday again."

Emily didn't answer. She was out of answers.

At the entrance to the Abbey was a pair of large wooden doors that formed a Gothic arch. When Emily opened the door on the right, a huge gust of warm, scented air blew out on the two visitors. The inside was something like a lobby, with a high, vaulted ceiling. On the wall to the left was a fireplace with a small fire crackling away. To the right was a Christmas tree, colorfully decorated with handmade ornaments: farm animals, shepherds, stars, wise men, angels, and miniature nativity scenes.

Directly in front of them, behind a large desk, sat the receptionist — a short Filipino nun wearing thick glasses and a permanent grin. On either side of the desk were archways, each leading to some other part of the Abbey.

"Good afternoon," said the receptionist. "And Merry Christmas! I'm Sister Julieta."

"Merry Christmas," said Emily. "My name's Emily and this is my daughter Heather. We're here to see Sister Sarah Ruth."

"Oh, yes," the little nun said with a chuckle. "Mother told me you'd be showing up on my watch." She sprang up from behind her desk and went to Emily and took her hands in both of hers, held them for a moment and then said, "Welcome to our Abbey. God bless you." She then did the same to Heather. However, when she looked into Heather's face, she added, "Oh my." She then giggled a bit and indicated for them to follow.

She led them past the Christmas tree, down the hallway to the right. It was dark at first, but then she turned right again and they found themselves in a brightly lit room whose walls were lined with books. Light streamed through a large, recessed window facing the south side of the Abbey. Along the bottom of the window, about two feet from the floor, was a window seat covered with cushions. There were also two wingback chairs on either side of the window, facing the center of the room.

"This is our reading room. I'll let Sister Sarah know you're here." And with that, the little nun was gone.

Emily sat in one of the chairs. Heather sat on the window seat and stared out the window. After a long silence, Heather said, "This is crazy, mom. This is all like a weird dream."

"But not a nightmare anymore?" asked Emily.

"I don't know."

"Would it have been any less weird if I had told you at age four, or eight, or twelve?"

"I don't know," Heather repeated. "I guess I always felt there was something off ... especially with dad. The thought occurred to me more than once that dad wasn't my real father. Just because of the way he's always acted towards me ... sort of awkward and distant. But then he was tall and blonde, and I was tall and blonde."

"And so was your grandfather — my dad."

"And so am I," a third voice interrupted. The two looked up to see a tall nun standing the arched doorway. She wore a traditional black habit, white wimple and black veil.

"Although the blonde part is hidden right now." She added and smiled at Heather. They both just stared at each other, as if looking into some strange mirror. Finally Sarah held out her hands.

Heather hesitated, but then went and embraced Sarah, leaning her head into the thick black cloth of her shoulder. When she raised her face, it was covered with tears. "A part of me was missing," she sobbed. "A part of me was gone ... all this time."

"I know," whispered Sarah as she stroked Heather's hair. "I know. Forgive me."

When Heather had collected herself, Sarah stood her at arm's length. "Let me look at you." Sarah's watery eyes took in her long-lost daughter. "Well, we do both take after the old man, don't we, Em?" Sarah then let go of Heather and went to her sister, embraced her, and said, "It's good to see you."

"It's good to see you too, sis."

The two women took each other in for a moment, then Emily said, "Well, I'm going to take a little walk to the chapter house and have some of that marvelous coffee and cake you ladies leave out for the tourists."

Heather was about to speak, but Emily raised her hand. "It's all right, Heather. I think you two should have some time alone. I'll be back in a while." And with that she smiled, and disappeared through the arch.

Sarah turned to Heather and suggested that they sit down. Heather moved back to the window seat and Sarah said, "Please, sit in one of the chairs. They're much more comfortable." She then took one of the chairs herself, flopped down rather abruptly, stretched out her legs and crossed her ankles. "Ah, that's better."

Heather settled into the opposite chair.

"You've come a long way in the middle of winter. You must be tired. I can run to the chapter house and get you some of that coffee and cake your mom was talking about, or some tea."

"No, that's OK. I'm fine. We stopped and ate on the way up."

Sarah folded her arms and leaned back in the chair. "So, is this as weird for you as it is for me?"

Heather smiled and said, "Yeah, I guess."

Sarah sighed and then said, "We do take after your grandpa Donohue. It's too bad you never got to meet him. I barely remember him myself. I mostly know him from pictures. Your mother and I were only children when he died. I was just a toddler really."

"My *mom*," said Heather with a tone of sarcasm.

Sarah looked Heather in the eyes. "She *is* your mother, Heather. That much is certain. Please don't blame her for this. Blame me, if you wish, but don't blame her. All she did was help. All she did is what I asked her to do."

"Why?"

"Because I wanted you to have a normal life ... with a mom and a dad ... normal experiences ... neighborhood friends, soccer games, Christmas morning ... and not be haunted by the specter of some strange nun locked away in a convent."

"Is that how you see yourself?"

Sarah smiled. "No. But I think that's how the outside world sees us much of the time. And I didn't want you to have to explain me to people. I wanted you to simply live.

"If I was wrong, I'm sorry. I'd just turned 18 when you were born. Your grandmother was clamoring for me to come back to the states and put you up for adoption. Then your mother stepped in."

Heather looked out the window. The clouds had parted and sunlight began to stream in, amplified by the thick, clear panes of glass. The shadows from the sash bars made stripes across the front of Heather's light blue hoodie.

She turned to Sarah and said, "Mom told me about all the grief Grandma D caused you. Why was she so mean?"

"It wasn't meanness for meanness's sake. At least I don't think so. It was pride. Pride run amok.

"Are you familiar with the seven deadly sins?"

"I've heard the expression."

Sarah grinned, "Well, I'm not going go all nunny on you and lecture you about them. You can get my sister the professor to do that. But I will say that pride is the worst of them. It's said it was pride that caused the devil to rebel against God.

"Your grandmother was consumed with pride. She was from a working-class family and was angry about having to do without things. Angered by lack of power and by her anonymity. I don't know what made her become that way exactly, but that's how she was.

"Your grandfather was an older man, of means. His family had made a small fortune during prohibition, by bootlegging liquor from Ireland.

"After your grandfather died, your grandmother lost all that connection. She had dad's money, but she wasn't dad. Without his smarts and level-headedness, she frittered it all away. Her pride consumed her. She became deranged ... longing for her past glory."

"Like Gloria Swanson in 'Sunset Boulevard,'" offered Heather.

"Exactly."

"That's what mom once told me," Heather said, looking pleased.

"But tell me about you, Heather. What do you like to do? What are you good at? Tell me about your friends."

With the mention of friends, Heather thought of Katy and her expression tightened.

"What is it?" asked Sarah.

"It's nothing."

"If something is bothering you, you can tell me. I promise it won't go any further. After all, I'm a cloistered nun. Who am I going to tell?"

Heather hesitated.

"That's OK," said Sarah. "After all, we've just met."

With this, Heather began to tell the story of Katy, the cabin, and the episode with Chad Robinson. She ended it by saying that she felt like she was losing her friend ... that something very vital was shifting ... what little bit of child that was left in her was being eroded away.

"I'm so glad you told me this. I'm so glad you trusted me with this," said Sarah.

"I'm just feeling less and less normal."

"Is that what you want to feel? Normal?" asked Sarah. "What's so great about being normal? Don't you want to be unique? Don't you want to be yourself?"

"But isn't that what you just said you wanted for me? A normal life?"

"I did, didn't I? Well perhaps I was wrong. Seeing you now, I think perhaps I was wrong this whole time."

Sarah gave Heather a long look then said, "Let me ask you a question. What made you put a stop to things with that boy ... Chad Robinson?"

"Because I didn't want to ... I didn't want to be involved in some weird threesome with my best friend and a strange boy."

"Was he attractive? Did you find the situation tempting?"

"Yes. I guess."

"But something stronger in you prevailed."

"Yes."

"That's what you have to follow, Heather ... the something stronger. That's the beginning of becoming who you are. It's not some kind of imposed moral high-mindedness. I know my sister and I know she didn't raise you that way. It's something deeper. It's the voice of God. Trust it."

Heather looked at Sarah then asked, "Why did you become a nun?"

Sarah laughed then sat forward and smiled. "It's because of the shoes." She laughed again, lifted her habit and pointed at the black lace-up boots she wore.

Heather laughed too.

"I'm sorry, dear. It's an old nun joke. We do have them, you know. I couldn't resist."

After settling back in chair, Sarah said, "I'll tell you the story some other time. But know this, I'm at peace. I'm here because I have peace. And the peace I have is indescribable."

Heather nodded. The light outside was getting dim.

Heather spoke, "I have one more question ... I have to ask."

"Who was your father?"

"Yes."

Sarah's face became very still. She looked out the window at the waning light then turned to Heather. "Your father was Chad Robinson."

Heather looked puzzled at first, then understood and nodded.

"Don't be too hard on your friend Katy. All things change. And true friends are hard to come by."

— Chapter 20 —

The chapter house at St. Hilda's was large and comfortable, with cream-colored stucco walls and a high, beamed ceiling. At the east end of the room was a huge fireplace. The south wall, facing the front of the Abbey, had five beautiful, tall, cut-glass windows. The other walls were lined with a four-foot high bookshelf and the area above the shelves was decorated with works of art. In the middle of the room were three long wooden tables, and in front of the fireplace was a large couch flanked on either side by two over-stuffed chairs.

When Emily entered the chapter house, there was a group of three nuns sitting by the fire. There was one very dark-skinned young nun who was at one of the tables speaking with some visitors who were also very dark. They looked to be East Indian. Emily guessed they were family members. And there was one older nun sitting alone at a table drinking coffee and savoring a piece of cake. Emily walked up to her, smiled, and said, "Good afternoon, Sister. I must say, I've been thinking about your Christmas cake all the way up here."

The older nun looked up and smiled. When she did, her face reminded Emily of Sister Wendy Beckett, the famed art historian of the 1990s. However, when she spoke, it wasn't with the delicate, cultured tones of the British nun of the BBC. Rather, it was a very flat mid-western voice that you could imagine yelling out some farmhouse door, *Come and get it!*

"I'm Sister Elizabeth. Call me Sister Lizzie. The cake and coffee are over there next to the far wall," she said waving a big knobby hand in that general direction.

"Thank you," said Emily.

"No problem. Oh, and Merry Christmas. Please come and join me if you have a mind to."

"Thanks," repeated Emily. "I think I will."

A few minutes later Emily returned with a mug of black coffee and a large hunk of red velvet cake with white buttercream frosting, topped with green sprinkles — St. Hilda's Christmas special.

"Load up while you can," smiled Sister Lizzie. "In a week it'll be back to flatbread and spinach soup ... for us, anyway. If you stick around for dinner, we got some beer sent up to us from St. Joseph's. It's the yearly Christmas exchange between us and the monks. We send them honey and jam, and they send us beer. I think we got the better end of that deal, don't you?"

Emily liked her. She was always caught off guard by how different all the sisters were. When she first visited Sarah at the Abbey, she expected all the nuns to be a bunch of reserved prudes. During all her visits she found that to be more the exception than the rule.

"I've seen you here before," continued Lizzie. "You're Sarah's sister. Where is she, anyway?"

Emily took a big bite of cake and washed it down with coffee. "She's talking to my daughter. This is her first visit."

"Oh," said Lizzie. "So does she know now?"

Emily gave Lizzie a long look.

"We all know each other's stories, dear," Lizzie added. "It happens when you're cooped up together."

Emily nodded, "Yeah, I see your point. And, yes, she does know. I told her this morning."

"Oh dear, that must've been rough."

Emily nodded again, "It was."

"Please excuse me if I'm butting in. Sorry. I don't get a chance to visit much, so I tend to run on at the mouth. Ya can take the girl out of Kansas, but ya can't take the Kansas out of the girl."

Emily and Lizzie both returned to their cake and coffee.

As Emily looked around, she noticed that most of the wall art were framed prints of well-known works. Her eyes landed on one in particular. It was of a mosaic from an old Church in Ravenna, Italy. "Christ Enthroned." On either side of the glorified Christ figure were two angels. Looking at the angels, Emily couldn't help but note that they were all exactly the same height.

"I see you admiring our art collection," said Lizzie. "All these prints came to us from Monsignor Shaw. He comes over from Burlington on the second Sunday of each month to say Mass. He's a big traveler. He loves Europe. He got most of these on trips he's taken. He buys posters at museums and churches and then gets them framed for us. Nice guy."

"They're very beautiful," said Emily. "I recognize some of them."

Lizzie nodded past Emily. "That one right behind you is one of my favorites."

Emily turned around to see a checkerboard of images on a dark red background. The title at the top read: "*Le Miracle icônes de Notre-Dame* (The Miracle Working Icons of Our Lady)." Each of the images was a different representation of the Virgin Mary, some where she was holding the baby Jesus, others where she was in prayer. In a couple, she was surrounded by angels, in another, the heavens, and in one she stood in front of a deep blue, white-capped sea.

As Emily studied the pictures, she recognized a few — Our Lady of Guadalupe, Our Lady of Perpetual Help — but many of them she did not. "That print is very interesting."

"He got that one at Lourdes. There was a seminar being held there on the miracles of Our Lady where they discussed all the miracles that have happened through the centuries ... the appearances to St. Bernadette and Juan Diego ... Our Lady of Fatima. One of the topics was miracle-working icons. Each of the images on that poster has a story behind it."

Sister Lizzie got up. "Let's take a closer look."

Emily got up, took her mug of coffee and followed Lizzie to the wall. When she got close to the poster she could see that there was a short description under each icon. She began reading aloud the one in the upper left for Our Lady of Kazan, *"L'icône de Notre-Dame de Kazan a été découvert en 1579 dans Kazanskaya en Russie. Selon la tradition, l'emplacement de l'icône a été révélé par la Vierge Marie à une jeune fille."* *

* The icon of Our Lady of Kazan was discovered in 1579 in Kazanskaya in Russia. According to tradition, the location of the icon was revealed by the Virgin Mary to a young girl.

"Ah, *vôtre français est très bon!*" Lizzie complimented Emily on her French. She had an odd accent Emily couldn't make out.

Emily quickly looked up, thinking to herself *these nuns never cease to surprise me.* "*Comme le vôtre. Où avez-vous appris?*" she replied, asking Sister Lizzie where she learned to speak French.

"Missionary work in Haiti for nine years before coming here," smiled Lizzie.

Turning her attention back to the poster, Lizzie rattled off a brief history of all of the images.

"Our Lady of Kazan was credited for protecting Russia from attacks by the Poles, the Swedes, and Napoleon. The icon was stolen in 1904. Many believed the Russian Revolution would have been averted, had the icon been left alone.

"Our Lady Stella Maris ... the Star of the Sea." said Lizzie indicating the Virgin in front of the white-capped sea. "Credited with protecting sailors.

"Our lady of Guadalupe ... I'm sure you know that story ... how she appeared to Juan Diego, a native peasant in Mexico.

"Our Lady of Czestochowa — interesting story. The original icon was thought to be painted by Saint Luke. It came to Poland in the 1300s. It's credited with staving off the invasion of the Swedes. I guess you gotta watch out for those Swedes.

"You see those two marks on her cheek? The tradition is that someone once tried to destroy the icon. They struck it twice with their sword. On the third attempt the fellow died.

"Our Lady of the Sign of Novgorod — another battle story. Apparently the icon saved the city of Novgorod from some kind of attack.

"Our Lady of the Gate of Dawn. One of my favorites." Here the icon was of the Virgin against a background of the stars and moon. "She looks so peaceful. She's supposed to have survived fire twice. She also survived communism. She has her own shrine in Lithuania.

"Our Lady of Perpetual Help — sort of the quintessential Catholic icon. The tradition is that the icon was taken by a merchant who set sail from Crete. During the voyage there was a great storm and the boat was sinking. The merchant venerated the icon and prayed to the Virgin for help, and the boat was brought safely to the Italian coast.

"Our Lady of Trojerucica, also known as our Lady of the Three Hands. You see the third hand there?"

Emily looked, and below the right hand of the Virgin Mary holding the Christ child was a third hand, made of silver.

"The story is that the iconographer, St. John of Damascus, had his hand cut off by iconoclasts and prayed in front of an icon of the Virgin for its restoration. In the morning he awoke and his hand was restored. In gratitude, he fashioned that hand you see out of silver and affixed it to the icon."

"What about the last one?" asked Emily.

The last icon on the poster was a depiction of the nativity. It showed the Virgin Mary seated with the Christ child. Over her head were seven stars and coming from within each star was an angel, shown from the waist up, as if they were looking from an open window.

As Emily studied the faces of the angels, she was suddenly struck. One of the angels looked exactly like Ron Cassiel, right down to the amber curls, green eyes, and the dimple on his chin.

"Is something wrong, dear?" asked Sister Lizzie.

Emily quickly wiped the look of shock off her face. "No, no. I'm fine."

Lizzie took the last swig of her coffee and nodded again to the poster.

"That last icon is the lost icon of St. John the Divine, also known as Our Lady of Faith, also known as Our Lady of the Angels, because of the seven archangels surrounding her.

"Just like the icon of Czestochowa was painted by St. Luke, this one's rumored to have been painted by the Apostle John himself. As you probably know, at our Lord's death, Jesus entrusted the care of his mother to his disciple John. At some point, St. John took the Holy Mother to live with him in Ephesus. According to tradition, that's where this came from. Of course, this is a reproduction — from somewhere in Greece I think." Lizzie bent forward and peered at the French description. "Hmm ... doesn't really say."

"And what are the miracles associated with it?" asked Emily.

"It's the faith-producing icon. It's credited with mass conversions. As missionaries brought Christianity from Greece into the Slavic lands, it's said that on seeing the icon, people were so overcome with a sense of peace that they welcomed the Lord into their hearts ... that whole tribes would recognize in the image that which they had always hoped for. They abandoned their sacrifice, warring, and pagan brutality, and embraced peace ... a much nicer story than her helping win a battle against the Swedes, don't you think?"

Emily nodded. "And what became of it?"

"No one's sure. The speculation is that she was hidden from the Turks, probably in some forgotten cave somewhere. Who knows? Just like the lost Ark, huh? There's a book from the seminar if you'd like to read it."

At this, Sister Lizzie went to a bookshelf about ten feet away and grabbed a book with a comb binding and light blue cover. She came back and handed to Emily. The cover was written in French. Translated, it read:

```
Seminar on the Miracles of Our Lady
          Lourdes, France
          September, 2004
```

Emily thought of Martin and his quest for phenomena. *He would enjoy this.*

"Thank you. It looks interesting, but I'm going to be taking off shortly."

"Oh, take it with you, if you want. We have a few copies."

Emily looked at the book in her hands. She flipped through the pages. She stopped on a page with a large photograph of the appearance of Our Lady of Zeitoun in Egypt. In the picture a glowing figure of the Virgin appeared over the dome of St. Mary's Coptic Church in Cairo.

"What do you think of all this, Sister?" asked Emily, indicting the picture. "Do you really believe it?"

"I don't necessarily believe in every instance, but I do believe these things happen," answered Sister Lizzie with a smile. "My faith is what keeps me whole, dear. Without it everything is empty and uncertain."

The two women went back to their seats. Emily continued quietly thumbing through the book, when suddenly there was some hubbub over by the fireplace. Emily looked up to see the three nuns that were previously seated standing on their feet.

They were all smiling and tittering, and pointing toward the door, as if the Pope himself had just entered the room.

Emily turned around to see her sister and daughter standing together at the public entrance of the chapter house. The three fireplace nuns quickly made their way over to the two and began introducing themselves, and fawning over Heather.

Emily looked back at Lizzie who said, "Like I said, we all know each other's stories."

After leaving St. Hilda's, Emily and Heather rode in silence for quite some time. Finally, Heather spoke up, "When we went into that place, I really didn't expect her to be that way."

"What way?" asked Emily.

"She's cool."

"Yes she is," agreed Emily.

* * * * *

That night Emily and Heather stayed in a hotel along Interstate 91 — a non-smoking room with two queen beds and cable TV. As Heather flipped through the channels, she came upon the movie "Sunset Boulevard," right at the scene where Norma Desmond, played by Gloria Swanson, comes floating down the staircase for her big scene. "I'm ready for my close-up, Mr. DeMille."

"I was just talking about Gloria Swanson with Sarah," observed Heather. "That's a weird coincidence."

"Perhaps it's not a coincidence" said Emily. "Perhaps it's a sign."

Heather continued to stare at the TV, then added, "You know, from what you and Sarah told me, I don't think it was pride that consumed Grandma. I think it was fear."

"Really?" said Emily. "Fear of what?"

"Fear of what she couldn't control. Fear of what she couldn't understand."

Part III
The Voyage of
A Estrela do Mar

In what torn ship soever I embark,
That ship shall be my emblem of Thy ark

— *John Donne, A Hymn to Christ* —

— Chapter 21 —

Devon, England, 1941 — Teatime

The two angels sat on a large veranda overlooking Torbay. It was a warm spring afternoon, and the sun sparkled brightly on the water and reflected off the colorful rooftops along Torbay Road. Mrs. Green, a kindly old widow, had just set out tea for the two and taken her leave.

Both wore wool trousers, dress shirts, and ties. It being a warm afternoon, they had placed their jackets over the backs of their chairs. Cassiel wore a green tie with narrow brown stripes; Raphael's tie was black with bright blue diamonds that matched his cobalt blue eyes and thick black hair.

"I like the tea this woman makes, and I like the view here," said Cassiel. "I hope you agree."

"Mrs. *Green*," said Raphael with a grin.

"She's a very devout woman ... belongs to the parish of The Assumption. She has a hard time seeing. I help her from time to time."

"Which includes the making of the tea, I imagine."

Cassiel smiled.

After adding some milk and sugar and stirring his tea, Raphael took a sip. "Yes, this is excellent."

There was a book on the table. Raphael picked it up and looked at the green embossed leather cover. The title in the center read "*Habitibus Angelos.*"

"I can't believe you put all this into a book. You're getting too directly involved."

"I want to ensure that it is safe," Cassiel said.

"When did you say the monks gave the icon to the man ... Klaus?" asked Raphael.

"Yes, his name is Klaus," answered Cassiel. "He received the icon two days ago. He is leaving with it now. As we speak he is on his way back into the dark country."

Raphael took another sip of tea and smiled. "Hmm, the English *do* know their tea."

"I believe this is something I am supposed to do," said Cassiel with a tone of urgency.

"And how will educating this Klaus about us help protect the image of Our Lady?"

"The humans of this age are befuddled by darkness. If Klaus knows we are with him, he will believe in his mission and will know he is safe."

Raphael looked out to the water again. "This whole thing is troubling. Why now, during these dark and dangerous times?"

"That's exactly why," answered Cassiel. "You know the power it has — power we helped give it. It needs to be seen safely to its end purpose. It cannot fall into the wrong hands."

Raphael shook his head. "I'm still uncertain we should be so directly involved. It is, after all, a human undertaking."

"The man has been surrounded by much prayer from the monks, but I believe he still could use our help." Cassiel took a long drink of tea. He thought a moment, then added. "I recall the story of this fellow named Tobit, when you yourself got quite involved."

Raphael pursed his lips, then nodded and said, "Point taken." He finished his tea and set down the cup. "All right. I will help you as you once helped me."

"Good," said Cassiel.

Raphael looked at the book again. "The pattern of the cover is in Angelic. Why?"

"Just whimsy, I suppose." answered Cassiel. "Those poems are some of my favorites."

"I see," said Raphael who then laughed. "I can't believe you wrote about the nipples."

"I was being thorough," Cassiel replied, with a chuckle.

"And why did you make it look old?" asked Raphael.

"The same reason I wrote it in Latin. The humans of this age expect it. An old, yellowed, leather-bound book written in Latin is more credible."

"I see ... Humans."

The two shared a chuckle at mankind's expense.

With this, Cassiel stood up and put on his jacket. He took the book off the table and looked to the east, to the land where the clouds had gathered and the sky was dark. Then he was gone.

— Chapter 22 —

German floatplane over the Adriatic Sea — 1941

Klaus was thankful for the din of the plane's motors as they flew over the shining Adriatic. It meant he didn't have to talk to anyone. The plane would take them to Venice, where they were to board a train for Berlin. As soon as they were on the train, he and his colleagues would have their own compartment, where they could talk about art and academics. Until then they had to endure the hovering presence of the Nazis.

On the return trip from Greece there was another officer who had joined the group. He was a tall man with a boyish face who, at the same time, wore an expression of someone who had seen a great deal — someone who could not be shocked by anything. He had dark, deep-set eyes, slicked-back black hair and a long upper lip. He frighteningly reminded Klaus of Hitler's propaganda minister, Joseph Goebbels, although he was younger, and much more handsome.

The man caught Klaus looking at him and smiled — a smile that unnerved Klaus, causing him to quickly turn his attention back out the window to the silvery Adriatic.

In Venice a boat came out to the plane to retrieve its passengers. The young, dark-eyed officer made it a point to take the seat on the boat next to Klaus. As he did, Klaus's colleagues watched cautiously.

"I am *Hauptmann* Hellmann," the man introduced himself. "I work for the *Einsatzstab Reichsleiter Rosenberg*. We are very interested in learning about your findings from your trip to Greece. I hope that you have all done a thorough job."

The *Einsatzstab Reichsleiter Rosenberg*, or ERR, was Nazi Germany's de facto ministry for the looting of precious art. For well over a year it had been officially sanctioned to take art, antiques, and other "items of cultural interest" from museums, churches, and private homes in all the occupied territories. Prior to that, ever since Hitler came to power, the Nazis had been doing the same unofficially. Even within Germany, the Nazis had confiscated thousands of works of modern art — what they called "degenerate art," claiming that viewing such works perverted the mind.

Klaus assured Hellmann that everything had been very well cataloged.

"Very good, very good. Even *Reichsmarschall* Goering is interested in your report. He has a keen interest in art." The young officer smiled again. In the light of the outdoors, Klaus could see that the irises of his eyes were a moldy gray color.

Klaus had indeed heard of Goering's interest in art. It was more of a mad obsession, really. He was known especially for pillaging wealthy homes in foreign cities and taking works for his own collection.

Once ashore, Klaus and his colleagues were taken to a small military building near the port. Even though they had been accompanied by German officers on their trip, each member of Klaus's team was to be questioned privately about the team's movements since they left Germany.

Klaus was told to go first. He was taken into a small room where he was seated at a table across from Hellmann.

"You may go, *Soldat*," said Hellmann. At this, the soldier who escorted Klaus in left the room.

Klaus studied Hellmann's unusual face again ... childlike yet almost sinister. It was a disconcerting combination. He was certain he was being singled out for some reason. Then he had a thought: *The icon!* Perhaps they found the icon in his luggage.

Klaus was nervous, but felt he could explain his way out of it. *It was just a souvenir, something the monks gave him as a gesture of friendship. He didn't realize it was wrong to take it. Certainly the government could have it.*

Hellmann held a lit cigarette in his hand whose ash had grown quite long. On noticing it, he extended it over the floor, pointed it down, and tapped it on its end. He then put it back up to his thin lips and inhaled. As he let out the smoke, he asked Klaus if he wanted one.

"No, thank you," answered Klaus.

In front of Hellmann was a large ledger. He closed it and moved it aside. "I apologize if I seemed a bit intrusive earlier on. It's expected of us to give the impression that we are always on the watch. It's really not like me to be that way.

"This is just a minor formality. We need to check everyone as they leave and enter Germany."

"I thought we were in Italy," Klaus said, trying for a modest joke.

"Hmm" Hellmann smiled. "Everything is Germany, my friend. Or will be soon enough.

"We have an interest in a few particular pieces we think may have been at the monasteries you visited. We will, of course, go through all of your photos and lists, but we were thinking we could perhaps save time if you or one of your colleagues could identify these pieces."

Hellmann reached down into a briefcase on the floor and pulled out an accordion folder. He undid the band, reached in and took out a small stack of drawings.

"I'd like to know, Professor Bronner, whether you saw any of these pieces while you were at the monastery."

He handed Klaus several pencil sketches.

"We're looking for famous works that we think may be in one of the Athos monasteries. Rublev ... El Greco ... those sorts of things."

"So you can have them for the Fuhrer's collection?" asked Klaus as he took the papers.

Hellmann ignored the question.

Klaus looked at the drawings. He recognized the first two pieces but hadn't seen them. When he got to the third, he was stunned. It was the icon of "The Lady."

Hellmann took note of Klaus's reaction. He seemed angry, excited, and a little afraid, all at the same time. "You've seen this?"

Klaus wasn't sure what to say. It was obvious that Hellmann had noted his reaction.

"I may have. It looks familiar," said Klaus, placing the drawings on the table.

"I have to warn you, Herr Bronner, it is not advisable to withhold information."

Suddenly, there was some commotion outside the room. The door opened and a couple of soldiers quickly came in. A tall man in an Italian colonel's uniform rushed in behind them. At this, Klaus stood up.

One of the soldiers lunged toward Klaus, but then went to his side, and moved behind the table. "What is this? He was just there! Where is he?" demanded one of the soldiers, with a look of astonishment.

The tall Italian brushed past the other soldier and looked around the room.

Klaus turned and saw that Hellmann was gone. He had vanished. There was no back door. He had just vanished.

The Italian told the two soldiers to leave the room. The first soldier protested, "I saw him! I saw him for a moment and now he's gone. How did he vanish? What is this? What is this magic!?"

The Italian noticed the drawing of "The Lady" on the table. He repeated the order for the soldiers to leave.

Once they were gone, the Italian turned to Klaus and smiled. Klaus was struck that he, like Hellmann, had a child's face, only the Italian had no trace of guile. His eyes were a pure green, his copper-colored curls poked out from under the rim of his hat, framing a face of absolute strength and certainty. His face was also strangely familiar.

The Italian waited a moment and then spoke, "There is no *Hauptmann* Hellmann, Klaus. The man you have been speaking to is an imposter." The Italian had just spoken to the soldiers in rough German with a thick accent. Now he spoke to Klaus with perfect diction and no accent at all.

"What is this?" demanded Klaus. "Who was that man? How did he disappear?"

"He wasn't a man at all." The Italian picked up the drawing of "The Lady" and held it up. "Do you know what this is?"

Klaus shook his head no. He wasn't sure what to think. He intuitively felt that this man was trustworthy, but he was frightened. Ever since the icon had come into his possession, he had felt a weight. He knew it was powerful. He could sense it when he looked at it, but now he realized it was also being sought after. And that his life might be in danger.

"It's an icon. A very powerful icon," Klaus said.

"Yes," said the Italian approvingly. "And you have it in your possession. I know this because I watched the monks give it to you."

"What is this?" Klaus asked again. "You weren't with us in Greece. Who are you?"

"My name is Cassiel." At this Cassiel removed his hat. Upon doing so, his hair began to grow. His curls grew over his ears and down around his neck. His face took on a supernatural glow. His green eyes became very large as he stared down at Klaus.

Klaus noticed the room becoming warmer. The walls became lighter as if reflecting the light from a fire. Yet there was no fire. The light was coming from the being standing before him.

"I am an angel."

Klaus didn't know what to think. He tried to force a smile, but his lips wouldn't move. He knew deep inside that this was no joke. And whatever this person was, he was very powerful.

"What do you want?" stammered Klaus. "Do you want the icon? It's in my luggage. My bags are in the room out there, if the Nazis haven't taken it."

"Your luggage is safe."

Klaus suddenly noticed that he was shaking. His legs felt as if they were going to buckle.

"Don't be afraid, Klaus. Please, sit down," Cassiel said, indicating the chair. "We haven't much time. The Nazi soldiers are slow but they will soon wonder what we are doing in here."

Klaus sat down.

"I cannot take the icon from you. It is a human creation and therefore humans must care for it. If the one posing as *Hauptmann* Hellmann had found out that you have it, as I'm sure he now strongly suspects, he could have only instructed the Nazis to take it from you. But that would have been tragic.

"The icon you have is very important. It is known to us as The Faith Icon, or *that which produces faith*. It's something the dark ones would rather remain hidden — or better yet, destroyed.

"But I will tell you more about that later. For now, you need to leave Germany — leave the continent, in fact. And you need to take the icon with you."

"Leave Germany?" Klaus asked incredulously, "But my work? And my family? I have a sister in Austria."

"Stefanie will be safe at her school. You can send for her at the end of her term. Now we must go."

"Now?" asked Klaus.

"It is the perfect time. You are already packed." Cassiel smiled. He put his hat back on and then said in his rough-accented German, "*Wachen*, come in here now!"

The two Germans soldiers clodded back into the room and half-heartedly stood at attention.

"What? You stand at attention that way because I am Italian?" snapped Cassiel. "I will have you know that I am very good friends with your General Friedrich. I am with the port authority here and, even though I am not German, I can make your lives quite miserable, trust me."

The two snapped to attention. "Very sorry, sir," they muttered simultaneously.

"That's better," smiled Cassiel. "The man who was here before, *Hauptmann* Hellmann, was impersonating a German officer. I believe he may have subversive motives. I wish to retain Dr. Bronner a little longer to try and determine what the imposter was after. I will be taking him to my office. He will catch a later train to Germany."

After explaining the situation to his colleagues and assuring them that everything was OK, Klaus left with Cassiel. But rather than heading to the port offices, they headed to the docks.

As the TL37 light utility truck rumbled along the cobblestoned waterfront, Klaus looked over at Cassiel. He noticed again how his face was like a boy's. The incident at the German military post had happened so fast, and seemed unreal. Now he was able to study the creature sitting beside him.

He was muscled in the same way as a man, but his skin was like that of a child. He had no trace of a beard. And, like his green eyes, his hair was a color Klaus had never seen before, not red, not brown. It was almost like shining metal.

Adding to his boyish appearance, he seemed to be quite amused driving the big Italian military truck — like it was some new toy.

"We are different from you," said Cassiel. "But we are also much the same."

Klaus turned his attention to the road. They were turning in the direction of a series of piers.

"We are not gods. We don't know all things. And we can't make humans do our will. We can only influence."

"Really?" said Klaus.

"Yes. Take, for instance, the shepherds at the birth of Christ. We told them about the birth, but they chose to go themselves. No one made them go into Bethlehem."

"Interesting," said Klaus. "Like the Annunciation."

"Yes!" answered Cassiel. "'Behold, I am the handmaid of the Lord; be it unto me according to thy word.' The Virgin acted by her own will."

They rode in silence for a while. Finally, Cassiel slowed down and turned on to a pier. Docked at the pier was a merchant ship, *A Estrela do Mar* (The Star of The Sea), whose home port was Lisbon.

Cassiel brought the truck to a stop and turned to Klaus, "But, we are *very good* at influencing.

"This is your ship. They are expecting a Dr. Klaus Bronner. You will stop in Lisbon and then head across the Atlantic to New York. Do not get off the boat in Lisbon. Keep a low profile. Do not share unnecessary information. Here. I brought you some books to read." Cassiel reached behind the seat, retrieving a leather satchel, and handed it to Klaus.

Cassiel quickly got out and walked toward some men who were standing next to the ship's gangway, about a hundred feet away. They recognized him. He approached and addressed them in Portuguese. As he continued speaking, he indicated Klaus. Feeling conspicuous, Klaus looked down and opened the satchel.

There were several heavy volumes, including a Latin-German dictionary, a Portuguese-German dictionary, an English-German dictionary, and, curiously, a Polish-German dictionary. There was one very old book that had a green embossed leather cover. The pattern was intricate. It was similar to the interlocking patterns of the Celts or Vikings, but much more complex — and much more elegant. He opened the book. It was in Latin. "*Habitibus Angelos.*" Lastly, there was also a copy of the Bible, and some documents held together in a thick binder. There was also a flashlight.

"The material in the binder will explain a lot," said Cassiel as he approached the truck. "You're all set. You are assuming the identity of one Klaus Bronner, MD — a physician from Frankfurt who was connected with the Nazi Party. In the last year or so he had taken possession of several valuable works of art."

On hearing this, Klaus looked up, rather surprised.

"What, did you think you were the only Klaus Bronner in Germany? The Klaus Bronner whose identity you are using died two days ago in a bombing raid. And since your specialty is art history, who better to assume the care of his art collection?"

"How convenient," said Klaus with a tone of suspicion.

"A coincidence we are taking advantage of. Something else we angels are good at. Another coincidence is that the visa you were given for your trip to Athos is unrestricted and still valid. If anyone asks to see it, it should suffice nicely. We cannot see the future, but we are very good at understanding signs that are full of portent. When you get to New York, I will come to you again.

"Oh, speaking of New York, I have one other book for you, I just got this," said Cassiel as he reached into his coat pocket. He then produced a copy of the "1940 Spalding-Reach Official Guide to Baseball."

"In addition to the English dictionary, this will help you adjust to your new life. Being able to talk baseball with the Americans will come in handy. I myself find the game quite enjoyable."

Klaus took the book and got out. He still didn't believe what was happening. However, he couldn't go back. By now the Germans at the post in Venice had reported the incident and a thousand questions were circling about Hellmann and the unnamed Italian officer. Were he to go back to the train station, he'd be questioned and the icon would be discovered and end up in the hands of the Nazis.

As Cassiel helped Klaus with his bags, he paused and looked Klaus in the eye. Again, he looked like a boy — almost timid this time. "May I see her?" he asked.

At first Klaus was perplexed. Then he remembered the whole point of the venture. He opened one of the bags and reached down. He pulled out something the size of a large book, wrapped in brown paper. He unwrapped the icon and gave it to the angel, who took it in his hands like a poor child receiving a gift on Christmas morning.

"The handmaid of the Lord!" said the angel. And he kissed the icon. He lifted his head and closed his eyes, as if in prayer. A wind began to blow and his hat flew off, skipping across the surface of the pier and over the edge and into the water. His coppery hair, now free, became fuller as it had back at the German army post. Light began to envelop him as if the sun were coming up behind his head. It hurt Klaus's eyes. He squinted, and suddenly Cassiel was gone. Then he heard the words, "You are safe. God bless your journey. Go."

Klaus looked over at the men by the gangway. They were still talking among themselves as if nothing had happened. When he turned around again, the truck was gone as well. Klaus and his bags were alone on the pier.

Remembering the icon, he looked inside his bag. It was there, neatly wrapped in the brown paper and nestled between his shirts as it had been before.

— Chapter 23 —

The first leg of the voyage, from Venice to Lisbon, took three and a half days. By the first night, *A Estrela do Mar* was leaving the Adriatic and making its way around the heel of Italy and into the Ionian Sea. It was a beautiful spring evening. The stars were out and the moonlight danced off the surface of the water as the ship headed southwest toward Sicily.

In his cabin, Klaus took a more detailed look at the books he'd been given. Of immediate interest was the binder. In it, he found documents related to the other Klaus Bronner. As Cassiel had said, Bronner was a doctor and a Nazi. Included in the binder were Bronner's financial statements, along with an ample purse of American money. According to the paperwork, Bronner had already shifted most of his money to banks in the United States. The account records and all other necessary information were attached.

In the pocket of the binder was a small diary. It was new. When Klaus opened it he saw the ink was fresh. He read the first page.

"My name is Klaus Bronner. I am a medical doctor from Frankfurt. I am writing this as I plan to leave Germany. I became associated with the National Socialist Party three years ago in order to preserve my practice and keep my family safe. However, the more I learned of the party and the more deeply involved I became, I realized that the opposite was happening. Things were growing more and more unsafe."

How did Cassiel get all this? wondered Klaus.

As Klaus read on, he learned that Bronner had amassed a great deal of wealth by buying art and other valuables deemed as worthless or "degenerate" by the Nazis — the same subject he had been thinking of during his conversation with Hellmann. He also learned that this very same collection of art was in the hold of the ship.

Also contained in the binder were carbon copies of pages from the ship's cargo manifest. There were seven crates in the aft hold of the ship that belonged to Bronner. Each was 20 x 6 x 6 feet. Each was numbered. According to the manifest, they contained furniture and household effects. However, on the back of the copies, in pencil, were listed the actual contents.

The list read like a who's who of modern northern European art — Marc Chagall, Max Ernst, Hans Grundig. There were also a few older pieces, including — Klaus couldn't believe his eyes — two paintings by Vincent Van Gogh.

As Klaus was reading the list, he heard voices, from the deck outside. He wasn't certain as first, but some of the voices sounded like children. Then one of them laughed, and he was sure — there were children out there.

He got up, put on his shoes and coat, and went out. When he stepped out on the deck and looked toward the bow, he saw about twenty people standing there, all looking up at the moon and the stars. There were men, women, and children of various ages.

One of the women noticed Klaus and tapped her husband's shoulder. He and the others quickly turned around.

Klaus moved forward. As he did, he began to distinguish their faces in the moonlight. The children seemed curious, the women frightened, and the men angry.

Klaus wasn't sure what language they spoke. He only knew a few words in Portuguese. *"Boa noite,"* he said with a smile. He thought it meant good evening.

A couple of the men seemed to relax a bit. *"Boa noite,"* one of them responded and Klaus could tell that Portuguese was not his native language. He figured he'd go out on a limb. *"Sprechen Sie Deutsch?"* he asked.

At this, many in the group froze. The men started mumbling among themselves. Klaus sensed right away that these people were no friends of the Fatherland. Finally, one of the men came forward and responded in German. "Yes, I speak German, although it is not my native tongue. We are from Poland. My name is Eliaz — Eliaz Balsam."

It then hit Klaus: They were Jews.

"My name is Klaus Bronner. I am from Austria. I am not a German." Then he added, "I am not a Nazi. I am running, too."

Eliaz turned to the group and assured them that it was OK. At which they all seemed to breathe a little easier.

He told Klaus that they were from Krakow. They had escaped Poland two years ago, and had been living in parts of Italy all that time, but that now there were too many Germans, and it was time to go.

Klaus told him he understood but, remembering the angel's warning, was reluctant to divulge too much. He only said that he had been targeted for some of the ideas he held and that, he too, had to leave. *Which was true,* he reasoned. *I'm leaving for holding the idea that there are angels and that I was told by one of them to leave.*

Klaus looked down at a group of the smaller children sitting on the deck. They returned the look. A couple of them smiled. It made him think of his own family back in Austria when he was small — long before any of the madness had begun.

He said to Eliaz, "Tell your friends that they have very nice families. Let's hope we all have a safe journey."

"Yes, Herr Bronner," responded Eliaz. "Let us hope."

And with that, Klaus bid them all a good night and turned to go back to his cabin. As he walked down the deck, he could hear a flurry of whispered conversation erupt behind him. He smiled to himself and went inside, grateful that they had gotten out.

* * * * *

By the following morning, the ship had made it to the middle of the Mediterranean and was heading west through the straits of Sicily. Klaus went out on deck and was amazed at the sight of Malta to the south. They were close enough that he could see the port of Valleta — the bastions of Fort St. Elmo, the spire of St. Paul's. He had read reports of the Germans bombing the island and could make out a number of buildings in ruin. Nevertheless, in the morning sun, it seemed like a magical city of gold rising from the sea. Seeing it gave him faith that he was doing what was right.

Klaus went to the mess hall for breakfast, where he was told to sit at the table with the captain and his deck officers. Breakfast consisted of toast, baked beans, eggs, and a couple of questionable-looking slices of bacon.

Except for one older officer named Matteus, no one really spoke German. So, for Klaus's part, the conversation consisted of a few introductory *bom dias* and then a lot of smiling and nodding.

Klaus looked around but didn't see any of the people he'd encountered on the deck the night before. "Where are the families?" Klaus asked Matteus.

Matteus was a grizzled old salt with curly silver hair, deeply brown and creased skin, and a three-day case of stubble. On Klaus's asking about the refugees, Matteus shot Klaus a look of disgust and asked with very rough tone, "You saw them?"

"Yes," answered Klaus. "Last night on the deck."

Matteus turned to the captain and said something in Portuguese. The captain replied, and Matteus turned back to Klaus. "The captain says they are to be let out at night to get some air. To have them on deck during the day is dangerous. The Mediterranean is teaming with Nazis. If they spot women and children roaming around the deck of a merchant vessel, we could get boarded."

"What about inside the ship?" asked Klaus. "Surely ..."

"They are to stay where they are!" snapped Matteus. "Until their time comes to be let out, they stay in the steerage quarters below deck."

— Chapter 24 —

Two nights later, *A Estrela do Mar* was docked in Lisbon. Remembering Cassiel's warning, Klaus stayed off the deck, despite the fact that it was a very warm night.

Since leaving Venice, Klaus had spent hours poring over the books Cassiel had given him, especially the binder of documents related to the other Klaus Bronner. He was fascinated by the collection of works his namesake had acquired. He wished to see them.

Since almost the entire crew was ashore, Klaus decided to venture into the hold of the ship to see if he could find the treasure. Since they were in port, he thought the hold would be open.

After only three days, Klaus's knowledge of the ship was still limited. *A Estrela do Mar* was a 350-foot long merchant steamer built in England in 1927. Even though her primary purpose was transportation of cargo, there were also a few passenger accommodations, including some very small steerage quarters on the aft tween deck. Klaus's quarters were with the officers', toward the bow.

Before leaving his cabin, Klaus grabbed the flashlight from his satchel. *The angel thought of everything*, he mused.

Klaus had been told to stay off the deck while in port, but in order to get to the aft hold, he had to cross the deck and get past the wheel house. There was a door that led from his cabin out onto the upper deck. Once on deck, he could be seen from the bridge, so he had to time his escape. Through the small window in the cabin door, Klaus could see Matteus's wild gray hair moving as he paced around the bridge. He waited until the gray head disappeared for a minute, and then took his chance. He opened the door and dashed across the deck to the wheelhouse and went through another door on the deck level.

Once inside, Klaus went down a short flight of steps and into steerage. To go aft, he walked past several closed doors, behind which he could hear voices. *The Jews,* he thought. He proceeded quietly and found his way to a ladder that he believed would lead down into the hold. He took his flashlight and peered into the darkness below.

"Looking for something?" came a voice behind him.

Klaus's heart jumped as he swung around and lifted his flashlight. It was Eliaz.

"*Scheiße!* You scared the hell out me."

Eliaz smiled. "I'm sorry. We heard a noise. I came out to investigate. What are you doing down here?"

"I have some property in the hold. I need something."

"I see," smiled Eliaz. "So you're going down there?"

"Yes."

"You're crazy. If they find you, they will shoot you."

"I will take that chance."

Eliaz laughed at Klaus's bravado. "Let me go with you ... to at least be lookout for you."

Klaus thought about it, and nodded.

The front of the aft hold was full of wooden barrels. *Wine,* thought Klaus as he reached the bottom of the ladder. He could smell it. *How long it had been since he'd had a good night of drinking?*

Behind the barrels were several large crates. *This must be them,* he thought.

Klaus searched for something to open the crates. He found a large pry bar for just this purpose. He had no idea which crates were his, so he chose one randomly. He began prying at the corner. The nails being pulled from the wood made a horrible screeching sound that resonated loudly. He tried to avoid damaging the crate. He knew that he would later need to pound it back together.

Klaus finally managed to loosen one side. He opened it and looked in using his flashlight, only to see more boxes about the size of fruit crates. Out of curiosity, he lifted the top off one of the boxes. It was full of yellow and brown chunks. He reached in and took a handful and held it to his nose. It had an odd moldy-smoky odor that he didn't recognize.

"Opium," said Eliaz who had walked up from behind.

Klaus was shocked. He looked down at his hand holding the raw opium. "Are we in the company of drug runners?"

"We are in the company of businessmen. I doubt the crew even knows what's in these boxes."

"So they just pull into New York and offload the opium, as simple as that?"

"New York?" Eliaz chuckled then scratched his beard. "They didn't give you many details about this trip, did they? I can't believe I know more than you."

"We are going to New York, yes?" Klaus asked with a tone of urgency.

"Eventually ... but first we are going to the Canaries and then to Havana."

"Havana? Cuba?"

"Yes. There we offload the Italian wine and the Turkish opium and take on Cuban sugar and tobacco. Then we go to New York"

"I see. I guess I *didn't* get the details. I took the ship because it was available. I thought we'd be going directly to New York."

"It's better we're not. The North Atlantic is full of rough frigid seas. If we're going to get sunk by a German U-boat it's better to die in warm water, eh?"

Klaus nodded.

A male voice shouted something in Polish from up above. Eliaz responded, presumably telling him everything was all right.

"I almost forgot you are Polish," said Klaus. "Your German is very good."

"I studied in Berlin ... rabbinical school. Long before the war, of course." Eliaz looked away. It was obviously something he didn't wish to discuss. "So what are you looking for down here, my friend?"

"As I said, I have some property in one of these crates."

"I see," said Eliaz. "Do you wish me to help you find it?"

"No, that's OK. It was stupid of me, really." Klaus looked at the all the crates. There must have been 15 or 20. "We will end up tearing them all apart, and they will throw us off the ship. I don't want to make enemies of these men. He looked down at his hand, still clutching the opium. He reached over and put it back into the box.

"Let's try one more." said Eliaz. "If it's not there, we'll stop. We've nothing better to do. The crew is in port — spending their money on drink and whores before heading out to sea."

They moved to a different part of the hold. Eliaz picked out a crate and put his hand on it. "Try this one."

Klaus went over, handed Eliaz the flashlight, and pried the corner. It came apart much more easily than the first crate. Cool air came from inside and a scent very familiar to Klaus— artist's oil paint. Eliaz shined the light inside and Klaus could see the face of a woman staring back at him. A woman wearing a white cap.

"This is it! This is it!" chirped Klaus. "We must remove the entire panel in order to go inside."

Eliaz helped Klaus remove the panel, and then shined the light over the works of art. Many were abstract. Klaus recognized the contorted faces of Otto Dix and the flying birds and flowers of Marc Chagall. Many he did not recognize.

"Where did you get these?" asked Eliaz in a flat tone.

Klaus wasn't sure what to tell him. He wasn't sure what to believe himself. The other Bronner's diary said that the art had been acquired legitimately. Klaus thought quickly.

"I bought these to save them," he told Eliaz. "The Nazis were going to destroy them. They call this degenerate art."

"I recognize some of these artists," said Eliaz. "I couldn't tell you the names or titles, but I know some of them. I would visit museums in Berlin. This one here ..."

Eliaz took out a painting. It was a of a farm scene. But instead of cows and sheep and chickens walking around the barnyard, they were shown as winged creatures, flying in the air over the barn, circling the bearded farmer and his fat wife, who were dancing against the backdrop of the sun.

Eliaz rested the first painting against the edge of the crate and then took out another. The second painting was a grotesque, almost comical exaggeration of a nude woman. She was lying on a large sofa and staring into space. Her pubic hairs were painted like little worms. Her eyebrows were thick sponges and her hair fell over her shoulders in geometric shapes. The painting was done in shades of orange and red and gray and black.

He picked up another. It was of a violinist dancing against an abstract background. He had a very big beard and was wearing a small skull cap on his head.

"Many of these are Jewish," said Eliaz. "You see here?" he said, pointing to the violinist's head. That's a yarmulke. These were painted by Jews."

Klaus shrugged and said, "I don't know. I bought them as a lot. I was told they were from museums. They were being sold because they were considered inappropriate for public display."

"Perhaps *that* one," Eliaz responded, pointing to the garish nude, "but most of these were thought inappropriate because they were painted by Jews. Many of these were probably stolen."

"I don't know," repeated Klaus. Of course, he knew full well what these paintings were and he resolved to correct matters as soon as he reached the United States.

"I don't want to be a party to any theft," Klaus said. "When I get to New York, I will have them looked at. Now we must put these crates back together, before the old Portugee finds us here."

"You mean Matteus?" Eliaz sneered. "He hates us. If it were his choice, we would have never been let on the boat."

"Why?" asked Klaus.

"He's a Nazi sympathizer," said Eliaz. "Many Portuguese are. They think it's inevitable that the Führer will eventually overrun their country, and they are hedging their bets."

The two pounded the crates back together. When they were done, Eliaz walked Klaus back to the ladder.

"I don't know whether I trust you," said Eliaz. "I'm sure you understand. I just hope you do the right thing with the paintings and whatever else you have in your boxes."

Klaus nodded, wordlessly. Then climbed the ladder and went along the passageway, up the stairs, and out the door. Before heading back to his cabin, he stood for a moment. After being in the hold for more than an hour, the outside air was a blessing. A salty warm breeze blew through Klaus's hair.

Then he felt a hard blow against his back, and was thrown forward. He hit the deck and his flashlight skidded away from him.

"What are you doing out here?" someone asked in Portuguese.

Klaus rolled over and sat up, resting on his elbows. He could see the outline of Matteus's wild hair against the moonlight.

"Herr Bronner?" asked Matteus.

"Yes," answered Klaus.

"I thought you were one of the Jews. What were you doing down there?"

Klaus got up. His eyes were now better adjusted to the light and he could see Matteus's sinister face studying him.

"Were you visiting the Jews, Herr Bronner? Perhaps you have a taste for Jewish cunt, huh?" Matteus let out a short cackle.

"You are a vile man. I'm going to bed."

Klaus then walked across the deck and picked up his flashlight. He checked it to see if it still worked. It did. He shined it in Matteus's face.

"Turn that off!" ordered Matteus.

Klaus waited a moment and then turned off the light. He opened the door to his cabin and went in. Matteus was yelling as he shut the door, "Stay off the deck, Herr Bronner. Next time I will be doing my patrol with a gun."

— Chapter 25 —

Two evenings later *A Estrela do Mar* was about 300 miles due west of Morocco, heading south to the Canaries. The air had grown warmer, and the heat was insufferable inside the ship.

Now that they were at sea and heading south, the threat of being stopped by Nazis was next to nil.

Klaus spent most of his time reading "*Habitibus Angelos*," learning about the characteristics of faith and the attributes of angels. Reading the part about men being enamored with their own intellects made Klaus wonder about the Germans. Did they see themselves in their own minds as gods? Is that how they became so deranged?

When he read how angels adore the Mother of God, it made him think of the icon. He had only looked at it a couple of times since Cassiel had left him on the dock. He was nervous to look at it, because it had such a great effect on him. He would lose himself in it. He couldn't hold a thought. But after looking at it, he was at peace. It made him realize things were not in his control. It helped him understand his place in life. He felt release and trust. He felt faith.

He went into his bag and found the icon. He took it out and unwrapped it. As he pulled back the brown paper, he saw her face looking at him. He saw her right hand indicating her son as he rested in her other arm.

I and my son love you, Klaus. You are chosen to help us. Be at peace. The words were not audible, but they rang inside Klaus's head as loud as any bell and he knew ... he knew he would be safe.

He studied the angels circling above the mother and child. He looked at each of their faces. The one furthest to the right was Cassiel, as if it were a photograph of him — his copper hair and green eyes, his uniquely dimpled chin. He looked at the others — innocent and mild, and yet absolutely strong.

As he stared at the icon, he suddenly heard the sound of children. Eliaz and his small community were heading out on deck. He was tempted to go and join them to escape the heat, but decided to let them have their time alone. Even though he had somewhat gained Eliaz's trust, he knew "the big, German-speaking man," was still a spooky thing to the others.

An hour later, Klaus heard the group making its way past his cabin to go aft, so he decided to head out into the fresh air.

When Klaus emerged on deck, he was delighted to see faint light on the horizon, and millions of stars beginning to show themselves in the southern sky. Above it all hung a waning moon in the shape of a giant slice. The air had cooled, and a breeze blew across his face as he looked out on the pink and silver ocean. Turning to the bow of the boat, he saw one lone figure standing. Eliaz.

"*Guten abend, Herr Balsam,*" Klaus said.

"*Guten abend, Klaus,*" answered Eliaz, not taking his eyes off the stars. Then he said, in English with an odd brogue, *"I ofen looked up at the sky an' assed meself the question, 'what is the moon, what is the stars?'"*

"Sorry," said Klaus, "I don't speak much English."

Eliaz smiled. "Well, you'd better start learning. After all, we're heading to America."

Klaus nodded his head.

"It's a line from a play by an Irishmen. Sean O'Casey. About a family falling victim to a reversal of fortune."

"You are in a pensive mood tonight, my friend," observed Klaus. Is everything OK?"

"I worry about our future in America. Even though we had no choice, it's a scary thing to leave everything behind and head off to a new land. A new life."

"But you have family there, yes?"

"Yes. Family I do not know."

"I think you will be fine. Like you said, you had no choice. When you have no choice, it is like God is guiding you, right?"

Eliaz turned to Klaus and smiled, "Yes. You are right, my friend. Now I should go and join the family that I do know."

As Eliaz turned to go, Klaus put his hand on his shoulder. "Wait a moment. I want to ask you something."

"What is it?"

"You said you studied to be a rabbi, yes?"

"Yes, Klaus. It is my plan to finish my studies in America."

"I'm wondering — what do your Hebrew teachings say about angels?"

"Why do you ask?"

"I've been reading a book that someone gave me before I left Venice. It's very old. It looks as if it's from the Renaissance or Middle Ages. It goes into great detail about the nature of angels. I was just curious what your tradition says."

"Well, the Torah itself says very little, other than the Bible stories you may already know. An angel appeared in the Garden of Eden, driving away the sinful Adam and Eve. Angels appeared to Abraham and Lot. An angel appeared to Gideon. Angels came to the prophets Ezekiel and Daniel. Mainly, they come to give instructions and warnings. The Hebrew word for angel, *malach*, means messenger.

"But beyond the Bible, there are other traditions.

"In our Kabbalah, we assign powers to the angels. They each have mystical power over things in our universe. It's part of the oneness of the temporal and the celestial ... spirit and matter. There is no division."

"I don't understand," said Klaus.

Eliaz rubbed his beard and studied Klaus's face for a moment. "You Catholics see everything as a closed system. And that which doesn't fit the system is viewed with suspicion or rejected as evil. But we see the physical universe as part of God. That which doesn't make sense now, will eventually make sense in time.

"That's why when someone like a Galileo or Copernicus comes along, you treat them with fear. But we see the scientific as part of God — no need for fear." Waving his hand at the night sky, Eliaz continued. "You asked about angels. Upon learning of the sun and the orbits of the planets, we didn't throw men into dungeons, we embraced the new knowledge, placing the care of each into the hands of angels.

"Michael presides over the sun; Gabriel over the moon; Raphael is over mercury; and Hanael over Venus; Kamael is over Mars; and Zadkiel, Jupiter; and Cassiel presides over Saturn."

Upon hearing the name Cassiel, Klaus's skin went cold. He then thought of the icon with the seven stars and Cassiel on the right.

"Thank you," said Klaus quietly.

The two men stood on deck, looking at the stars. The sun was now beyond the horizon and the sky was a brilliant shower of sparkling light.

"I have one more question, Eliaz. I hope you don't think it too strange. Do you know anyone who has ever seen an angel?"

Eliaz held his answer for a long moment, then said, "I had an old uncle, back in Poland. He claimed to have seen an angel once. He told me the story when I was a boy. I don't remember much. The one thing I do remember was him saying that the angel had a face like both a child and a man at the same time. I don't know what he meant by that, but it was always very curious to me."

"Yes," agreed Klaus. "It is very curious."

Klaus thought very hard about what he was going to do next. Eliaz probably already knew too much. He knew about the art. He suspected it was stolen and he was probably right. Yet, Klaus liked Eliaz, and he needed to talk to somebody or he would go mad.

"I have something I'd like to show you," said Klaus.

Klaus took Eliaz into his cabin. He found his copy of "*Habitibus Angelos*," and showed it to him.

"This book is about angels. In it, it describes angels as you say — the face of a child and man at the same time. They are also said to be very tall, and all the exact same height."

Klaus handed the book to Eliaz. "And this cover — these patterns — they show up throughout the book as decorations, but I think they are more than that. I have no idea what they mean."

Eliaz took his time looking at the book. "It's in Latin. That's one language I'm not familiar with, I'm afraid."

He paid special attention to the cover.

"I've seen these kind of designs before ... on one of the scrolls at the synagogue in Krakow ... the Book of Daniel."

"It's interesting," said Klaus. "It reminds me of Nordic or Celtic scroll patterns, but much more complex and less random."

"Like you said, there's a meaning to it," Eliaz said, as he handed the book back to Klaus. "It's not just decoration.

"So are you starting to believe in angels, Herr Bronner?"

"As you say, science and faith do not necessarily contradict."

Klaus looked at the book in his hands. The patterns on the cover were mesmerizing, like the stars he had just been looking at. It seemed so infinite and profound.

Harry Steven Ackley

And yes, I do believe in angels, He thought. *I must.*

— Chapter 26 —

Once they were out on the Atlantic, the rules eased a bit, and Klaus and the other passengers were allowed to roam more freely. In the southern Atlantic, the heat sometimes became so unbearable that the passengers were allowed to stay out on the deck all night. Late at night, and sometimes early in the morning, Eliaz and Klaus would have lengthy conversations about angels, and art, and America. And baseball.

It turned out that, in his correspondence with his relatives in America, Eliaz had heard much about the sport and about the great Brooklyn Dodgers. He was planning to go to a game soon after his arrival.

Klaus would spend hours with Eliaz, pouring over the book Cassiel had given him, familiarizing himself with statistics, schedules, and the history of the players.

Over the remainder of their voyage, Klaus even gained the trust of Eliaz's fellow travelers. There were three families, including Eliaz, his wife, and his two children. And four other adults — three young women and an older man. Seventeen people in all.

Among the young women was Rachel, Eliaz's younger sister — a very attractive girl with dark brown hair and piercing blue eyes. Eliaz' and Rachel's parents had been killed by German troops.

As the shores of the western hemisphere got closer, an excitement began to grow. Everyone on ship seemed brighter. The mood was heightened even more when, on June 10th, the

Portuguese celebrated their national holiday. Routine work was called off for the day and ship rules were relaxed. In the late afternoon, when it cooled off slightly, there was dancing, dining, and drinking on the deck of the ship.

At the celebration, Rachel and the other young women danced with the sailors to the music of an accordion, a violin, and a guitar. As the sun got lower in the west, Rachel's sensuality came alive. During the course of the voyage Rachel had grown even more beautiful ... she'd become thinner and her skin had turned a lovely brown from the tropical Atlantic sun.

She danced barefoot on the deck, her partially unbuttoned blouse blowing in the wind, her breasts moving up and down with the rhythm of the dance. Every man's heart was beating a bit faster at the sight of her.

When the music ended she stopped, staggered and fell into the arms of one of the sailors. She was drunk and dizzy from the dancing and heat. She laughed and kissed the young sailor on the lips.

Eliaz and one of the other men came forward, pried Rachel from the young man's arms, and escorted her over to a place where she could sit.

"A little too much to drink," said Eliaz to the sailor. "Too much to drink," he repeated.

One of the older women then sat next to Rachel and proceeded to button her blouse.

Everyone chuckled — except Matteus, who was watching from a distance. Matteus glowered at Rachel.

Night came, but the air remained muggy. Klaus sat up in his bed trying to read. The windows to his cabin were wide open. Suddenly, he heard a loud clank on the deck outside. He went to his window, poked his head out, and looked up and down the promenade but could see nothing. He was about to turn to go back to his bed when he heard a familiar voice say,

"You fucking Jew bitch. You scream and I will throw you overboard." It was Matteus.

Klaus grabbed his flashlight and carefully went to the door that led out onto the forward deck. He looked through the round window but it was a cloudy sky with just a hint of moonlight shining through. He could barely see the surface of the ship where hours earlier there had been sunshine, dancing, and merriment.

He eased himself out the door and onto the deck and stood there silently, facing the back of the ship. Then he heard the faint sounds of a whimper and then the muffled grunts of a man. The sounds were coming from his left on the starboard side. He began walking down the length of the ship. As he got near one of the funnels, the sounds grew louder.

Coming around the back side of the funnel, he saw Rachel's bare legs and Matteus's dark body moving up and down between them.

In shock, Klaus stood for just a moment. Then he heard Rachel whimper again, pleading, with tears in her voice, for Matteus to stop.

Klaus switched on the flashlight and shined it at the two of them. Matteus quickly turned. Klaus flipped the flashlight around in his hand, lunged forward, and hit the side of Matteus's head with the butt end. Matteus collapsed between Rachel's legs and she scooted back away from him.

Matteus's head fell forward. He tried to prop himself back up but Klaus fell upon him, bashing his head onto the deck.

Klaus felt rage overtake him, thinking of his young sister at school back in Vienna, almost the same age as Rachel, and of the rest of his family, now all dead. He hated predators like Matteus. He hated the Nazis who had destroyed his world. He slammed the head against the deck again and again until he felt the man's warm blood on his hand.

Then Klaus felt another hand, grabbing his shoulder, pulling him back. He realized what he'd done and backed off and got to his feet. He turned to see Eliaz flanked by two of his fellows, staring at him. Rachel was crying in the arms of one of the men.

"He was a pig," said Klaus. "A pig!"

Eliaz embraced Klaus. "You are a good man, my friend. We saw she was missing and went to search for her. But you were the one who saved her."

They stood at arm's length and Eliaz smiled. "Now I have two things on you ... you are an art thief and a murderer."

Klaus looked down at Matteus's dead body and nodded awkwardly, knowing both accusations were, in a way, true.

Then Eliaz added, "But you are also a hero and your secrets are safe."

The men threw Matteus's body overboard. They looked at the blood on the deck. It was a mess — impossible to clean in the darkness.

Klaus looked to the southwest. There was a break in the clouds where the stars were shining through. Silhouetted against the starlight was a singular tall figure who then suddenly disappeared. After he was gone, a heavy warm rain began to fall on the deck, washing the blood away.

No one but Klaus, Eliaz, Rachel, and the two other men knew what happened. In the morning, when Matteus was discovered missing, the crew all assumed that he had fallen overboard in his drunkenness. No one cared. Klaus later found out that Matteus was only taken on board as a favor owed by the captain to a relative. "We will get along fine without him," the captain assured Klaus at dinner. "And good riddance," added another officer.

— Chapter 27 —

Upon arrival in Cuba, the crew of *A Estrela do Mar* went to work unloading and loading cargo. The process was to take a day or two. On the first day in port, the passengers were allowed off the ship to stretch their legs and see a little bit of Havana.

Klaus decided to take some of his American cash and go exploring. The first thing he wanted to do was to try the famous Cuban cigars he'd heard so much about. He visited the *Partagas* and *Particulares* cigar factories and stocked up with a few boxes. After that he ventured into Old Havana. He thought of going to the casinos, but after having been at sea for so long, he opted to stay outside and take a walk along the *Playas de Este*, the beaches of East Havana.

The beach in Havana was perfect. It felt wonderful to have the warm sand under his feet. The soft whoosh of the waves against the shoreline was calming, compared to the constant mechanical hum of the ship's engine and the wind whipping across the deck.

Looking out at the deep blue water, Klaus could not believe what he had done. *What were his colleagues at the university thinking? What had they been told about his disappearance? What did his sister Stefanie know? As soon as he reached New York, he would wire her school and let her know he was safe.*

Looking up the beach, Klaus saw a beautiful young woman in a light blue summer dress walking his way. She walked barefoot, holding her shoes in her hand. A puff of wind carried her dress up her thigh to reveal a smooth, tan, and shapely leg.

She grabbed her hair to pull it away from her face and Klaus could then see that it was Rachel. At that point, she was about fifty yards away. She saw him looking and smiled and walked toward him.

"I like your dress," said Klaus in his best, broken, Polish. With Eliaz's tutoring, along with the Polish dictionary Cassiel had given him, Klaus had managed to learn a few phrases during the voyage.

"Eliaz bought it for me," answered Rachel as she strolled up to him. "He bought this one and a yellow one for when we get to New York. I got so skinny at sea that my old dresses no longer fit. The prices are very cheap here."

Not quite sure what she had said, Klaus looked down at the sack he was carrying and smiled, "I bought cigars.

"And where is your brother?" he asked.

"He's back that way with his wife and children," said Rachel, indicating the direction behind her with a nod. "He's probably watching us," she added, with a laugh.

"I told him I wanted to have a little time alone before we went back to the ship. Let's walk."

As the two walked down the beach together, Klaus was unsure what to say. Besides the language difference, Rachel was only 18 years old and he was almost 30. They were from two different countries, two different religions. Two different worlds. She was only a year older than his sister Stefanie.

They walked past a group of boats that were pulled up on the beach. Rachel took Klaus's hand and led him behind the boats. She pulled him toward her and looked up into his eyes. "*Danke*," she whispered, and then kissed him on the mouth.

He was unsure how to respond. Eliaz was his friend. She was too young. Yet, she was strikingly beautiful.

Just then the sound of voices interrupted. Men speaking Spanish were approaching from the other side of the boat.

The two stood apart quickly as a group of four older men walked past and looked at them. One of them made a joke at which the others chuckled and they all moved on.

Klaus and Rachel looked at each other. Rachel reached up to him on her tiptoes and gave him one more kiss. "*Danke. Danke, mein held,*" she said. And the two began walking back up the beach.

— Chapter 28 —

Before *A Estrela do Mar* left Cuba, Klaus got permission from the captain to go into the hold and have another look at his paintings. He took both Eliaz and Rachel with him, and opened the same crate they had opened weeks earlier. All was as they had left it.

"Take whatever you want," said Klaus. "Whatever you and your friends can carry is yours. I don't want any Nazi blood on my hands. I don't want to be a part of any Nazi thievery."

Eliaz knew Klaus was sincere, but only chose the two small paintings they had looked at when they first opened the Crate, those of the farmer and his wife, and of the violinist.

"And what about you, my dear?" he asked Rachel. "Please, take something to remember me by."

Rachel stepped inside the crate and looked around. She was shorter, so she was able to enter without having to duck her head. She first looked at the painting of the woman in the white cap, then moved it aside.

She looked at a few other paintings. She found the painting of the woman with the worm-like pubic hair, and laughed. She turned to Eliaz and said in Polish, "And I was beginning to think our friend Klaus was a bit of a prude. I guess I was wrong."

Eliaz translated and they all laughed, though Klaus turned quite red in the face.

Finally, Rachel brought out from the back of the crate a canvas about 2 feet square. On it was an angel shown from the waist up, dressed in a bluish-white gown.

"The Rembrandt Angel," said Klaus in a hushed but urgent tone. "This is the other Van Gogh."

Eliaz looked at Klaus curiously. "If it's by Van Gogh, why is it called The Rembrandt Angel?"

"It's a study by Van Gogh of an older work by Rembrandt, 'Jacob Wrestling with the Angel.'"

"Ah," said Eliaz. "That story I know.

"Jacob wrestled with the angel through the night. As dawn broke, the angel said, 'let me go.' And Jacob replied, 'I will not let you go until you bless me.'"

Klaus looked at the face of the angel with its eyes half closed. Its face was serene and youthful — like that of a boy and a man. It brought to mind the original painting where the depiction was much the same. He wondered whether Rembrandt or Van Gogh had ever been visited by one of the creatures.

"It's very beautiful," said Rachel to Eliaz, "but much too important for me to take."

Eliaz translated for Klaus.

"You can have it if you wish," said Klaus. "I want you to take it."

"But how can I carry such a masterpiece through immigration? I can't just walk onto Ellis Island carrying a Van Gogh. They will seize it and lock me up as an art thief."

"I can keep it for you, if you wish," said Klaus. "Where will you be in New York? I will find you." He then smiled at Rachel.

"We will exchange our information before we disembark," said Eliaz.

"*Danke, Herr Bronner,*" said Rachel. "I will call it my Hero Angel." She reached up and kissed Klaus on the cheek. "Just as you are my hero."

"We will take these three to remind us of you and your kindness," said Eliaz. "But the rest are yours. They are yours for a reason. It's for you to figure what that reason is." Eliaz nodded at the canvas that Rachel held up and said "May God and his angels be with you."

Klaus thought privately to himself, *that is what I am afraid of.*

* * * * *

Less than a day after pulling out of Havana, the coast of Florida came into view and all the passengers were on the deck to get their first glimpse of America.

After an hour or so, people started filtering off.

Klaus and Rachel were among the few left on deck. She stayed to look after some of the children who didn't want to go back inside.

Rachel seemed troubled. Klaus asked her how she was doing. She responded, but Klaus couldn't quite make out what she was saying. He did understand the word *smutny*, which means sad. Then he had an idea.

"Stay here," he said. "Stay here and I will show you something that will lift your spirits."

Klaus went to his cabin and retrieved the icon.

He brought it back to the deck and went to Rachel's side, where he proceeded to unwrap the brown paper.

When Rachel saw the icon, she gasped. "She's beautiful."

Tears began to well in her eyes. It was not the effect Klaus had intended.

"What's wrong?" he asked. "I thought this would bring you joy."

Rachel pointed to the image of the virgin and said, "Miriam. See looks like my friend Miriam in Poland."

Klaus understood enough to know that the image reminded her of a friend. He assumed that it was a friend that had been left behind.

Just then one of the children screamed with laughter.

Rachael and Klaus both turned at the same time to see the children on the deck surrounding a young woman. The woman was playing a game with them. All of the children were joyous and engaged. The woman was dressed in beautiful blue and scarlet robes that looked to be middle-Eastern. Yet, as she joked with the children, they understood her completely. She obviously spoke Polish.

"I see we picked up a new passenger in Cuba," said Klaus.

Rachel turned to Klaus and said, "It's the girl. It's the girl in the painting." She pointed at the icon.

The two looked at the icon and, indeed, it was the same woman.

"It's The Lady," said Klaus in a choked-up voice. "It's the Blessed Mother!"

They looked back to the lady who was now lining up the children for some kind of race. She bid them to run toward Klaus and Rachel. As they did so, with their backs turned away from her, she stood and smiled at the two adults. Then she vanished.

— Chapter 29 —

New York City, June 1941

Among the papers in Dr. Bronner's binder were arrangements to have the crates unloaded and taken to a warehouse on Long Island. Once in port, Klaus had to sign some papers. Beyond that, Klaus was unsure what to do. Cassiel said he would contact him.

Once customs was cleared, Klaus took a cab to The Waldorf Astoria on Park Avenue. He had been told it was the best, and after almost a month at sea, he was ready for the best. On arriving at the hotel, he wired his sister Stefanie's school in Vienna, assuring her he was safe and that he would call her soon.

He bathed for close to an hour, put on clean clothes, went to dinner and drank an entire bottle of French wine, followed by two glasses of an exquisite cognac, accompanied by one of his Cuban cigars.

Klaus then stumbled back to his room, removed his shirt and pants, fell on the bed, and slept for ten hours.

Klaus awoke around noon the next day to the sound of a driving summer rain outside his window. His head throbbed. He went to the bathroom and drank three full glasses of water. He looked at himself in the mirror, wearing nothing but his underwear and T-shirt. He thought of coffee, and immediately the aroma of hot coffee came to his nostrils.

He walked back into the bedroom to find Cassiel sitting in a gold velvet wingback chair, with his long legs propped up on an ottoman. He wore a cream-colored summer suit with a light green shirt. On the small table next to him was a silver pouring service with the steam of hot coffee rising from the spout.

"Enjoy yourself last night?" asked Cassiel with a smile, as he extended a cup of coffee with cream to Klaus.

Klaus took the cup and sipped. It was delicious. He had never tasted coffee like that before. *The coffee of angels,* he mused.

Klaus had a thousand questions for Cassiel — about angels, about the book, about the stolen art now in his possession, about the fate of his sister, his colleagues, his life back in Europe, what his mission was, how he would survive in America, and, most importantly, about the icon and The Lady he had seen on the ship. But the question that first came to his lips was, "Why me?

"I am not a holy man," said Klaus. "I murdered a man. You were there, you saw it. And when I got off the ship, I didn't run to church and pray to God. I went out and got drunk. Why me? Why was I the one given the icon and put on the ship? Why not a saint? Why not one of the monks at Athos? I don't understand."

"Matteus was evil," said Cassiel. "You saved the girl Rachel. He would have killed her after he had his way.

"And as for you being holy, have you ever thought, that might not be all there is to it? Have you ever thought that God might see things differently? Look at Moses and David — a stutterer and a reckless boy. And perhaps it's not all about you either. Perhaps there are others, holier than you, who have been praying for you — people who see more in you than you do."

"Who would that be?"

"Your brother Ernst."

At this, Klaus fell silent.

"Do you know how your brother died?" asked Cassiel.

"He was killed in Northern France, fighting in the German army. That's all I know."

"He was defending a family of civilians, the Giroud family," said Cassiel. "His unit was going through the countryside looking for Resistance fighters. The German officers suspected the Girouds of aiding the French Resistance. They were innocent.

"The officer in charge knew they were innocent, yet he still planned to torture and kill them. He fancied their large house and wanted to use it for his outpost. Your brother was ordered to assist in the torture, but he refused, and was shot as an example. That is how he died. Just as you would have fought Matteus to the death to save Rachel, if you had to."

Learning the truth about Ernst, Klaus bowed his head. "You don't know that I would have fought to the death."

"I believe you would have," said the angel.

"Your brother prayed for you every night, Klaus. He loved you and believed in great things for you. Oftentimes, the prayers of others, not your own, have the greatest effect on your life.

"I should add that Ernst's efforts were not in vain. After seeing your brother murdered, his fellow soldiers turned on the officer and the family was spared."

Klaus stood in the elegant hotel room in his underwear, with disheveled hair, looking down at his bony white toes sunken into the plush dark carpet.

He started to speak, hesitated, then said, "Are you able to ... to?"

"To see Ernst?" Cassiel finished the sentence. "No. At least not in the way you mean. We are aware of him, but we don't communicate as you mean.

"Angels are intended to minister to those on Earth. That's why The Lady is so important. She will bring faith. And that faith will restore the relationship between our two kinds of beings."

Cassiel got up and walked to Klaus, placing his hands on his shoulders.

Klaus looked into the manchild's face. Tears began to well in his eyes. He felt an overwhelming sense of unworthiness. He still didn't understand why he was there, but he began to reconcile himself to what was happening, and to feel some sense of peace.

"Rest for now," said Cassiel. "Knowledge will be given when it is necessary. You are to keep The Lady safe, so she may one day be revealed to all and bring true faith to a world that needs it."

"I saw her," said Klaus. "I saw her on the ship when I was with the Jewish girl Rachel. We both saw her."

"Indeed," said Cassiel. "It does happen. It's something even my kind doesn't really understand. The Lady reveals herself to whom she wills, when she wills. But it seems she particularly appears to children. She's always loved children for their joy and innocence. Were there children when you saw her?"

"Yes," said Klaus.

"You are blessed, Klaus. Whether you choose to believe it or not, you have been blessed for a purpose."

Part IV
Faust's Art Collection

Oh gentle Faustus, leave this damned art,
This magic that will charm thy soul to hell

— *Christopher Marlowe, Dr. Faustus* —

— Chapter 30 —

Mar del Plata, Argentina — Early December, the Present

Laura Espinoza stood naked by the poolside, skimming leaves off the surface of the water with a white pool net. Admiring her 23-year-old body, Kevin appreciated that, at this time of year, the absence of clothing was *de rigueur* for young women in this part of the world. In late December, the high heat of summer had arrived in Argentina.

There was something more sensual about watching Laura than actually having her. She smiled back at Kevin's stare and walked to the pool house, where she leaned the net against the wall. Then she went back to the pool and dove in. She swam underwater its full length. Kevin watched her brown body glide under the blue water.

At the other end she emerged near Kevin, who was lying on a chaise chair, drinking his morning cocktail and clutching a book he intended to read. He had already tasted every inch of Laura's flesh many times, but seeing her walking up the pool steps, dripping in the mid-morning sun, revived his interest, a sensation that he, now in his sixties, needed to savor.

She went to him, leaned over and kissed him, dripping water on the cover of his book. Suddenly his cell phone went off, with a ring tone that filled him with dread.

He stole a quick caress of Laura's waist and breasts, kissed her again and then indicated that he needed to take the call. She nodded with a delicious smile and walked past him into the house.

"Yes?"

"Hello, Kevin. It's been a while."

"Yes, it has." answered Kevin thinking, *but not long enough.*

"There's been activity at your uncle's old house. It's even been in the news. But I doubt you pay much attention to the New York news down there in your little South American paradise."

Kevin took a long drink from his glass. "I searched every inch of that place. There was nothing there when we sold it."

"You were mistaken" shot back the other voice, in a short but even tone. "And you failed to get any information from the new owner, didn't you?"

"My secretary died trying," Kevin answered nervously. "What about the wife? It's been over twenty years. In all this time..."

"We can't touch her. She's protected. And we can't enter the house. You know all this."

Kevin waited.

"We can't enter the house, but you can. You need to get to her. What could soon happen could be very damaging to us."

"Why me?" asked Kevin, knowing this was an argument he wouldn't win. "I'm an old, drunken playboy. I'm of no use to you."

"You underestimate yourself. You know the story. You have the inside information. You know what needs to be done.

"I've taken good care of you, haven't I ... filled your life with poolside drinks and beautiful senoritas?"

Kevin looked around, knowing full well he wasn't there. But still, *he knows where I'm at and what I'm doing.*

"Get yourself to New York, Kevin. Miss Espinoza will wait until you get back."

"OK," answered Kevin flatly, resenting that someone had such control over him.

"And one last thing," said the voice. "Mrs. Cuthbert seems to have an ally these days. Her name is Emily Campbell. She's a college professor. She's being watched by the others, so she must be important. Perhaps you can find something out about her from Mrs. Cuthbert. I'll fill you in more when you get to New York."

* * * * *

After landing at JFK, the first thing Kevin did was check the warehouse on Long Island.

The last time he'd been to New York was five years ago, when he came for a business meeting and to sell some art. That was in the early fall. He couldn't remember when he'd last been there in winter. It might not have been since the year his Uncle Klaus died, more than twenty years ago.

Compared to the Argentine summer he'd just left, New York was a penetrating cold. He sat in the back of the limousine and looked out the window at gray buildings, rundown houses, and piles of slush as he rode along the parkway in Queens. He hoped the trip would be over quickly and he could get back to the warmth of his garden, his pool, and the soft caresses of Laura Espinoza.

He wondered about his mission. Why was this icon so important? It was just a painting. All it ever did for him was cause trouble and uncertainty. Looking at the icon made him feel powerless. It made him question his purpose in life. It made things feel out of his control. He didn't like those feelings. He didn't want religion. He didn't want visions. He didn't want to ponder the meaning of existence. He just wanted to have fun ... pleasure and comfort.

As he rode along, he thought back about how it all started.

— Chapter 31 —

August 1985

Kevin Peters, 31 years old, looked out the window of the 747 as it flew over the Rocky Mountains. The big brown mountains, whose tops were covered with summer remnants of snow, looked like photographic negatives of rectums, thought Kevin. *Where do I come up with this shit?* he asked himself. *I should be a writer.*

Kevin was on his way to Boston, where, in a week, he would begin the MBA program at Harvard Business School. Until then, he was planning a short visit with his Uncle Klaus in Manhattan. Kevin barely knew his uncle. He had visited him only once as a child. Kevin's mother, Stefanie, and her brother weren't very close.

The story went that they'd had a falling out when his mom met and fell in love with Kevin's father on the ship when they were making their way to the U.S. during World War II. Kevin's dad, Glenn Peters, was a robust California engineer who had traveled to England to assist with some secret project for the British military. The return voyage from England to New York was a scary one. Even though the ship was a luxury liner flying a Swedish flag, German U-boats swarming the North Atlantic. Such desperate times drove Kevin's parents into each other's arms.

After arriving in the U.S. Stefanie, then 18, stayed with her brother Klaus in New York only briefly. She madly corresponded with Peters who, because of the strategic military necessity of his civilian job, didn't join the service when the United States entered the war. Stefanie, longing for the protection of his Americanness, left New York as soon as she could, married Peters, and worked very hard to become as un-European as possible.

Uncle Klaus, on the other hand, dealt with the situation differently. He bought himself a big house on the Upper West Side and became a recluse. According to Kevin's mom, Klaus never left the city and rarely went out of his house. Even though he was Austrian, he was embarrassed by his German accent.

How he was able to survive financially, no one really knew, not even Stefanie. It was a touchy subject in their family. Finally, in the late 1940s, Klaus came out of hiding and became involved in the New York art scene. Rumor had it that he made a small fortune off pop art. That he'd seen the potential in abstract expressionism and had bought up a lot of early works by Pollack, DeKooning, Rothko and others.

But all Kevin could remember, from his one visit as a child, were the *old* paintings that lined the walls of the brownstone — that's where his uncle's true passion was. Religious works ... paintings of angels, Christ and the Virgin Mary, and scenes from the Bible.

He also remembered the one his uncle called "The Lady."

Kevin was eight years old when he first visited Klaus. His sister Greta was five. The year was 1962. He later learned that the trip was supposed to be a kind of fence-mending for his mom and Klaus. Kevin's father didn't go.

As the 747, now over the prairie, raced through the air, Kevin remembered that trip. It was the first time he had ever flown in an airplane — a great luxury in 1962.

* * * * *

Our Lady of West 74th Street

New York City, 1962

Kevin and Greta screamed and giggled as they climbed up Uncle Klaus's wide staircase of polished dark wood. Their house in California was a modern, large, rambling ranch house in the Palo Alto hills. By comparison, the narrow, four-story stone house in the city of skyscrapers and noisy cars seemed like something out of one of the old movies their mother watched.

They loved the way their voices echoed off the walls.

"Children, please stop!" shouted Stefanie. "You need to be quiet."

"It's OK, it's OK," said Klaus, with a smile. "This place could use a little noise."

Klaus and Stefanie stood in the entryway of the brownstone on West 74th Street. They hadn't seen each other in almost twenty years, since she'd left New York to marry Glenn Peters. She'd aged, to be sure. She now had the curves of a woman. But California had treated her well. She had a smooth golden complexion. Her thick blond hair was pulled back in a ponytail. All traces of the Austrian school girl were gone.

"The kids are excited," she said with a smile. "We've made all kinds of plans to see the sights — the Empire State Building, the Brooklyn Bridge, the zoo ... maybe tickets to the Ed Sullivan Show. I wouldn't mind seeing a baseball game."

"I don't know if I can stomach the Yankees," smiled Klaus. "I'm still really upset about the Dodgers."

"Oh yes," said Stefanie. "I forgot about that. Sorry."

"No need to apologize," said Klaus. "Everything is moving to California. That's where it's happening! Hollywood, palm trees, the beach!"

"You should come out sometime. It will do you good."

"Perhaps someday," said Klaus. "In the meantime, we are here and you are my guests.

"Speaking of seeing the sights, I took the liberty of getting us tickets to a matinee performance of 'The Magic Flute' at the Metropolitan opera. It's geared for a young audience, with a question-and-answer session afterward. Do you think the children will enjoy it?"

"I'm sure they will," said Stefanie with a smile.

Suddenly, there was a yell from the top of the stairs, "How far up can we go?" shouted Kevin.

Klaus answered, "Go ... Go! Explore!"

The two kids erupted with laughter and headed up to the third story.

"Don't knock anything over!" added Stefanie.

The house was fascinating — so many places to hide, closets and alcoves, high beds with room to crawl under.

Kevin was older and faster than Greta. When he got to the fourth floor he decided to hide from her. "You have to find me!" he yelled.

Laughing, he ran into the back bedroom on the south side of the house. Rather than finding a bed and dresser, he found a room that was filled with paintings. However, they weren't hung on the wall. Rather, they were stacked vertically in large racks. *Wow*, he thought to himself. *This is way out!*

The paintings were like none Kevin had ever seen before, not like the medieval and religious paintings in the rest of the house. Rather they were full of color —splotches of red and blue and purple, stripes and crescents, boxes and circles.

There was a huge desk near the window. It was strewn with papers and pencils. There was also an old black typewriter. On a table off to the side, there was a microscope. Kevin's mom had explained to him that his uncle's job was to take care of old paintings — that he worked for a museum. This must be his office, Kevin thought.

Just then Kevin heard Greta's giggling from down the hallway. He ran to the closet in the corner of the room and opened the door, and again he entered a new world. The closet had been made into a small chapel. On the side walls were very old paintings of saints with halos around their heads. The ceiling curved up in the middle in a half circle, and painted on its surface were angels. But these weren't like the little fat angels he'd seen on Valentine's Day cards. They were serious looking men — all intently watching him. The angels were surrounded by golden stars against a background of dark blue, painted to look like the night sky.

"Where are you?" shouted Greta's voice from nearby.

Kevin pulled a small chain that turned on a ceiling light and shut the door. He turned around, and that's when he saw The Lady for the first time. There was a painting of the Virgin Mary holding the baby Jesus. She was surrounded above by seven angels peering out from seven stars. The image made him feel comforted.

"Where are you?" Greta's voice was now in the room outside. Thinking she might see light coming from under the closet door, Kevin pulled the chain again and the closet went dark.

"Where are you, Kevin?" Greta's voice now sounded agitated. Kevin began to snigger.

"That's not very nice. She's your sister," said a calm female voice from within the closet. Kevin quickly flipped on the light again and turned around. There, for only a moment, stood the most beautiful person he had ever seen. She was dressed in red and dark blue robes. Her face smiled. She was The Lady from the painting.

The door opened and Greta burst into the closet. "I found you!" she exclaimed. Kevin quickly turned around again, and the woman was gone.

* * * * *

Harry Steven Ackley

August 1985

That was over twenty years ago. When he'd mentioned it to his uncle, he'd been told that The Lady shows herself rarely, and that Kevin was blessed to have seen her at all. His mother privately told him that his Uncle Klaus was a little nutty and that Kevin should stay out of his office. He could tell, even then, that his mother didn't care much for her brother's religious beliefs. Perhaps it was a factor in the distance between them. Despite his mother's warning, Kevin snuck back into the closet a few times during his stay, but he never saw The Lady again.

After the visit in 1962, as far as Kevin knew, his mother only saw her brother Klaus two more times. The first was when she went to New York to see an old schoolmate who had moved from Vienna. The other time was about five years ago, when she and Kevin's dad were having marital troubles. Other than that, Stefanie and Klaus only corresponded occasionally — Christmas cards and so on — and that was it. His mother tried to get Klaus to come to California to visit, but he never would. There was always some excuse.

Since graduating from UCLA seven years ago, Kevin had worked as a junior accountant for an electronics company. *Seven years as a subordinate.* Determined to go father, he applied and was accepted to Harvard Business School. It was he who suggested that he visit Klaus before starting his term. He was curious about his uncle, about the whole Austrian thing and about World War II. He wanted to learn more about that side of his family. Up until then, he only knew about the Peters — a bunch of Presbyterians from Iowa who had settled in California around the turn of the century. He wanted to know more about the Bronners — his odd old uncle, his grandparents, and the family torn apart by war.

He was also was curious about The Lady. Even though he was now 31, he still wondered, *was she real, or just a childhood hallucination?*

It was mid-August when Kevin arrived at his uncle's house. The humidity was stifling, far from the dry, warm summer that he'd left in Palo Alto. However, the tree-lined street of old brownstones, with its shady canopy of green leaves, was so different from the spacious modernism of suburban California that Kevin welcomed the change.

He walked up the steps and stood before the door with its dark wood and thick glass pane, and breathed deeply before ringing the bell.

When his uncle opened the door, Kevin was struck by how dashing he looked. In the years since his first visit, Kevin's mother had skewed the memory of the man to the point where Kevin remembered him as a lunatic nutty professor — lost in his world of art and religion. Kevin had imagined a frizzy-haired old man with thick glasses showing up at the door, unable to make coherent conversation.

Klaus was anything but that. Rather he was a slim, distinguished-looking man in his early seventies. His wavy, sandy blond hair was combed back, reminding Kevin a little of the Hollywood actor Joseph Cotten.

"Kevin!" said his uncle. "Welcome! Come in! Come in! You must be boiling out there."

On stepping inside the house, Kevin was soothed by cool scented air — a mixture of leather, spice, and old books.

The place looked very much as Kevin remembered it from his childhood. As you entered the house there was a foyer. From there, you walked straight ahead, down the hallway, back to the kitchen. To the left was a grand living room, lined with bookshelves and furnished with a massive coffee table, two wingback chairs, and a large green sofa, all strategically placed in front of an elegant marble fireplace. To the right was the great wooden staircase. The walls were still covered by old paintings of saints and angels and the kings of forgotten kingdoms.

"This is just as I remember it," said Kevin in a soft voice. "You have a fascinating home, Uncle Klaus. I feel like I'm inside a Sherlock Holmes novel or something."

Klaus chuckled, "Yes. My tastes are a bit Old World, I'm afraid. It's something your mother always found a little disconcerting, I think. Tell me, how is she doing?"

"She's doing well. It's been difficult since the divorce, but she's managed all right. She keeps busy with her women's groups. Greta's close by, so that makes it easier."

"I'm sorry about your parents," said Klaus.

"That's OK. It was a few years ago." Kevin shrugged. "It happens."

"I heard Greta's in grad school at Berkeley, yes?" asked Klaus.

"Yes. She's studying political science."

Klaus smiled. "She's not becoming one of those radical activists, is she?"

"I don't think so, Uncle Klaus. She's more of a bookworm really. Anyway, she and mom see each other at least once a month. They like to meet for lunch in San Francisco."

"That's good," Klaus nodded. "Someday I would like to go to San Francisco."

"You should go. Now that I'm on the East Coast, I can house-sit for you sometime." Kevin smiled.

After having some iced tea and catching up, Klaus showed Kevin to his room. It was on the second floor, right above the kitchen. Its window looked down onto the garden and a nice little cobblestone patio with a fountain in the middle. The garden walls were lined with trellises blooming with climbing roses. Great ferns and other plants filled the flowerbeds.

The bedroom had its own bathroom and walk-in closet. It was wonderful. *Why on earth did the old man stay here all by himself?*

"Pardon me asking, Uncle Klaus. But don't you get a little lonely here all by yourself? It's such a huge house."

"That's quite all right, Kevin. I don't mind you asking. I do have house guests from time to time. Visiting lecturers and researchers from the museum, art buyers and so forth. I like to entertain visitors. I also have a woman who helps me with the cleaning and also a gardener. Sometimes it can be quite a busy place." Klaus smiled. "Anyway, I will leave you to settle in."

After Klaus left the room, Kevin stripped down to his T-shirt and underwear and threw himself on the big bed. He couldn't believe his good luck. He felt that the world was at his feet.

* * * * *

Two days later, after spending the afternoon bar-hopping in Greenwich Village, Kevin came back to the house to find his uncle not at home. As Kevin climbed the stairs to his room, the sound of his footsteps made him remember The Lady in the closet. Rather than stopping on the second floor, he continued, all the way to the fourth floor.

He went to the door he remembered as Uncle Klaus's office and opened it. When he entered, he was shocked to see that the entire room had been converted into a chapel. The windows facing the south were now covered in beautiful, rose-colored glass. The walls and ceiling were painted with angels and scenes from the Bible. The room's light fixture had been replaced with a beautiful chandelier. A great oriental carpet covered the floor.

On the eastern wall of the room was a giant carved wooden altar, and in the center was the icon of The Lady, illuminated by a single votive candle. Looking into her eyes she seemed to smile at him, welcoming him back after so many years. As he continued to stare at icon, her face took on an almost three-dimensional quality.

She's so young in the picture, thought Kevin.

Kevin wasn't sure what to make of it all. His family wasn't really religious. They went to church on Easter and Christmas, and for weddings, baptisms, and funerals. That was about it. To Kevin, church was mostly about singing songs he didn't know and listening to old men dressed up in strange gowns droning on, *ad nauseam*.

This was different. This was, for lack of a better word ... cool.

Suddenly, Kevin sensed he wasn't alone. He quickly turned and looked behind himself. Standing in front of the doors of the walk-in closet was The Lady — who was really more of a girl. She looked exactly as he remembered, only younger. She was no more than a teenager. She wore a dark blue gown covered by a scarlet robe. Her hair was covered by a large red scarf. She smiled and slowly nodded her head as if in a greeting. She then asked, "Where is your sister?"

Kevin was about to answer when he heard the front door open and close downstairs. He glanced away for only a moment. When he turned back, she was gone.

Quickly, Kevin left the room and hurried down the stairs. Halfway between the second and the third floor, Klaus caught him coming down the stairs. He only looked at him. That's all that was necessary.

"I'm sorry, Uncle Klaus. I'm sorry. I remembered going into that room when I was a kid and my curiosity got the best of me. I'm sorry. I should have asked your permission."

"It's OK. It's OK. What did you see?"

"I saw her again. I saw the girl. She hasn't aged. She was exactly the same. Who is she? What is she?"

Klaus ran past Kevin up the stairs. He went to the fourth floor and went into the room. Kevin followed close behind.

When they went into the room, everything was different. It was an office again. It wasn't quite the same as it had been in 1962, but the desk was still there. The racks along the walls were there, although the paintings were different. There were a few bookshelves that hadn't been there before. The typewriter was now an electric. But it was still just an office.

Klaus went to the walk-in closet. It was locked and he had to open it with his key. Inside, everything was the same as it had been when Kevin visited over twenty years ago ... the paintings of the angels, the small altar at the back of the closet, and *The Lady*.

"This is crazy," said Kevin breathlessly. "When I was here just before, that was over there and this whole room was decorated like an ornate church. Those windows were different. This is too weird."

"You need to calm down, Kevin. You need to calm down and let me try to help you understand what you saw. What you saw today, and what you saw years ago."

Kevin and Klaus spent the next couple of hours sitting in the living room and talking. Klaus explained to Kevin about the icon and about its special powers. He explained that there had been times when The Lady briefly appeared. It had happened a few times since the icon had been in Klaus's care.

"It seems to happen when children are near," said Klaus. "That's probably why she asked about your sister. She remembered you."

"What should we do then?" asked Kevin.

"What do you mean?"

"I mean this is major stuff. Shouldn't you call the Vatican or The New York Times, or something?"

Klaus shook his head and said, "No, I am simply to protect The Lady until I'm told what to do."

"Told? By who?" asked Kevin.

"I think I've said enough for now," answered Klaus. "You need to get ready to leave tomorrow."

— Chapter 32 —

August 1985

The day after Kevin left for Boston, Klaus went for a long walk in the park. He was troubled that Kevin had seen The Lady and uncertain whether he should have shared with him as much as he did. *What else was he to do?* he thought. *He had seen her. What did it mean?*

Klaus soon found himself approaching the fountain with the giant aberration of an angel in the middle that Cassiel and his fellows found so amusing. He had questions for Cassiel, and he knew that, if he wanted to find him, this is where he would show up. He didn't quite understand it, but he knew the place was some kind of hub of activity for Cassiel's kind.

As Klaus approached the fountain, Cassiel was already there. Curiously, he was taking a picture of a mother and her two young girls. He noticed that the mother and one of the girls had brilliant red hair. The other girl, the younger of the two, had straight blond hair which reminded Klaus of Stefanie when she was child — a lifetime ago. *The younger one must take after the father,* thought Klaus.

After handing the camera back to the mother, Cassiel turned and approached Klaus.

"You're a photographer now!" joked Klaus.

"One of my many talents," answered Cassiel with a laugh.

The two walked away from the fountain along the path toward the boathouse. On seeing Cassiel, Klaus was always struck by how unchanged he was — the boy and the man combined together into a timeless being — a being able to glimpse eternity and reflect it back through his bright green eyes.

"You are concerned about your nephew," said Cassiel.

"Yes," said Klaus.

"Your perception serves you well, old friend. You should be concerned. He's a very confused young man ... smart and quick but with misplaced priorities. He loves the things of this world. Money, pleasure, power. Not uncommon at his age. But he is also volatile. His actions are unpredictable and he's vulnerable to influence. Do you plan to see him again?"

"Perhaps at Christmas. I told him that if he doesn't go back to California, he was welcome to visit. He is, after all, my nephew."

"I know. Something my kind has no experience with, I'm afraid. I simply have a myriad of brothers." Cassiel smiled.

The two stopped along the lake as they neared the boathouse. They watched the swans and ducks on the water and the children running along the bank.

"Cassiel, Kevin told me that when he entered the room where I keep the image of The Lady, that the entire room had been transformed, not just the closet, but the entire room. He described paintings on the walls, lighted candles, incense, a chandelier, and windows of colored glass. I've never heard of anything like that."

Cassiel's face looked troubled. Then he said, "She remembered him from the time before and she was welcoming him back. For some reason, he has a connection with the house and with the outcome of it all. Beyond that, I don't understand it any more than you."

"Perhaps he will be the one to bring all this to completion."

"You mean like some sort of heir apparent?" asked Cassiel.

"Perhaps," said Klaus.

"It doesn't work that way. God chooses whom he wills to complete his tasks ... like King David or Daniel. He might use Kevin. But for all we know he might use that red-haired girl back there."

Klaus nodded.

"Be careful with Kevin, Klaus. I have an uneasy feeling about him. Watch him."

"I will."

Cassiel put his hand on Klaus's shoulder and gave him a slight shake. "I have some good news for you."

Klaus looked up, "What's that?"

"Do you remember when you first arrived and I told you about your brother Ernst and how he saved the French family from the Nazis?"

"Yes," said Klaus. At the mention of his brother, Klaus's countenance changed. His eyes lit up with keen interest.

"The Giroud family," continued Cassiel. "Not long ago Mrs. Giroud passed away. Her husband died a few years before. Not having need of the house, but wanting to see that it continued to honor the memory of their parents, their children donated the property to a group of French nuns who were trying to start a school for teenage mothers.

"If your brother hadn't done what he'd done, that never would have happened.

"You see, Klaus, we never know how God will work. But we can trust that, in the end, he will."

— Chapter 33 —

Boston, Early Autumn 1985

The first few weeks at school had been overwhelming. The boy from suburban California sitting next to the old money of New England and the super-rich sons and daughters of oil sheiks and Asian CEOs. *What the hell was he doing at Harvard anyway?* Kevin asked himself.

The one place of refuge Kevin had found was Felder's Pub. He had discovered the place by accident one night when he was roaming downtown Boston. It was a Wednesday night, right after the semester had begun. A jazz quartet was playing. The music reminded Kevin of the In Your Ear club in Palo Alto, where he used to go listen to blues and jazz groups as a teenager. Felder's quickly became Kevin's place to escape.

Kevin studied the dark orange hue of the liquid in his goblet as he sat at the bar one evening. Scaldis Amber Ale contained a whopping 12 percent alcohol. On top of that, he'd also had a few shots of Maker's Mark. Kevin was feeling no pain.

Sitting a few stools to his right at the bar was a pretty young thing wearing a short white skirt, a pink tube top, white sandals and not much else. Her silky black hair flowed down her back, the curve of which Kevin's eyes followed all the way to her slim ankles and perfectly manicured toes. She was the living embodiment of the word "sex."

He wasn't sure whether to smile and say something stupid, or just forget the whole thing — the only two options that occurred to him.

As Kevin was about to speak, a large bearded man, wearing overalls and a Hawaiian shirt, who looked to be a cross between Colonel Sanders and Jerry Garcia, bellied up to the bar next to him. "I'll have a V.O. on the rocks, Myron" he said to the bartender.

"Sure thing, Doc," the bartender replied.

After the bartender moved off to get Doc his drink, Kevin turned to him and asked, "Have you ever seen anything really unusual in your life, like ghosts, or angels, or apparitions of the Virgin Mary or ... that sort of thing?"

Doc studied Kevin through thick glasses. After a long pause, he answered, "Only once, when I was a kid growing up in the Antelope Valley in California. Do you know where that is? It's where they land the Space Shuttle."

"I'm from California too," said Kevin, a little too enthusiastically. "I'm from Palo Alto!"

"Good ... good," answered Doc with a chuckle. "I've been there once or twice. Nice place. Lotsa trees as I recall."

"Yes ... YES! That's it!" Kevin now realized he was a lot drunker than he'd thought, so he shut up.

"The only time I think I may have encountered an angel," said Doc, "is when I was a boy. I was on the side of an irrigation canal out in the desert somewhere. I was all by myself, running along the top of the canal, when suddenly I slipped and went tumbling down the bank. Right when I was about to hit the water, I felt a hand grab the back of my shirt and pull me up. When I looked around, no one was there. It was a very weird thing."

The bartender came back and set down Doc's drink. "Here you go, Doc. Let me know when you're ready to start and I'll shut the music off."

"Thanks, Myron. Sure thing," said Doc.

"Wait," said Kevin, "You're with the band?"

Doc took a long drink and exhaled. "That's the stuff." Then he turned to Kevin and answered, "Yep, Dr. Gone's ICU. We're a blues group. Been playin' around Boston for the last ten years or so. I used to have an all-girl back-up band. We called ourselves Dr. Gone and the Night Nurses. That was a lot of fun." He smiled. "Well, I better get going."

"OK," said Kevin. "Nice to meet you."

"Nice to meet you too, kid."

"Kevin."

"Kevin," affirmed Doc. "Uh, none of my business, but when you're done with that, you oughta consider switchin' to water. At least for a while."

Doc then smiled, took his drink, and headed to the front of the room, where his band was setting up.

"Yep. Yep, he's probably right," said Kevin, sliding the remains of the goblet away. "Bartender ... Myron, can I have a glass of water please?"

"You got it, pal," said Myron who, in one smooth motion, set down a tall glass of ice water and whisked away the beer.

"Thank you," said Kevin. "You are a gentleman."

As Kevin lifted the glass to drink he noticed that the beautiful brunette in the pink top was still there. She was politely fending off some old hippie with long hair and a big walrus mustache. Kevin watched, drank his water and tried to gain his bearings when, to his left, someone said, "You seem quite attracted to her."

Kevin turned and saw a tall thin man in a gray suit, sitting two stools away. He was in the shadows, and smoke obscured his face. His cigarette hand reached over the bar and hovered above an ashtray. He held the cigarette vertically and tapped the end of the filter, dropping a giant ash.

The cigarette went back to its owner, who then took a large drag. The light from the cherry illuminated one of the strangest faces Kevin had ever seen. If it weren't for the man's stature, Kevin would have thought it was a kid playing dress-up in his father's clothes, yet ... a very sinister-looking kid.

"What's not to be attracted to?" asked Kevin.

"Indeed," said the man, as he exhaled. "I heard what you asked the musician a few minutes ago. Interesting question. One thing I always find interesting are the kind of thoughts that come to mind when we've had a little too much to drink. I think that's when our real questions come out, don't you?"

"I suppose," said Kevin who then took another long drink of water and looked over to the girl. She had successfully lost the walrus mustache man, and was trying to pay her bill.

"Perhaps a conversation for another time," said the man. "Right now, I suggest you go and assist the lady in pink. She's a bit short on cash."

Kevin shot a quick look at the man.

"Trust me. Go!"

Kevin straightened himself up and slid over to where the girl was madly fumbling through her purse. He smoothed the front of his shirt, put on his best Harvard smile and asked, "Can I be of some help?"

The girl looked up, smiled with her beautiful teeth and batted her big brown eyes. "Oh, could you? I swear I thought I had another twenty in here."

Kevin reached for his wallet. "Please. Allow me."

"Thank you," said the girl. "My name's Marissa."

And suddenly Kevin didn't feel so drunk. He turned around to look at the man and he was gone. There was only smoke dissipating in the air.

*****

Six weeks later, Kevin sat in the Harvard financial aid office being told, in essence, that, if he didn't come up with an additional $4,300, he wouldn't be unable to come back in the spring. Some funds he had expected weren't materializing, and his grant money wasn't going to be enough.

He told the woman that he was doing well in the first semester and that he would figure out a way to get the money. "How long to I have to pay?" he asked.

"We need the full amount by the end of the semester, Mr. Peters." said the smug woman behind the desk.

"Very well," said Kevin and he got up to leave. After walking out of the room and closing the door behind him, he let out a very frustrated, "Fuck!"

An hour later, Kevin was back on what he now called his *lucky stool* at Felder's. Not only had he rescued the young damsel that night, despite his blood alcohol content he'd had some of the best sex he'd ever experienced.

It was the middle of a weekday afternoon, and the bar was empty. He was on his third beer, combing his brain for ways to come up with the money he needed. He and his dad were on the outs, and his mother was already stretched. He'd sworn that when he came to Harvard he would do it on his own. He had everything lined up; or so he'd thought. Then, because of some stupid technicality, there was $5,000 that wasn't coming through. *Shit!*

There was his Uncle Klaus. He could ask him. But he barely knew the man. And he was afraid. The things that had happened at Klaus's house during those days before he came to Boston seemed unreal. Even though Kevin said he'd visit during Christmas, he was afraid to go back there. He was afraid how it might change him. He didn't want to be like his uncle. He wanted to live and have fun. He wasn't going to let some religious experience take over his life.

As he looked toward the front window at the far end of the room, smoke began to waft across his vision.

"My friend," said a calm low voice from behind. "Do you mind if I join you?"

Kevin turned and looked at the man. He was even more surreal-looking in the light of day than on the night that Kevin had met the beautiful Marissa. His face would have been almost cartoonish, had it not been so eerie. It was as if Kevin were looking into some timeless portrait painted centuries ago.

"Not at all," said Kevin.

A girl was working the bar this time, a very curvy, curly-haired girl who jiggled in all the right places and wore a permanent smile on her lips.

"Stoli on the rocks, please," said the man.

"I don't even know your name," said Kevin, who turned and extended his hand. "My name's Kevin."

"Pleased to meet you," said the man, who took Kevin's hand and squeezed. His skin was smooth and cold, but his grip was firm. Even though the fellow was quite lanky, Kevin felt that, if he wanted to, he could have ripped his arm right from the socket. Shaking his hand and looking into his emotionless gray eyes sent a chill down Kevin's back.

"My name is Hellmann, Dr. Arlen Hellmann."

"Doctor? You mean an MD type doctor, or one of those stuffed-shirts that stands at the front of the lecture hall and pontificates, while I shell out twelve grand a year?"

"Is that what they're charging now? My goodness, it's a wonder anyone can afford to go to college anymore."

"Yeah, well, if I can't find some extra income pretty soon, I may be done," said Kevin, who then took a big gulp of beer.

"Hmmm. Well to answer your first question, I am a medical doctor of sorts ... more of a researcher really. A scientist. And secondly, I may be able to help you with your financial dilemma."

Kevin noticed his glass was empty and motioned to the bartender for another beer. He didn't trust this Dr. Hellmann, but he was desperate. "OK," he said, "I'm listening."

"Why don't we find ourselves a table," said Hellmann, getting to his feet. It was then that Kevin was struck by the man's full stature — a good foot taller than himself.

The girl came over with Kevin's beer. She smiled flirtatiously, put down a napkin and set the goblet on top. "Thanks," said Kevin. "We're going to sit at a table."

When he looked down to grab his glass, he saw written on the napkin, "Kelly." And a phone number.

"My," said Hellmann, looking down at the napkin, "This *is* your lucky stool."

* * * * *

That afternoon with Dr. Hellmann, the conversation eventually led around to Kevin's uncle and his art collection and to the icon, in which Hellmann seemed to take a keen interest.

Weeks later, Dr. Hellman gave Kevin the idea that Klaus wasn't exactly who he seemed. "I looked into the matter and it seems your uncle may have had some affiliation with the Nazis during World War II," he told Kevin. Klaus Bronner, MD. Hellmann showed him the paperwork. Klaus had lived in Frankfurt. He'd had a family. No wonder his mother was so hush-hush about it all.

It was then that Hellmann began to disclose to Kevin his true objectives.

Our Lady of West 74th Street

— Chapter 34 —

New York — December 1985

The day that Kevin arrived in New York for Christmas break was bitterly cold. It hardly snowed yet that year, which oddly made everything seem even colder. The entire city was shades of dark brown, gray, and steel blue. The sky was shrouded with thin, high clouds, dulling the already dim winter sun.

Kevin arrived by train at Grand Central and then took a bus to the Upper West Side. He looked out the window at pedestrians braced against the cold, hurrying to get somewhere warm and safe. It made him wish he were back in Palo Alto, having a beer with his friends on University Avenue. There was something he dreaded about going to his uncle's. It didn't feel right. *It's Christmastime*, thought Kevin. He should be home with his mom and sister and their dog Garbo — a big hairy mix of yellow lab and golden retriever. Their mom named the dog Garbo because the movie "Grand Hotel" was playing on TV the night his dad brought her home. That was over ten years ago — a very happy day.

The bus stopped on Central Park West across from the Dakota Apartments. Kevin wasn't ready to face his uncle, so he decided to walk around Central Park a bit. The park was practically empty. He ended up at Bethesda fountain. Kevin then remembered the summer before. How his uncle had told him about the fountain being the meeting place for angels. He also remembered his uncle's description ... the angels being tall and hairless. He dismissed the thought.

He was looking up at the bronze, winged woman towering over the dark green pool of frigid water, when a young man appeared suddenly to his right. As the man got closer, Kevin felt intimidated by his height. Kevin was 5-foot-5, and became nervous standing next to tall men. Sitting down was fine, but standing, especially out in the open, made him feel vulnerable.

Kevin quickly looked around to check if there was anyone else he could call on for help if the man tried anything. There was no one.

But when he looked back at the man, he suddenly didn't feel threatened anymore. The man looked rather melancholy. His wet, red curls dangled over his face, a face which looked almost like that of a little boy. Kevin felt a kind of empathy for the man.

The man moved to within about five feet, then looked up at the statue.

"Do you think that's what they look like?" asked the man.

"What who look like?" asked Kevin.

"Angels," smiled the man with a nod towards the statue. "Do you think that's what they look like?"

"I don't know," answered Kevin. "I've never met an angel."

The man smiled again and asked, "Are you sure?"

"Well, I've never met one that I've been aware of."

The man just looked at Kevin. Kevin suddenly felt sad ... guilty for what he was planning to do. A gust of wind blew up and the cold penetrated him. He couldn't stand being next to the tall man any longer.

"Nice talking to you," said Kevin. "But I have to go."

Kevin turned and walked off. When he got about fifty feet away he almost looked back, but he was strangely afraid he would see that the man had disappeared.

* * * * *

Kevin was to stay for four days at his uncle's house. After that, his plan was to return to Boston. He wasn't sure when he was going to take the icon, but it made the most sense to do it right before he left. By the time his uncle discovered it missing, he would be long gone. That way there would be no absolute way to pin it on him — it could have been the gardener or the housecleaner who took it. However, this also put him into a position where, for four days, he had to pretend to be enjoying the holiday with his uncle.

Unlike Kevin's visit in the summer, Klaus was very quiet. They went out for dinner on the second night at a small Italian restaurant on Columbus Avenue. The red walls of the place were adorned with pictures of famous opera singers from times gone by — Enrico Caruso in his Pagliacci costume, Maria Callas as Carmen, Robert Merrill as Valentin in "Faust."

As Kevin stared at the last picture, his uncle asked, "Do you know that one?"

Kevin answered, "That's Robert Merrill. He sings before the Yankee games, right?"

Klaus gave a weak smile. "The Yankees, yes ... well, nobody's perfect."

Kevin returned the smile, took a big bite of pasta and washed it down with wine.

"Do you know what opera that's from?" asked Klaus.

Kevin studied the photo and guessed, "Don Giovanni?"

"Faust," said Klaus. "The story of a man who sold his soul to the Devil."

"I see," said Kevin. "I thought "Faust" was a play."

"It was," said Klaus. "It was a play written by an Englishman, Christopher Marlowe, during the Renaissance. 'The Tragical History of Doctor Faustus.' Then there was also a very long-winded German version written by Goethe. Charles

Gounod, a Frenchman, made it into an opera in the 19th century."

The two men sat silently for a moment, then Klaus said flatly.

"'Oh gentle Faustus, leave this damned art,
This magic, that will charm thy soul to hell,
And quite bereave thee of salvation.
Though thou hast now offended like a man,
Do not persevere in it like a devil.'"

Kevin shot his uncle a questioning look.

"Some words of warning to Faustus," explained Klaus. "From the play."

Two days later, Kevin was preparing to leave. His uncle had said his goodbyes and left the house early, simply instructing Kevin to lock the door behind him, and telling him where he should hide the key. As Kevin packed his bags, he noted how quiet the house was. It seemed all too easy.

During his stay, Kevin had not gone into the room where the icon was kept. Like an attacker avoiding looking into the face of his victim, Kevin did not want to see the face of The Lady. Yet, with all his bags packed, it was time to act.

He set his suitcase in the hall and slowly walked up to the fourth floor, each footstep echoing through the house. But unlike the happy clomping of he and his sister in 1962, this was a dreaded sound, like a man climbing to the gallows.

When he reached the door to the room where the icon was kept, he stopped. For a moment he felt compunction for what he was about to do, but then the compunction gave way to pity for his uncle. He was a fool for worshipping an object made of paint and wood. He was doing him a favor by getting rid of it. And then he remembered what Hellmann had told him —

about Klaus's Nazi past, and that Klaus himself was an art thief. The icon itself might very well have been part of his plunder.

Having thus reasoned his way through it, Kevin turned the knob and entered the room. It was as he remembered it from the last time he'd been there — a normal office. He'd already convinced himself that the vision he'd had last summer was the result of the heat and too much to drink.

He went to the closet and, after easily picking the lock, opened the door. Inside were the images of the angels on the ceiling and the icon at the far end, again, just as he remembered. However, everything seemed duller. He picked up the icon and, without looking at it, tucked it under his coat, pinning it against his chest with his elbow.

Kevin quickly exited the room, closing the door with his free hand. He then hurried down the stairs. His heart was racing. He would turn the thing over to Hellmann and his problems would be over. And he really didn't care about his relationship with Klaus or whether he'd ever see him again. He grabbed his bag from the second floor landing and proceeded to the first floor.

As he went down the last flight of stairs, he saw in the living room a pair of very long legs in wool trousers, stretched out in front one of the wingback chairs before the lit fireplace. When he reached the bottom of the stairs, the man in the chair spoke to him.

"Hello, Kevin."

He recognized the voice, but could not place it. Then the man leaned forward and turned around. It was the man from the fountain.

"Who are you?" asked Kevin. "How did you get in here?"

Then his uncle's voice came from the direction of the kitchen.

"I let him in."

Kevin felt his heart sink and, as he did, he also felt a warm wetness at his side.

Klaus came from around the corner and stared at Kevin. At the same moment, Cassiel stood up, turned, and faced him as well.

"My name is Cassiel. I am an old friend of your uncle's."

Kevin looked at the man. He couldn't have been any older than himself.

"*Old* friend?" said Kevin, who then added nervously, "Well, you look remarkably good for your age."

"You're wet," said Cassiel.

His uncle then came forward, grabbed Kevin's arm and reached under his coat. He took the icon and stepped backward, looking into its face.

"Tears," he whispered. He then moved closer, showed it to Kevin and said more forcefully, "Tears! You have no idea what you are doing! You have no idea what this is!"

The face of the virgin was wet. He could see a small bead of water form on the surface at the bottom of her right eye. He watched it as it ran down the length of the painting, across her hand and over her robe and then, before it could fall from the edge, it disappeared.

Kevin felt his side. It was soaked.

He looked back up at the icon and noticed the angel, the one furthest to the right. He looked from the angel to Cassiel, then back to the icon. It was the same face — exactly the same person.

Kevin was afraid. It was all true. The vision he'd had the summer before — seeing The Lady.

"I never asked for this," was all he could think to say. "He came to me."

"Who?" asked Klaus.

"His name is Hellmann," said Kevin.

— Chapter 35 —

New York — December, the present

Sure, he'd been willing to steal the icon. The thing spooked him. To get it out of his uncle's house should have been easy. He'd been promised he would be paid handsomely, and was given thousands in advance — a fortune at the time for a young grad school student.

But he'd been caught. He remembered his uncle yelling at him, with tears in his eyes: "You can never come into my house again — never!"

After he failed, Kevin thought his business with Hellmann would be over, but it wasn't. Only then did he realize the true nature of that person. Throughout his life, Hellmann, or whatever his real name was, continued to have some kind of hold over Kevin, mysteriously showing up throughout the years.

And it all kept going back to the icon. *The Lady*. Why? Why was she so important to a creature who seemed to have everything?

* * * * *

The limousine pulled up in front of the warehouse, and Kevin got out. He entered his security code, opened the door and went in. Since the night Vince and Dana died in the car accident, much of the art had been sold. Kevin had often considered selling the whole lot to get it out of his life.

However, there were still many pieces that had been part of his uncle's original connection — pieces that could be traced back to the war and possibly the Nazis. He didn't want to raise any red flags, so he sold it off slowly and quietly, and always through a third party.

The two pieces he intended to sell this time would cause a riot in the art world, but could make him over 100 million dollars. He went to the back of the warehouse and, after moving a few things out of the way, found what he wanted. Lying on a shelf against the back wall were two flat metal cases, each about two feet square. Kevin took the top case and, after unlocking the latch, opened it. Staring up at him was the stern face of an old Dutch woman.

The painting was one of several by Van Gogh all with the same title: "Head of a Peasant Woman with White Cap." This version (also known as painting F65) had been missing for decades. Its last estimated value was $43,000,000. It and the Van Gogh in the other case were worth more than the remainder of the collection combined. If Kevin could sell them both successfully, he could disappear and close this chapter of his life for good. But first he had one last task to perform. He had to connect with Amy Cuthbert and try to find that cursed icon.

Kevin closed the first case and moved it aside. He then opened the other.

He looked down upon a face filled complete serenity, Van Gogh's study of Rembrandt's blessing angel. He studied the expression ... no passion, no anxiety ... just calm observance. And Kevin imagined that's how unfallen angels were: calm, passionless ... watching humans contort their way through their lives, reacting to their pain and temptation, wondering why in the world they make things so hard for themselves.

Looking at the painting made Kevin wonder: *Was he damned?* He didn't feel damned. But he didn't feel peace, either.

The painting of the angel had originally been set aside by his uncle for friends he had met during his Atlantic crossing, friends who never came to claim it. Kevin looked over at the wall next to where he was standing, and saw some other paintings covered with a sheet and loosely tied together with a rope; paintings that had been reserved for the same friends. There was a large note pinned to the sheet that said, "Save for Eliaz and Rachel Balsam."

Kevin learned the story of the Balsams from his uncle's diaries, which he obtained after Klaus's death. They were brother and sister. Jewish immigrants his uncle had befriended on his voyage to the States in 1941. Klaus knew that some of the paintings in his collection might have been art that was confiscated from Jews by the Nazis. The story goes that he had offered the Balsams the paintings as a peace offering. Klaus had also noted a special fondness for Rachel and how he had saved her from being raped during the voyage.

After his uncle had settled in New York, he tried to find the Balsams to give them the paintings, using an address and phone number he had been given. When he called, he was told he had the wrong number. When he went to the address, he was almost murdered. A tall, blue-eyed, German-speaking man was not welcome, poking around a Jewish neighborhood in 1941.

He wrote in his diaries that he tried over the years to find them, but repeatedly failed.

When Kevin told the story to his sister after Klaus's death, she insisted that he hang on to the paintings, in case the Balsams ever showed up. But Greta had long since been out of the picture. Kevin had bought out her interest in the collection years ago. She didn't know its true value. He had, essentially, stolen it from her.

After Klaus died and Kevin got his first look at the warehouse, he went through everything with a trusted appraiser whom he paid handsomely and swore to secrecy. On discovering the Van Goghs, he had the special cases made for them for added protection.

Kevin went over to the bundle of art and untied it. In addition to the Van Gogh angel, there were two other paintings left that were meant to be collected by the Balsams. One showed a farmer and his wife flying around in the air with farm animals. *Weird,* thought Kevin. And one of an old Jewish violinist with a yarmulke and exaggerated payot. *OK, I can understand why a Jew would want that,* Kevin thought, with a smile.

The appraiser had told Kevin about the Nazi pillaging of art during World War II. That meant that these were probably confiscated works. He looked back over at the Van Gogh angel and said to himself aloud, "OK, I can understand why the Nazis would take these, but why would they take the one of the angel? It wasn't painted by a Jew and it's not particularly offensive."

"Perhaps, given their crimes, they found the sight of angels upsetting," came a familiar voice from behind him.

Kevin turned around to see Hellmann, looking very much like he had at Felder's Pub in 1985.

Hellmann let out a long, smoke-filled hiss and looked down at the Van Gogh angel. He didn't say anything. He just glared.

"You shouldn't smoke around the art. It could damage it." said Kevin as he closed and locked the case.

"Hmmm," said Hellmann with a passive tone. Standing next to Kevin, Hellmann loomed over him. He looked down at Kevin with a cold, expressionless face, and Kevin felt his insides grow numb. It was as if, all of a sudden, his life had no purpose.

"So," said Hellmann, "It looks like I need your help again after all. As I said on the phone, there's been new activity at your uncle's old house. I trust you read the news article I sent you."

"Yes."

"So, as I suspected, the object is still there.

"I really didn't plan to drag you into this. I was hoping to be able to flush out Mrs. Cuthbert using other resources. However, I'm afraid my associate, Mr. Onock, jumped the gun a bit in his effort to contact Mrs. Cuthbert. You remember Mr. Onock?"

"Yes," said Kevin, with a look of distain.

"Mr. Onock used your name and mentioned your brief association with Mr. Cuthbert as a way to try and gain Mrs. Cuthbert's trust."

"And?"

"Well, not all of my kind are equally as skilled in such things. Sensing her wariness, he told her that you yourself would be in touch.

"Also, as you know, we can't get into the house. You can call it a matter of spiritual logistics."

"So what do you want me to do, exactly?"

"Offer her your help. You know the story of the house and you know that what's happening there now is all real. I'm sure you can gain her trust. You're a charming fellow. Good with the ladies.

"Offer her legal help, seduce the poor woman, do what you must, but find the icon."

Hellmann then produced a manila envelope and handed it to Kevin. "Here, this may be of some use."

"What is this?" asked Kevin as he opened it.

"A leftover piece of a possible strategy from twenty years ago ... before Mr. Cuthbert met his untimely end."

As Kevin looked at the pictures of Dana and Vince Cuthbert, he grew angry. His beautiful young secretary used to seduce and to blackmail. And he knew that he too had played a part in it all.

"Perhaps it will prove of some use with the widow," added Hellman. "In any event, it's another playing card in your deck."

Part V
A Sign from God

A great sign appeared in heaven ... a woman clothed with the sun

— *The Apocalypse of Saint John* —

— Chapter 36 —

Emily Campbell's House — The Present

When she pictured her mother, Emily often thought of tomatoes. Annette Donohue had had bottle-red hair, red lipstick, and red finger nails. *She's a spicy tomato. And if you squeeze her, red acid will ooze out and burn your skin.*

The red tomato was yelling at Emily. "What the hell do you think you're doing? You're just going to make a bad situation worse! This is the stupidest thing you've ever done!"

Emily felt hate and pain at the same time. The ones you love hurt you the most, goes the old saying, and isn't it true?

"This is our family," responded Emily.

"People will know. They'll figure it out," her mother shot back.

"Who cares? It doesn't matter."

The tomato became black and huge. It spread its wings like a giant bat and roared. It flew to Emily and reached out to grab her.

"Mother!" shouted Emily.

* * * * *

Emily sat up in her bed. She looked around her bedroom and saw that it was still night. She was sweaty. The clock said 3:12 a.m.

It had been a while since Emily had had a nightmare about her mother. She hated it when she did. She wished she could let the bad memories of the woman rest and only hang on to the good. There actually was some good to her — at least there used to be, before Emily's and Sarah's dad had died, before Sarah had gotten pregnant. There had been a time when her mother was actually fun to be around.

Emily tried to go back to sleep but couldn't. At 4:30 she got up and made coffee. There were three and a half more weeks before school resumed in January. Emily had vowed she'd get much accomplished on Martin's book during the break. Heather was up in Rochester with Terry, and wouldn't be home until the next morning. Now seemed like a perfect time to get started.

The trip to St. Hilda's, especially her conversation with Sister Lizzie, had changed Emily's attitude about certain things. For so long she had tried to adopt a scientific approach — if it can't be proven, it isn't true. And people who believe in such things are weak.

But Lizzie wasn't weak. And her sister Sarah wasn't weak, either. In fact, sometimes it seemed like the non-believers in her life were the weak ones — Martin and his continual sarcasm, her mother and her desire for success and accolades. People like Lizzie and Sarah were the calm ones. Even Amy Cuthbert, in the midst of the ordeal at her day care center, managed to maintain a casual attitude about what she'd seen and heard. She didn't care whether Emily and Martin believed her story. It was what it was, take it or leave it.

She thought about her conversation with Ron Cassiel. He too had a confidence and a mystery about him. She wondered what it would be like to be held by him. To feel his hands on her waist and his lean body pressing against hers. It had been so long since she'd been with a man.

Emily thought about going online, and maybe connecting with Henry471 from White Plains. Heather was out of town. Perhaps now would be a good time to meet up for a drink.

She elected instead to flip on the TV for a while. She turned to the news. On the screen behind the commentator was a picture of an old painting — a stern-looking woman with frightened eyes and square-tipped nose. To Emily the woman in the painting looked a bit like her mother. She turned up the sound.

"The two lost Van Goghs have not been seen since they disappeared in Europe decades ago. For years they were suspected to be part of the Nazi plunder of World War II.

"The two paintings, coming up for auction at Sotheby's this week, have thrown the art world into a frenzy. Speculators estimate that their combined worth could top 100 million dollars."

100 million dollars, thought Emily. Van Gogh died in anonymity. The woman who posed for that painting was most likely a pauper who died young from hard labor and malnutrition. *And now she's worth tens of millions.*

As the commentator continued to speak, another painting, this one of a glowing angel dressed in a bluish white gown, came on the screen. Emily was struck by the face. Though not an exact duplicate of Ron Cassiel, it resembled him: tranquil, androgynous. And the hair was like his. Odd that she was thinking of him only moments ago.

Emily turned off the TV and went to the dining room table, her de facto desk and command center. And there again she was confronted with the subject of angels — her unfinished section of Martin's book.

She already had enough material. There were several firsthand accounts, including the singing at the day care center. There were also sightings of angels reported at the scenes of traffic accidents and hospital-room deathbeds. There was one story of a man who claimed that an angel had saved him from drowning when he was a child. He had slid down the dirt banks of a large irrigation canal and came to a sudden stop just before reaching the water. He swore that someone had grabbed him and held him back, but when he looked around, no one was there.

There was also one recent story similar to Amy's, where a group of elders at a Protestant church in Denver were singing a hymn at the end of a prayer meeting. When they stopped singing, the hymn continued. They reported the sound exactly as Amy had — a high chorus of crystal-clear voices, singing unearthly harmonies.

Emily now needed to consolidate it all into a concise narrative and turn it over to Martin. She also needed to suggest some pictures. Each chapter, where appropriate, was allowed to include two or three photos or illustrations.

She laid out all her material on the kitchen table and fired up her laptop. While waiting for it to boot, she looked at the cover of one of the books from the library. On the cover was Rembrandt's "Jacob Wrestling with the Angel" — another androgynous being looking down on Jacob with a kind of curiosity, almost cradling Jacob rather than grappling with him. And the bearded Jacob in his rust-colored robe, his eyes closed, fighting like a blindfolded child trying to strike a piñata.

Emily's eyes then moved across the table to the cover of "*Habitibus Angelos.*" She had decided during the course of her review that it really didn't pertain to what she and Martin were doing. Nevertheless, it was a curious book. She hadn't yet bothered to wade through the Latin in the last part of the book, about the return of the angels. She picked it up and turned to where she had left off.

"*Apparent coram angelis, cantu loquar, audiatur*" — "Before the angels are seen, their singing will be heard."

A description followed.

"*Aetherias voces, ut vitrum stellae caligine coruscans*" — "Their voices are ethereal, like glass, like stars sparkling in the darkness."

Well, how else would angels sound? thought Emily. *That's how I would write it.*

Yet, weary of her own cynicism, she admitted aloud, "OK, I don't know what to think. There's too much similarity."

She was becoming less convinced of Martin's theory that there was some matching psychological profile for all these case studies. Martin was trying to make an academic splash — his last before his retirement. These people were as different as apples and oranges. The only things that were the same were the stories they told. Emily wasn't so sure she wanted to be part of Martin's project anymore.

Emily turned another page and found a business card tucked in the crease of the book.

```
             Klaus Bronner, PhD
  Consultant in Art Appraisal and Restoration
```

When Emily read the address on the card, she couldn't believe her eyes. It was the address of Amy Cuthbert's house.

She remembered Amy's words ... *the man who used to own the house before we did — an old German guy. I think his name was Klaus something.*

Just then the phone rang. The voice on the other end sounded horrible. It was Martin.

"Hello, my dear," he said, in a weak, raspy tone.

"Martin," Emily responded. You sound awful. Are you all right?

"I'm afraid not, dear. I'm at St. Francis."

Our Lady of West 74th Street

* * * * *

On the 8th floor of the Ansonia apartment building on New York's Upper West Side, 90-year-old Rachel Balsam-Bennett sat in a comfortable chair. She stared at the television in wonder as the face of the angel came into her life once again. *Where had it been all these years? What had happened to Klaus?* A thousand questions flooded her mind.

Rachel picked up the phone next to her chair and dialed a number. After a moment she spoke, "Milo, I need your help. Please come over as soon as you can."

After hanging up the phone, the flood of memories continued.

She remembered the fights she'd had with her Uncle Benny when Klaus called the house. She argued that Klaus wasn't a Nazi, but it was no use. She pointed out that Klaus wasn't even German, that he came from Austria, to which Benny responded, "So did Hitler!"

Months after her arrival she learned that, using the address Eliaz had given him, Klaus had come looking for her, and that he had barely escaped unharmed. Men in the neighborhood had surrounded him on the front steps. Many wanted to kill him. They warned him never to come back, or he would be shot.

She tried going to Eliaz for help, but he had changed. He had his sights set on the Jewish Theological Seminary. A relative of theirs had a connection and was going to help to get Eliaz admitted. The last thing he needed was to be associated with the likes of Klaus. She remembered him telling her that things were different now. His words were, "We were on a ship at sea. Now we're on dry land in a new world — a world now at war with Hitler and Germany. Let him go, Rachel. Let him go."

But she couldn't let him go. He had saved her life. He had been bigger than the hate of his countrymen and had killed the anti-semite. Why couldn't her family do the same? Why couldn't they muster at least a grain of magnanimity and give the man a chance?

A few years later she met and married Christian Bennett, a successful New York businessman and a Protestant. Her family complained, but there was nothing they could do. Bennett had the means to insulate her from them and their small-mindedness. He was tall and handsome like Klaus, but he wasn't Klaus. There would never be another Klaus, *so why not?* she reasoned.

Then there was that fateful day at the opera. It was the summer of 1962. She and Christian were taking their son Philip to a matinee of Mozart's "The Magic Flute" at the Met. They had balcony seats.

Before the lights dimmed, she looked down to the orchestra section and there he was. Twenty-one years had passed, but she recognized him as if she'd seen him yesterday. Klaus and a young blonde, with two children, a boy and a girl, were moving into their seats. Even though she was married with a family, it stung deeply to see Klaus with another woman.

She thought of trying to find him at intermission, or to seek him out afterward, but she decided that she would only be tempting fate. She had a family and a husband. So, in the end, she did as her brother suggested, and let him go. But never completely.

— Chapter 37 —

Upon arriving at the hospital, Emily learned that Martin had been diagnosed with acute coronary artery disease. He was scheduled for surgery early the next morning — angioplasty and stint placement. Until then he was under close observation. He was supposed to rest.

"Dr. Campbell!" he managed to squeak in a cheery tone when Emily entered the room.

"How are you, Dr. Ellis?" said Emily softly as she came to Martin's side. He was pale and looked helpless.

"I'm a mess. But you know that already. Too many bags of Cheetos and vodka martinis through the years, I suppose. Sit ... sit."

Emily pulled up a chair.

"So, how did the big ski vacation go?" asked Martin.

"It was intense," Emily said with a sigh.

"Really? How so?"

Emily sat back in the chair. She studied Martin's face. He had been a good friend for the last twelve years — from the time she first came on as an associate. He'd mentored her, scolded her, and provided a shoulder to cry on, especially when her marriage was unraveling. Yet she was uncertain what to tell him. He was supposed to remain calm.

"Are you sure you want to hear about all this now?" asked Emily.

Martin nodded yes.

"I believe I've told you about my sister Sarah," said Emily.

"The nun. Yes ... the one who is the big family secret. Frankly, Emily, I never understood why it's all so hush-hush."

"I took Heather to meet her. Over Christmas, while we were up in Vermont."

"Good. It's about time she met her aunt, don't you think? How did it go? Is that what was so intense?"

Emily took a deep breath. "The thing is, Martin. Sarah is not Heather's aunt. She's her biological mother. I'm Heather's aunt."

Martin furrowed his brow and studied Emily's face for a long time. "Oh my," said Martin. "Oh my."

Emily then went through the entire story with Martin. He knew part of it already — Emily's tyrannical mother, the school in Europe. He'd just never heard about the adoption. No one knew. No one still living knew, except Emily, Terry, Sarah, Heather, and now Martin. And the nuns.

After it was all out Martin just laid there, staring at Emily. Finally, he smiled and said, "You did the right thing, dear. The truth is always the right thing."

Changing the subject, he asked, "So how's our Mrs. Cuthbert? You saw her again, yes?"

"Yes," answered Emily. "Look, Martin, I'd just as soon not use her in the book. She's under a lot of pressure from this stupid investigation. She's a nice person. She's been through a lot."

"That's not the Professor Campbell I know," said Martin.

Emily sensed what was coming; some sort of halftime speech about keeping your edge and not losing sight of the vision. The problem was, she wasn't sure of the vision anymore. "I guess I've been through a lot, too," said Emily. "My mind is clouded. I need a break."

"Hmm," rumbled Martin. "Are you starting to believe in things? Did the visit with the nun ..."

"Let's just let it go for now, Martin. I need a few days to think. To get my objectivity back, OK?"

"Fair enough."

Martin looked Emily hard in the face. "You know, dear, I'm not as much of a hard-ass as you think. And finding myself lying flat on my back, staring death in the face like this, I'm not so sure what I do and don't believe, myself."

Emily's eyes widened. She'd always viewed Martin as the old absolutist curmudgeon of atheism. For him to express any uncertainty whatsoever was a twist.

"If I don't make it," Martin started, but Emily held up her hand to signal *don't even go there*.

Martin waved her off. "If I don't make it through this, you write the book how you see fit.

"I give you my permission to do whatever you want. We have the contract with the publisher. Just write the book."

With that Martin started to fade a bit. The two just sat there in silence for a good ten minutes or so. Then there was a knock at the door.

The door slowly opened and a young priest entered the room. "Hello, I am Father Luis."

Emily and Martin both looked up. Father Luis was a short Hispanic man with glasses, all dressed in black except for the little white square collar below his Adam's apple. Emily hadn't seen so much clerical garb in such a short amount of time since her days as a Catholic school girl.

"Hello, Father," said Martin.

"I understand you are scheduled for surgery in the morning. I was just wondering if I can be of any assistance to you."

"Well, I think I'm gonna pass on the last rites, if that's what you mean," said Martin with a smile. "But I wouldn't mind a chat. We can talk a little hagiography, eh?"

"Oh, yes." said Father Luis as he stepped further into the room. Emily got up and offered him her chair. Before leaving, she kissed Martin on the forehead.

"Be good, old man," she said.

"Never," smiled Martin.

"You're gonna get through this. Then you can finish your book yourself."

"I'll do my best."

With that, Emily made a quiet exit. As she left the room, Father Luis wished Emily a Merry Christmas, to which she smiled and said thank you. As she closed the door, she heard Father Luis ask Martin, "Say, do people ever tell you, you look like Santa Claus?"

And Martin's answer, "No! Really?"

Looking down the hall, Emily saw a room with an open door. In it a doctor was holding the hand of an unconscious old woman. He appeared to be taking her pulse. *Was she dead?* wondered Emily. As she watched the two of them, the doctor looked at Emily and smiled. He was a very tall man with coal black hair, olive skin and penetrating blue eyes. *She'd seen him before. He was the man who sat next to her on the bus.*

Then she saw the woman open her eyes and sit up. Not the way a sick person would. Rather, like a child. She sat up and scooted back in the bed a bit. Then she swung her feet over the side, slid to the floor and stood, the doctor holding her hand all the while — like the two of them were about to dance. *She's so much shorter,* Emily noted with a smile.

Suddenly, someone shouted from down the hall behind her. "Room 404! 404 now!"

Emily turned to see two nurses rushing toward her.

"Excuse me, Ma'am," said one as she bumped past her.

Emily followed them with her eyes. They were heading to the room where she'd just seen the doctor and patient. The old woman was now lying on the bed. Her face was still and ashen.

Tears began to well up in Emily's eyes. *What's happening? What is happening to me?* She turned and walked quickly toward the elevator. As she waited for the doors to open, she whispered, "Please, God, save my friend Martin."

Not knowing where else to go, Emily went to her office at Vassar. The students were all home for Christmas break and the place was desolate. Even though it was only 1 o'clock in the afternoon, it seemed like dusk. The sky had darkened and there was another snow storm on its way in.

When she got to her office, Emily saw that she had a voicemail message. She put the phone on speaker, pushed the requisite sequence of buttons, and listened.

"Hi, Em. This is Vicky Branham in Berkeley. I have questions about some of the sources you're using for the book. Marty's not answering his phone or email, so I thought I'd try you. I would have called your cell, but my phone got clobbered by a four-story drop to the pavement and I lost all my contacts. It's a long story.

"This is quite a collection of characters you guys have assembled. There are some real loo-loos in here.

"Give me a call when you get a chance and pass the word along to Marty. Merry Kwanzaa-Kah and all that jazz."

Loo-loos, thought Emily. After what she'd just seen in the hospital, she wondered, *was she herself becoming a loo-loo?*

Emily sat in her office thinking about the book. Thinking about what Martin had said. *You write the book how you see fit.*

At that point she couldn't care less about the book. She just wanted Martin to live. She wanted things to be right with her daughter. The pot of stew that was her life was at a boil and she longed for the slow simmer of simplicity.

Emily looked at the picture on her desk — Sarah and her in their pink and yellow summer dresses — their doting mother grinning into the camera. *The camera,* she thought. Then she remembered where she had seen Cassiel before.

* * * * *

Bethesda Fountain — Central Park — August 1985

The recently widowed Annette Donahue was walking back from the boathouse with her two daughters when 8-year-old Emily piped up and said, "Look at the big angel, mom!"

Annette and Emily's little sister Sarah both turned around to look at the giant winged statue in the center of the fountain. "Oh yes," said Annette, "God's angels are watching over daddy now, my dear."

"But that's not a real angel," added Sarah.

"Well, no," said Annette, "It's a statue of an angel."

"But that's not what angels look like," said Sarah. "That's a woman! Real angels are men — big tall men. I've seen them in pictures."

"You mean like your daddy?" asked Annette.

"No," answered Sarah. "Daddy was old."

"A woman can be an angel," protested Emily. "Huh, mom?"

"Oh, a woman can be anything she wants," Annette agreed.

"There. See?" gloated Emily.

Sarah frowned, then persisted, "Angels are big, tall men with handsome faces. Like that man over there," she said, pointing at a tall man a few yards away ... a man with copper-colored curls that fell down over the collar of his light green shirt.

Both Annette and Emily turned and looked at the man, who smiled at them — one of the warmest and friendliest smiles they had ever seen.

"Well, how about we ask your angel friend to take our picture together?" Annette said, humoring Sarah.

The man agreed, and the three Donahues assembled in front of the fountain with the grand winged woman in the background, rising over their shoulders.

* * * * *

Emily was staring at her reflection in her office window — staring into the duplicate of her mother's face — when behind her another face suddenly appeared from nowhere.

"We have always found the statue quaint," said Cassiel. "That's why we meet there.

"Your sister was right, by the way. But you know that now."

Oddly, Emily wasn't frightened or even shocked. She knew. She knew ever since that snowy night in front of Blodgett Hall that there was something different about him. And she suspected what he was the moment she saw the icon at St. Hilda's with his face peering at her from his place in heaven.

"*Habitibus Angelos*," said Emily. "It was no accident that it came into my hands, was it?"

"No," said Cassiel.

"It has something to do with Amy Cuthbert I think."

"Yes."

"But you can't tell me what."

"No. The truth is, I'm not exactly sure myself. We see time unfold just as you do."

Emily had been talking to Cassiel's reflection. Finally, she swiveled around in her desk chair and looked up at him.

"Yes, that's what the book says, doesn't it? *Angels are constrained by the confines of human time. They are immortal but they cannot know the future.*"

"Exactly," said Cassiel.

"But there are things the book doesn't say," asserted Emily.

"There are many things the book doesn't say," agreed Cassiel. "What is it you want to know?"

"What about the others?" asked Emily. "What about devils and the forces of hell? If all this business with Mrs. Cuthbert is so important, won't there be others trying to disrupt it?"

"That's a good question. And one that's better answered by an illustration rather than in the written pages of a book. If you will indulge me, professor?"

Cassiel walked over to Emily's whiteboard and picked up a marker. He began to draw. Then he stopped and picked up another color and continued. He switched to another color, and then another. He drew with amazing speed and accuracy and, when he was done, backed away.

There before Emily was a beautifully detailed depiction of heaven and hell. Starry heavens filled with winged angels, then white clouds with God's giant hand poking through into a great blue sky. In the middle were hills of green grass, and purple snow-capped mountains in the background, and a stream winding through the center. On the hills were men, women, children and an assortment of animals. Then, below the Earth, red flames. And in the midst of the flames, serpent-like creatures with horns and menacing faces.

"I believe this part down here is what you're alluding to in your question, yes?" asked Cassiel.

"Well, yes," smiled Emily. "The big hand of God is a little Monty Python-like, but yes, that looks right."

"Too much time in the UK," agreed Cassiel with a smile.

"Now, consider this," he said, and he wiped the whiteboard clean.

"The battle between good and evil is not like some game of football on a vertical playing field. Rather, good, or heaven, is the center of reality." And as he spoke the center of whiteboard began to glow, the room grew darker as the shape took on a three-dimensional quality. Colors blended and swirled within.

"Heaven is in the center and the center of heaven is God. And yet God is in all things, and in him all things are given their existence."

Emily continued to stare at the light. It was so peaceful. She didn't want to do anything or be anywhere else. She only wanted to go into it and disappear from this life into what she now perceived as real life. Suddenly the ball disappeared and she was jerked back to her office and all was normal, except for the fact that a very tall celestial creature was standing a few feet away.

"Not yet, my dear, not yet," said Cassiel. "You have a few years left in this place first."

She stared at him for a long moment, getting her bearings. "So, if that is what heaven is like, then what is hell?"

"It is nothing," answered Cassiel. "Heaven is all truth, and all light, and all reality. And hell is nothing. And yet there are things that do exist inside the nothing. Your poet Milton hinted at this.

Without dimension: where length, breadth, and height,
And time, and place, are lost; where eldest Night
And Chaos, ancestors of Nature, hold
Eternal anarchy, amidst the noise
Of endless wars, and by confusion stand.

"So you're saying, rather than fire and brimstone, there's darkness and confusion?" asked Emily.

"Something like that, yes.

"*The heart is restless until it finds its rest in thee.*

"Hell is that restlessness."

"St. Augustine," said Emily.

"Yes," said Cassiel.

"You're just a quotation machine, aren't you?" she said, with a weak smile. "And where does this business with Amy Cuthbert fit it?"

"If what I think is about to happen is true, a great many more will move toward that true rest of which Augustine spoke."

"I believe you."

The two of them sat for a moment. Emily was a little surprised that Cassiel was still there, that he hadn't done his disappearing act yet.

Finally, Emily said, "There's another one of your kind watching me isn't there? I saw him in the hospital and I saw him before Christmas on the bus in the city, right after we first met with Amy."

"Yes," answered Cassiel. "Raphael."

"Raphael?" Emily repeated. "The Archangel Raphael?"

"Yes, well, the whole Archangel thing is something humans came up with, but, yes, he's that same person."

"What is it you want?" whispered Emily.

"We want to return. We want the world of man to change so it can receive our kind again. There was a time in history when angels and men interacted more freely. Now it is almost impossible. You've become too smart for us. Too smart to believe. Too wise in your own estimation."

Emily thought for a moment then asked, "What about the book? '*Habitibus Angelos*?'"

"Just my way of providing a road map for an old friend. I never imagined that it would end up in the hands of that same red-haired girl from decades ago. God's sense of irony, I suppose."

"Was your friend named Klaus?" asked Emily.

"Yes."

For some reason, Emily had grabbed the book before heading to the hospital to see Martin. Now she knew why. She reached into her bag and pulled it out. She opened to where Klaus's old business card was wedged between the pages. She took the card and handed it to Cassiel.

He looked at the card, then said, "You're very close, Emily. You have to keep following the signs."

"Why can't you just tell me what's going on?" said Emily. "I'm tired. I don't have the energy right now for a cosmic shell game."

"Why doesn't my kind just tell you everything then?" asked Cassiel. "Have it all done, no more veil; no more charades? It's because it's not our place. This is your story, not ours."

"But it *is* your story," replied Emily. "You said yourself that you want to return. Like it's your destiny or something. You're more wrapped up in this than anyone."

Cassiel gave Emily a passive look, "As I said, follow the signs." He handed the card back to Emily who tucked it back into the pages, and closed the book.

She studied the cover for a moment. "And the cover ... what does it mean? It's not just decoration, is it?"

"No. It's written in Angelic. It's different from human language. The shapes represent thoughts and the way they interlock and crosscut each other determines their context. But it's not really syntactical — it's dimensional ... it's difficult to explain."

She handed the book to Cassiel.

"Will you read it to me? I want to hear how it sounds."

Upon holding the book again, Cassiel smiled, that same warm smile he'd smiled by the fountain years ago. "They are poems of praise, something similar to your Book of Psalms. But Angelic is not spoken. It's sung."

Cassiel closed his eyes and lifted his head. He didn't need to look at the book's cover. He knew it by heart.

Cassiel began to sing. He sang the way it had been described. Crystal pure sounds, so tranquil and calming, like the vision he had shown her on the whiteboard, only heard with the ears rather than seen with the eyes. As he continued, Emily's office began to glow a warm orange, as if reflecting soft firelight. Cassiel became a pillar of light, too bright to behold.

As he concluded, the room went dark. Cassiel was gone. Emily was asleep in her chair.

— Chapter 38 —

Amy sat at her kitchen table with Kevin Peters and an attorney, Mark Gardner, as her son Nick leaned against the counter. They were going over their strategy regarding the investigation.

"All you have to do," said Gardner, "is sign this statement saying that it was never your intention to indoctrinate anyone and that, going forward, you will be more careful in what you say to the children."

"And that's it?" interjected Nick.

"That's pretty much it," answered Gardner.

Amy looked at the paper in front of her. After weeks of theater, it all came down to this — a one-page *mea culpa*. A little bit of embarrassment and a slap on the hand.

"Unbelievable," Nick quipped. "Two weeks ago these people wanted to burn us at the stake."

"What changed their minds?" asked Amy.

Kevin smiled, "Let's just say, when they found out that you suddenly had some legal muscle on your side, they lost their taste for a prolonged fight."

"Hmm," said Amy. "Let me study this tonight and I'll bring it with me to the deposition tomorrow. Will you both be there?"

"Mr. Gardner will. I have some other engagements," said Peters.

"I'll be there too," added Nick.

"We wouldn't have it any other way," said Kevin.

"I hope it wasn't too much trouble taking the time away from your work," added Kevin.

"No," said Amy. "It's the week after Christmas. A lot of people take their kids out during this time of year anyway. For the few that come, I asked the parents if they could make other arrangements. So, we'll be all closed up tomorrow."

"Excellent," said Kevin.

As Kevin and the attorney began packing their briefcases, Kevin turned to Amy and asked, "I heard rumors that you've giving interviews for a book that's being written by a couple of college professors — a book about paranormal phenomena."

"How did you hear that?" asked Nick. "Have you been investigating us?"

"No need to get upset," said Kevin. "Background checks are routine in these types of cases."

"We need to make sure there are no surprises when we go downtown tomorrow," the attorney explained.

"But how would anybody know that?" asked Amy. "I only met with Emily twice. It was informal. She told me it was all off the record until, if and when, she and Professor Ellis decided to use my story in their book."

"*Emily?*" said Kevin. "It sounds like you've gotten close to her."

"I've really only just met her," said Amy. "She seemed like a nice person, that's all."

"Well, until this matter is settled, I would advise not talking to her," Kevin said with a frown. "As you say, you've only just met her."

Amy studied Kevin's face for a bit. She sensed all along that he had some other agenda, but she wasn't quite sure what it was. To this point, she'd hesitated asking him about what happened with Vince. However, upon learning about him poking into her affairs, she felt less compunction about doing so.

"Nick, would you mind waiting out front with Mr. Gardner for a moment? I have something I'd like to ask Mr. Peters in private."

Nick gave a questioning look to his mother but then replied, "Sure. We'll be out in the living room, waiting."

After Nick and Gardner had left the kitchen, Amy turned to Peters and said, "I have to say, Mr. Peters, when I first received the phone call from your friend Mr. Onock, I was a bit taken back."

"That's quite understandable," said Peters. "It's been a long time. Over twenty years."

"Yes," agreed Amy. "He mentioned something about an object. That there was possibly something in this house that people might be after."

Peters smiled and shook his head. "Yes, well, I'm afraid Mr. Onock got his information wrong. The object in question was a piece of artwork missing from my late uncle's collection. It has long since been found. My intentions for reaching out to you were purely sentimental. I spent many hours in this house as a child during numerous visits to the city. And I have to say, it does possess unusual, almost mystical qualities. Does it not?"

Amy gave Peters a wary smile and responded, "Yes, I suppose it does." There was something vaguely familiar about Peter's missing artwork story, but she couldn't put her finger on it.

"The phone call from Mr. Onock also got me to thinking about Vince and the circumstances surrounding his death. I have to confess, one of the reasons I decided to accept your help was so I could talk to you — to find out what you knew."

As Amy spoke, Peters stared at her with a troubled face. Then his expression lightened. "Ah yes, well ... that doesn't surprise me. Of course you'd want to know."

Peters thought for a moment then continued, "Well, what I have to say about that isn't going to be pleasant, Mrs. Cuthbert."

"I figured as much," said Amy.

"The night your husband and my secretary died, they had been sexually involved."

Peters looked at Amy for a reaction. When there was none, he continued, "They had had an encounter at my storage unit on Long Island. I learned later that it was a blackmail attempt by my secretary."

"Really?" asked Amy. "How did you learn that?"

"Weeks after the accident, I was contacted by the man Dana had hired to secretly photograph the encounter. I have no idea how he got my contact information. I guess Dana gave it to him. He wanted payment."

"And what was the reason for the blackmail?" asked Amy.

Peters smiled and said, "Your husband was rich, Mrs. Cuthbert. He was on the leading edge of the Internet revolution. He had just made millions and was poised to make more."

"Hmm," huffed Amy. "And the photos?"

Peters hesitated.

"You paid for them, didn't you, Mr. Peters? And you still have them, don't you?"

Peters fidgeted then answered, "I didn't want them to get out. I was very fond of Dana."

"I'd like to have them," said Amy.

"Are you really sure you want to see them?" he asked.

Amy just looked at the man.

"I'll see that you get them," Peters nodded.

After Peters and Gardner were out the door, Nick asked his mother, "What was that all about?"

"Just some questions I had for Mr. Peters about his meeting with your father back in the early '90s."

"Why are we accepting this guy's help anyway, Mom?" asked Nick. "Why don't you hire your own attorney?"

"I was curious about Mr. Peters," said Amy. "Besides, I checked out Mr. Gardner. He's legit."

Amy thought a bit more, then added, "When your dad died, they searched for Peters to try and get some info on what his secretary and your father were doing in his car out in the middle of Long Island. They couldn't find him. Then twenty years later, he shows up wanting to help me. He said he'd read about the story in the news and feels a connection with the house.

"Bullshit! This guy wants something. He knows something about this place. And I just want to know what that something is."

Later that evening, Amy received a call from Emily Campbell.

"Hello. Amy?"

"Yes."

"This is Dr. Campbell ... Emily."

"Hi," said Amy quietly. "What can I do for you? How was your trip? Weren't you and your daughter going skiing or something?"

"Yes. Thanks for asking. It was good. Heather went to Rochester to see her father after we got back. She's coming home tomorrow."

After an awkward pause, Emily continued, "I just wanted to let you know that, I think you have enough on your hands right now, so I'm not going to draw any more attention to it. I'm going to leave your story out of the book. As a matter of fact, I'm considering pulling out of the project entirely and just letting Martin be the single author."

"Really?" said Amy. "Well, whatever you want to do is fine with me. It looks like this situation with the city is coming to a close anyway.

"Do you remember that phone call I told you about?"

"Yes," said Emily. "You said it kind of spooked you."

"Well, it turns out, this Mr. Peters actually showed up. He explained that he'd had some similar experiences in the house when his uncle Klaus was alive. He offered to provide some legal help ... to just settle the whole thing. I tell you, once this is over, I think I'm going to sell the place. I really can't explain what's kept me here, but there's nothing I can do anymore. I'm just tired."

At the mention of Peters' uncle Klaus, Emily remembered the business card. Her voice took on a different tone. "Are you sure?"

"I think so. I don't know. Honestly, I just want this thing to be over. The deposition is tomorrow."

"Really?" asked Emily. "Well, I'm picking up Heather at La Guardia tomorrow around noon. We talked about spending some time in the city afterward. It's our little tradition to go see the Christmas tree at the Met each year. We need to do it before they take it down. Maybe we could meet up later. You could tell me how things went."

"I'll think about it," said Amy. "Look I have to go. I have your number. If things go smoothly and quickly, I'll give you a call."

"OK," said Emily.

Amy hung up and thought, *Odd that Emily would call right after her conversation with Peters — his warning her not to speak to her.* Emily had had a tone of concern in her voice that worried Amy. *There's been too much of that,* she thought ... a*ll the more reason to get this over with and move on.*

Amy looked over at Nick who, smiled and said, "Well, so much for not talking to the college professor."

— Chapter 39 —

Emily hadn't visited her parents' gravesite since she'd buried her mother seven years ago.

On the day she was to pick up Heather at the airport, Emily left early and took the Taconic State Parkway down to Hawthorn, to the Gate of Heaven Cemetery. The Gate of Heaven was a Catholic cemetery where many notable Catholic New Yorkers had been laid to rest, including the great Babe Ruth. Emily's dad, Timothy Donohue, had loved the Yankees and, after his death, when there was still plenty of family money, Annette bought a pricey gravesite for her and her husband as close to the Babe's as she could get.

Emily arrived at Gate of Heaven at around 10 o'clock in the morning. The grounds were covered with snow, but the narrow road that led to her parent's grave was clear. She parked, got out and crunched through the snow to the large marble headstone marking the final resting place of Timothy and Annette Donohue. It occurred to Emily how, once you know where a gravesite is, it's not something that you forget.

She thought back to the two burial services that had occurred there. Her dad's on a sunny spring day in 1985, and her mom's, during a cold, biting rain in early November, over two decades later. Her dad's funeral had been well-attended, with many old Irish friends and business associates. She remembered the wake on the evening before — her father's dead, cold, body lying in their living room. He looked almost artificial to her. She remembered sitting with Sarah on the huge brown leather couch in their father's study while well-dressed men and women stood around with drinks in hand and spoke in low tones about the suddenness of her father's death and all the unfinished business he'd left on his plate.

In contrast, her mother's burial was a sparsely attended affair. Since Sarah was at the St. Hilda's, Emily and Terry had to see to the arrangements. Her mom's sister Renee, another strained relation, came from Baltimore, but that was the extent of family members who were there. On the day of the funeral Sarah showed up, but she wore a large hat and a scarf, and stood a distance away. She left promptly after the burial. That was the last time Emily had seen her sister outside of the Abbey.

It was odd that Sarah had asked to meet there.

Emily looked at the monument in front of her.

Timothy Patrick Donohue
March 19, 1923
April 16, 1985

Annette Rosemary Donohue
August 24, 1944
November 3, 2007

The information for her father was almost thirty years old now. It had faded and given in to time, becoming like what the letters on a headstone should look like. Her mother's were newer. They still had their edge. Emily reflected on this and thought that the death of her mother still, indeed, had a bite to it, whereas her father had faded into the past. His memory had grown happily vague. Her mother's was still fresh and stinging

But all was different now. The encounter with Cassiel had thrown everything into a new light. Perhaps now was the time to talk to her mother ... to talk to her as she'd never been able to do when her mother was alive

"What was so important?" asked Emily. "What was so damned important that love and gentleness had to be pushed aside? Would it have hurt you to have been a little more kind and patient? Would being so have really changed the outcome of anything? And what if it had? Might not have things even been better? Wouldn't it have been better to have a family filled with love, than a family torn apart for the sake of pride and propriety?"

Emily stared at the grave as if waiting for an answer. When none came, she continued, "Your granddaughter, whom you barely knew, at whom you turned up your nose, made an observation and I think she was right. She said it wasn't pride, but fear. What were you afraid of, Mom?"

This time an answer did come. "Uncertainty," came her sister's voice, from behind.

Emily turned and saw Sarah walking toward her in the snow. She was out of her habit, wearing brown corduroy slacks, a pair of insulated boots, and a large, dark-green wool coat. Her head was covered with light-blue knit cap. In her hand she carried a small wreath.

Emily smiled broadly and said, "I haven't seen you in civvies since the last time we were here."

Sarah smiled back and said, "we keep a small wardrobe at the Abbey for just such occasions."

"How did you get here?" asked Emily.

"Lizzie drove," answered Sarah. "She said she was going to go and see if she could scrounge up a donut and a cup of coffee somewhere. I told her to meet us at your car in an hour."

Sarah moved next to Emily in front of the grave. She put her arm around her sister and looked down at the monument.

"Mom was afraid of uncertainly ... of what she couldn't control. It's the way a lot of people are. Fear of health problems, money problems, upheaval in the family. But the thing is, we can't control any of that. Not really.

"In a way, I was like her. That's part of the reason I became a nun. I wanted certainty. I loved the regimen and the finite answers. After I became pregnant, everything seemed chaotic.

"So, even though it wasn't money and social standing that I craved, I still coveted control, like mom did."

Emily stared at her sister's face ... her deep blue eyes and perfect skin that was quickly turning red on her cheeks and nose. "You've never told me that before."

"Yeah, well maybe I never really understood it myself until recently," replied Sarah, who then knelt down and placed the wreath on her parents' grave. She crossed herself and then stood up.

"But that's not the reason I remained a nun. I remained a nun because it brought me peace. And ironically, the peace comes from knowing that you can't control everything. That, regardless of how the world changes around you, there is one who is in control and that is where we need to entrust our fear rather than trying to manage it on our own.

"It's a simple idea. Many have said it before, but it's true. *Consider the birds of the air ... consider the lilies of the field ...* that sort of thing." Sarah smiled at her sister again. "Let's walk. The chapel is not far from here. It should be warmer in there."

As the two walked along the path to the chapel, Emily thought about the idea of certainty. How in her own way, she too tried to control everything by dissecting and unraveling ideas and beliefs until they meant nothing. *All truth is relative,* and by believing so, she mastered it. "Perhaps the need to control things is an impulse common to everyone," she said. "And some, like our mother, just let it take over."

"Perhaps," said Sarah.

The two went inside the Our Lady of Peace chapel. On entering, Sarah blessed herself by dipping her fingers in the font and making the sign of the cross. At first Emily wasn't sure what to do, but realizing her old habit of resistance to such ritual was no longer being true to herself — it was only yesterday she had encountered and angel — she did the same.

Even though they had the place to themselves, they sat in the back, and for a few minutes just admired the light and the furnishings and the image of the Blessed Mother. Emily waited for Sarah to speak. While waiting, she thought of Martin and silently prayed for him.

"Thank you for bringing Heather to see me," Sarah began. "I can't tell you how I've longed to see her all these years."

"I should have told her a long time ago," said Emily.

"Things happen when they do for a reason," said Sarah. "You've done a tremendous job with her. She's grown to be a wonderful person."

"Thanks," said Emily.

"I would like to stay in touch with her. But I want to make sure that's OK with you first."

"Of course it's OK," said Emily.

"I will never try to replace you. You are her mother and you always will be. But seeing Heather has brought something back to me that was missing and I don't want to give that up."

"What's that?" asked Emily.

"I don't know, exactly. A feeling of being connected, I guess. Not connected to the outside world so much, but being connected to the continuance of life. When I die, she'll go on. Perhaps it's a selfish feeling, but it makes me happy."

Emily put her hand on Sarah's back and massaged her a bit. Something about her being out of uniform made it seem OK. For the first time in a long time, Emily felt like a big sister again.

"It's not selfish, Sarah. It's natural. You're her mother. And your gift to me is that I'm her mother too, and I get to share in that same feeling."

They sat again in silence. Then Emily spoke, "Is that the only reason you wanted to meet?"

"Yes," said Sarah. "I needed closure to the past and permission to embrace the future. I've been in a kind of limbo these last fourteen years. Now it's time to move forward."

"I think that's true for us all, Sarah."

The two got up and left the chapel. After doing so, they walked down a corridor past a long wall of crypts. In the distance, Emily noticed light reflecting oddly off the surface of one of them.

She stopped and looked at it. There was a pear-shaped shiny spot on the pink marble plaque. Emily read the name engraved on the outside.

Klaus Bronner
December 10, 1911
July 27, 1993

Emily was about to speak, but it was Sarah who said, "Klaus Bronner ... that sounds familiar." Sarah then reached out her hand and touched the spot and held it to her nose. "Myrrh," she said. "It's a sign."

"You ain't kidding it's a sign," said Emily.

On the way back to the car, Emily told Sarah the whole story of Amy Cuthbert and Klaus Bronner and the house on West 74th Street.

When she was done with her story Sarah responded, "What's going on in the house on West 74th is very important. I don't know what it means either, but it certainly is exciting.

"But that name ... Klaus Bronner ... I know it too. I've heard it before.

Emily thought for a moment.

"I may go to see Amy this afternoon, after I pick up Heather at the airport. You could come too, if you wish. I can take you to the train afterward, or even drive you back to the Abbey."

Sarah shook her head. "Thanks for the offer, but I think this is something for you to do on your own. Have fun with Heather. Tell her I love her and, whenever she's ready again, we'll see each other."

Emily hugged her sister and said, "I'm sure she'll be ready soon."

When they got to the parking lot, Emily saw a new black Scion coupe parked next to her car, with a spectacled nun sitting behind the steering wheel. As they approached, the driver's side window went down and Lizzie shouted, "'Bout time you two showed up. I was about to freeze my tizzories off!"

Emily shot her sister a curious look and asked, "Tizzories? What are tizzories?"

"It's some inside-nun humor." smiled Sarah. "Believe me, being in on the joke is not worth taking vows."

Emily turned to Lizzie. "That's a nice new car you got there."

"Oh yeah," answered Lizzie. "It was donated to the Abbey a couple of months ago. A dealer in Montpelier was getting rid of last year's models and needed a write-off. Six-speed manual transmission, 180 horses, zero to sixty in seven seconds. Pretty spunky ride for a couple a nuns."

"*Donated?*" said Sarah to herself with a furrowed brow. Then she looked up, "That's it!"

"What?" asked Emily.

"I remember now," a man named Klaus Bronner left a huge amount of money to *La Maison Giroud* a few years before I started school there. That's how they were able to build the performing arts center and the gym. There's a big monument on the grounds commemorating his generosity. I believe he was an American too. I wonder if it was the same man?"

Emily smiled, "I'm sure it was. I'm done giving credit for such things to coincidence."

Emily pondered the snow-covered cemetery for a moment. She then turned to Lizzie, sitting in her little black car, and asked, "How come you aren't dressed in street clothes?"

Before Lizzie could answer, Sarah interrupted. "It was just my thing. I thought a nun wandering around a Catholic cemetery might be a target for attention. I didn't want us to be bothered. Plus I just wanted us to feel like two normal ol' sisters again."

"It'll take more than white linen and black wool to ever change that," said Emily.

— Chapter 40 —

Rachel Balsam-Bennett and her personal assistant, Milo Zeffren, a beefy, balding man in a dark blue suit, stood in the vault of Sotheby's waiting for the auction director and two armed guards to return with the painting. Ms. Allen, an assistant to the director, stood with the two as they waited.

"This is extremely unusual," asserted Ms. Allen. "If it weren't for the Bennett family's ties to the auction house and the art community ..."

"I assure you, Ms. Allen," said Rachel, "I quite understand the difficulty my request presents. I have my reasons for wanting to see the painting."

Just then the others returned. The director held the painting in his white gloved hands. He brought it to the table and gently set it down.

Rachel stared down at the calm face on the canvas. *Her hero angel.* It had been 73 years since she'd last seen it in the hold of *A Estrela do Mar.* She thought back on that day and of the handsome man who had stopped her rape and killed her assailant.

"Turn it over please?" asked Rachel.

Ms. Allen and the director looked at each other and shrugged. The director then carefully turned the painting face down. The backside looked no different from any other old stretched canvas.

Without looking down on the painting, Rachael said, "if you lift the canvas in its upper right corner, you will find the words, "My heart will always dwell on what might have been. Love, Klaus. That's Klaus with a K."

The director did so and, sure enough, written in dark pencil, were those exact words.

The two looked at Rachel with astonishment. "How did you know?" asked the director.

"Because the painting is mine," answered Rachel. "It was given to me by its former owner.

"He wrote it in English because we had just arrived in America," Rachel remembered with a smile. "I remember him asking me in his thick German accent, 'We speak English now, yes?'"

Rachel looked at Ms. Allen. "So, seeing as how the ownership is now in doubt and, as you mentioned, the Bennett family's ties to the auction house, I request that you postpone the auction of this piece until I have had time to talk to its current owner and, hopefully, arrive at a mutually acceptable arrangement."

About twenty minutes later, as Rachel and Milo were leaving Sotheby's, she turned to him and asked, "Did you get the information?"

"Yes," he answered. "The house is on West 74th, between Amsterdam and Columbus. Bronner died in 1993, but he'd lived there since the early '40s."

"My God," said Rachel. "All this time, and he was only two blocks away.

"Did you learn anything about his wife or children?"

"Ma'am?" asked Milo.

"His wife and children. He had a family, didn't he?"

"No, ma'am," said Milo. "He was alone all his life. The house was left to his niece and nephew. They sold it over twenty years ago."

Rachel looked at Milo with large, misty eyes, and said, "Let's drive by. I want to see where he lived."

— Chapter 41 —

Kevin sat in a parked car on the north side of West 74th Street. He had a perfect view in his rear view mirror of Amy Cuthbert's house across the street. Her meeting downtown was scheduled for 11 a.m. To ensure that she got there and that her son went along as well, Kevin had arranged for Gardner to pick them up in a car. At 10:10, Gardner arrived, and five minutes later they were on their way. Kevin grabbed a black backpack and got out of the car.

As Kevin walked across the street, he thought back to the first time he had arrived at the house, in 1962 — 52 years ago. He would never have guessed then that the place would factor into his life for so long. But why shouldn't it? There are people who spend their entire lives living in the same house ... going to the same church ... shopping at the same stores.

A black limo, parked in front, initially gave Kevin pause, but he dismissed it. Such a sight was common in this neighborhood.

As he neared the house, he heard footsteps behind him. He knew who it was. He stopped on the sidewalk. "Yes? What is it?"

Kevin turned around and looked at Hellmann. He was surprised by Hellman's expression. No longer cool and confident, he seemed worried.

"I wanted to give you one last bit of information. Once you have the thing, you must destroy it."

Kevin's entire face wrenched up in disbelief. "What? I thought you wanted it! I thought that was the whole point of this!"

"I can't take it. It is a human thing. You must take it and destroy it, preferably burn it. I will know when it's gone."

"This is insane. All these years, and you want me to destroy it?"

"Yes. Then our business will be over and I won't bother you again."

Kevin thought about the vision of the young lady. He could still see her soft, kind face. She had seemed so real. What would happen to her if he destroyed the icon? Yet, he knew the influence Hellmann had over him. He knew that if he didn't destroy it, the nightmare would only continue. It would continue for the rest of his life.

"I will take care of it," Kevin told Hellmann.

"Good," said Hellmann with a nod. "How do you plan to get in?"

"It's one of my many talents," answered Kevin. And with that, he proceeded up the front steps.

When he got to the door, he turned around and, as usual, Hellmann was gone. It occurred to Kevin that Hellmann was a coward — manipulating, planting ideas, making threats, and then disappearing — like some sort of decoy in a set-up, leading people into an ambush and then fading into the background.

After quickly picking the lock, just as he opened the door, Kevin heard another voice — a small crackly voice. "Excuse me."

He turned and was surprised to see little old lady standing at the bottom of the front steps. Behind her, leaning against the limo, was a large bearded man in a blue suit.

"Yes?" answered Kevin in an abrupt tone.

"I'm sorry to bother you," said the woman as she placed her foot on the first step. At this, the bearded man rushed forward and supported her from behind. On the seeing the man's full frame, Kevin softened his stance.

"I'm sorry to bother you," repeated the woman, "but are you affiliated with the day care center?"

Kevin was unsure what to say. He was nervous to be standing there, on the steps of a house where he had no business, having a conversation with an old lady while her goon driver propped her up.

"I'm helping Ms. Cuthbert out with some business matters," answered Kevin. "What can I do for you?"

With Milo's help, Rachael continued to make her way up the steps. "It's just that, I knew the man who used to live here. We were friends. I was just curious if I could poke my head through the door ... for sentimental reasons."

Rachel finally made it to the top of the stoop and stood next to Kevin. She looked into his eyes and said, "His name was Klaus."

Upon hearing the name of his dead uncle, Kevin froze. A dozen thoughts ran through his head. *Who is this woman? What does she want?*

"How did you know him?" asked Kevin.

"We were on a ship together coming from Europe during the war. We became friends. My name is Rachel, Rachel Balsam-Bennett. This is my assistant Milo."

Kevin studied the old woman's face. He then looked to Milo, standing there expressionless ... *her muscle*. Suddenly, it dawned on him ... *the painting*. Somehow the old lady had learned the story of the Van Gogh. She was here posing as Klaus's long lost friend trying to scam him out of his millions.

"You're here about the painting, aren't you?" asked Kevin.

"Excuse me?" said Rachel.

"Oh come on," said Kevin with a despising grin. "Somehow you found out about the Van Gogh. It doesn't surprise me. My uncle had lots of friends in the art world. I'm sure he ended up letting the story slip to a few people over the years. About the poor Jewish girl from the boat ... and now, just as the painting is about to be auctioned, here you are."

"Your uncle?" asked Rachael. "You are Klaus's nephew?"

"Please," said Kevin in a sarcastic tone.

At this, Milo stiffened himself, went to the step just below Kevin, and said on a flat low voice, "You need to watch your tone, sir. You have no idea who you are addressing."

Even though he was a step down, Milo stood taller than Kevin. Kevin stepped back, in deference to Milo's size.

Kevin softened his tone and said to Rachel. "You need to tell your muscle man to back off, Miss Balsam, if that is, in fact, who you are. If you're after the painting, you'd better have a whole army of lawyers on your side. It was left to me. I own it."

Rachel shook her head and said, "How could a foul little man like you be related to such a kind man as my Klaus?"

"Kind?" asked Kevin. "You're not much of a Jew, are you? Klaus was a Nazi. He tortured and murdered your people. How can you say he was kind?"

"A Nazi?" said Rachel. "You don't know what you are talking about. He saved my life. He saved my life from a Jew-hater bigot. He was no Nazi."

Kevin then remembered the story from Klaus's diaries ... his uncle's description of Rachel ... his recounting of the murder on the ship. He knew then that this really must be the woman. As for her 11th hour arrival on the scene, it then dawned on him that there were forces at work to keep him from his task.

"You have go," said Kevin. "I can't talk to you now. Call me tomorrow and we will discuss the painting."

"I don't want your painting," said Rachael. "My late husband built three corporations from the ground up. He was a partner in multiple shipping lines and in air transportation. I wasn't going to sell it. I wanted it because your uncle gave it to me. And I loved him."

With that, Rachel turned and began to descend the stairs. Milo turned back and said in harsh whisper, "You'd better hope we don't ever run into each other."

Once inside the house, Kevin proceeded straight up the stairs to the fourth floor. He went to the room that had been his uncle's study. It was now a bedroom. He assumed it belonged to the boy. The south wall was lined with computer equipment — monitors, mixing consoles and sound equipment. *Maybe the kid is making music videos or something*, thought Kevin.

He went into the closet, but nothing was there — just clothes and some old sports equipment. He figured as much. He had swept every inch of the place when his uncle died — the attic, the basement, every closet, cabinet, and cubby hole. Nothing was there.

After years of thinking about it, Kevin had concluded that, if it was here, the only place it could be was in the walls. Kevin set down the backpack and opened it. Inside was a device that looked like an oversized game controller. It was something developed by a company in England — a through-wall reader. It used ultra-wide-band radar to see objects and activity on the other side of walls. It was primarily created for the military, for rooting out terrorists in hiding. It was probably overkill for what Kevin was doing.

Kevin flipped on the device and the screen came to life. He held it to the wall and began moving it slowly up and down. As he did, he could see the wall studs and the faint shapes of solid objects in the next room. After scanning Nick's room, he moved to the hallway. He did the bathroom at the end of the hall and then proceeded to the second bedroom. The fourth floor yielded nothing, so he moved to the third.

On the third floor, he began with the south-facing room again, then moved to the next room. When he began scanning the wall, he saw a shape moving on the other side of the wall, in the hallway. It was a brighter yellowish-red color — a heat-producing life form — a human. "Hello!" shouted Kevin. "Who are you? Who's there?"

Was it the Balsam woman? Kevin wondered. Remembering the difficulty she had climbing the front stairs, he dismissed the idea. He went into the hallway. No one was there. He went to the front window at the end of the hall and looked down. The limo was still parked outside. *Had he locked the front door?*

He went back into the bedroom and scanned walls again. When he got to the wall facing the hallway and scanned, he saw the shape moving to the stairs. He could now see the outline more clearly. It was The Lady.

Kevin burst out into the hallway and ran to the stairs. There was nothing. She must have gone down, he thought. Still holding on to the scanner, he trotted down to the second floor landing and shouted, "Are you there? Are you there? Please show yourself to me. I won't hurt you."

He rushed into each of the second-floor bedrooms. No one was there. He then began to hear singing. At first it sounded like children. Faint. Coming from a remote part of the house. But then the sound began to swell and the voices changed. Suddenly the voices were clear and strong like the sustained ringing of bells. But not cacophonous at all. Rather, it was like sweet ringlets of water interacting with each other, like soft rain on the surface of a pool.

He came back out into the hallway and shouted again, "I don't want the icon. I don't care what happens. I just want to see you again. Mary!"

He started down the stairs to the first floor, then he heard her voice. "Kevin."

He turned around and looked up to the top of the stairs. There, standing on the landing was The Lady. She looked just as she did when he saw her in 1985 and in 1962 ... just as she did when the children at the day care center saw her ... just as she did when she comforted Amy when she was pregnant with Nick ... just as she has throughout the ages.

As Kevin stared at her, the front door shut with a loud bang. Then Milo's voice at the foot of the stairs shouted, "Hey you! You made Mrs. Bennett cry!"

The noise startled Kevin. He dropped the device he was carrying and lost his footing. He felt himself fall backwards, slowly, as if time itself were being slowed down. He looked into the face of The Lady once more. Her expression wasn't of concern or shock, it was simply love. As if what was happening wasn't tragic; it was just a part of what she already knew.

"Forgive me," he said as he fell further. "God, forgive me."

"You have always been forgiven, Kevin," her beautiful voice said. "Just embrace it. Move toward it and all will be well."

Kevin then felt himself going up instead of down. Lifted to the third floor, the fourth floor, and up through the house into something so wondrous that he never could have imagined it.

* * * * *

Across the street, Hellmann and Onock sat in front of another brownstone, staring with anger and hatred at the day care center, an impenetrable fortress for over 70 years.

At the moment of Kevin's death, the seven angels began to appear on Amy Cuthbert's steps. First Cassiel, then Raphael, then the others. The seven stood there staring back with their expressionless faces. They had won.

Hellman and Onock continued to glare at the gathering of angels until they could no longer tolerate the reflection of heaven in their eyes. Suddenly, the world of men became painful as well.

"So now we return to shadows," hissed Onock.

"Return?" questioned Hellmann. "We have never left. *Hell hath no limits, nor is circumscribed in one self place. For where we are is hell, and where hell is there must we ever be.*"

Onock gave Hellmann a puzzled look.

"Marlowe's Dr. Faustus" said Hellmann with a slight grimace. He then, for the time being, faded back into the long familiarity of nothingness.

Harry Steven Ackley

— Chapter 42 —

The Twelfth Day of Christmas

Every Christmas season, The Metropolitan Museum of Art displays an elegant Christmas tree and Neapolitan crèche in its medieval hall. Ever since Heather was young, Emily has always taken her to New York to see it during the week after Christmas. *Why should this year be any different?* she thought. *So their world had been turned on end. Heather had found out she was adopted; Martin is on the operating table and may die; and the events that had taken place in her office the day before had her — a former atheist — praying to God and looking for angels around every corner.*

When Emily picked up Heather at the airport, she asked how things had gone with her dad.

"Fine," was all Heather said — her code word for signaling that she really didn't want to talk about it.

Emily then told her about Martin. Heather responded with genuine concern, and asked Emily whether she still wanted to go into the city. "It's OK with me if we don't go," said Heather. But Emily still wanted to go. She wanted to go as if it were their first time.

As they drove onto the expressway, leaving La Guardia, Emily made an announcement. "I've decided to get a new car."

Heather turned abruptly in her seat. "Really? Wow! What brought that on?"

"I still can't afford it," said Emily with a roll of the eyes. "But I'm really tired of sitting in a cold car for twenty minutes every morning."

"I think that's great, mom. Just don't get an SUV. Get something sexy."

"I was thinking about a Scion coupe," said Emily.

"Cool," agreed Heather. "Something to jumpstart the social life."

"Exactly," said Emily with a smile.

For their visit to the Met, Emily and Heather's usual plan was to see the tree, stroll through the collections a bit, and then have lunch at their favorite hot dog joint — Gray's Papaya on the corner of West 72nd and Broadway. Even though Heather was now a vegetarian, she decided to keep the tradition — for Christmas, telling her mom that she'd opt for a piña colada and bagel instead of a hot dog. After that, they would perhaps see a movie, or do some shopping. If time permitted, Emily would then give Amy Cuthbert a call to see how things went at the deposition. She also needed to check in with the hospital. Martin's surgery had been scheduled for 9 a.m. It was probably over by now. She worried how he was doing.

The museum was crowded when they arrived. People were milling around the great tree, looking at the crèche and the numerous angels decorating its branches. Many were snapping pictures with their cell phones and sending them out over the Internet.

The thought of the digital images floating through the ether made Emily remember the comment Ron Cassiel had made that first day in her classroom. *Everything is ultimately ethereal.*

She studied the painted faces and curled hair of the antique angels adorning the tree. *In some ways they got it right*, she thought. *The smooth hairless skin and flowing hair ... the absolute serenity of their faces.*

Emily turned and looked at her daughter. She was studying the crèche — Mary and Joseph looking in amazement at the one who had come into their lives, the animals peering out from the shadows.

"So what do you think?" asked Emily

"What do you mean? It's the same as it was last year. It's the same every year."

"It is," answered Emily. "But then it isn't. It means something more to me now."

Heather gave her mom a curious look then smiled. "Yes, I suppose it does to me too."

Emily's phone rang. It was her default ringtone — *Who are You* by The Who. She took it out and saw that it was a Poughkeepsie number. *Martin*, she thought. She pushed the button to answer and held it to her ear.

"Yes?"

"Hello. Dr. Campbell?"

"Yes."

"This is the nurse's station at St. Francis hospital in Poughkeepsie. We were told by Dr. Martin Ellis to give you a call to inform you of the outcome of his surgery."

Emily suddenly became very scared. She didn't like the tone in the nurse's voice. "I'm listening."

"Dr. Ellis came out of surgery about twenty minutes ago. Everything went fine and he is expected to make a full recovery."

Emily felt a huge weight lift. She thanked the nurse and then hung up. Then she looked up at the angels on the tree and said "Thank you" aloud.

"What is it?" asked Heather.

"It was St. Francis hospital. Martin's going to be OK."

* * * * *

Our Lady of West 74th Street

A couple of hours later, after having way too much pineapple and coconut juice, Emily and Heather stood on the corner of West 72nd Street and Broadway trying to hail a cab. The plan was to head to Greenwich Village for some window shopping and perhaps a cannoli and a cappuccino before heading home. As for seeing Amy, Emily was having too much fun with her daughter. She figured the visit with Amy could wait till another day.

Just then Emily's phone rang — the default ring tone again.

Emily tapped the screen and answered. "Yes?"

As she listened, her face turned serious. "Wait ... wait! Slow down. He's dead?"

A look of horror came to Heather's face. She mouthed the words, *"Is it Martin?"*

"No, no," said Emily. "It's Amy Cuthbert."

"It happened while we were at the deposition," said Amy. "He was searching the house for something. I'm sorry I ever trusted him."

"OK," said Emily. "So who found the body?"

"An old lady ... apparently she'd been tailing him about some piece of art that she claimed belonged to her. The police questioned her and then let her go."

"And this all happened when?" asked Emily.

"Late this morning ... while we were at the deposition."

"OK," said Emily. "We happen to be in the neighborhood. We can be there in a few minutes. Just hang on, OK?"

Fifteen minutes later, Emily and Heather were sitting in the front room of Amy Cuthbert's day care center with Amy and her son Nick.

Amy poured everyone a glass of her favorite dark red Malbec — even Heather, saying they could all use it. A freshly lit fire was crackling away in the fireplace.

Amy and Nick had arrived home from the deposition with Mr. Gardner to find the police outside the front door, she said. They were stopped from going inside and told that a Mr. Kevin Peters had died in the house. Apparently an accident — he had fallen down the stairs.

"They also informed us that an elderly woman, a Mrs. Rachel Balsam-Bennett, was in the house at the time," said Amy.

"Apparently Mrs. Bennett had been tailing Peters over the matter of some stolen art. Her personal assistant, some fellow named Milo, was with her. Her reasons for coming here to confront Peters were a little vague. It had something to do with this house once belonging to Peters' uncle ... they had been lovers or something a million years ago. I didn't quite understand that part.

"Anyway, the door was unlocked, so they let themselves in. When they entered the house, Peters was at the top of the stairs, talking aloud to himself. They called to him and it startled him. He lost his footing and fell."

Amy looked over to the great staircase. "He broke his neck. That's why there's no blood. The police confirmed it was an accident."

"They were just covering the body when they finally let us come in," added Nick. "He actually looked kind of peaceful."

Amy took a long sip of wine and set her glass down on one of the day care activity tables. On the table was a large manila envelope. Her eyes lingered on it.

"What's in that envelope, anyway?" asked Nick. "I saw the lawyer hand it to you when we left the deposition."

"Just some papers from Mr. Peters," answered Amy. "Stuff from 1994, a few months after your father and I moved into the house."

Amy let out a big yawn. "Sorry. It's been a day full of lawyers, and cops, and testimonies. I'll just be glad when everything gets back to normal. How about some more wine?"

Emily nodded yes. Heather declined, saying one glass was enough.

"Nick, how about going into the kitchen and cracking me another bottle of the Malbec?"

"Sure thing, Mom."

As Nick was getting out of the chair, he noticed something. "What's that?"

He went to the corner of the room closest to the entrance hall, bent down, and pulled something out from under the chest of drawers where they stored DVDs for the kids. It was Kevin's scanner.

Nick studied the object for a while and then said, "I know what this is. This is like an X-ray wall scanner. It can see through walls."

Nick looked up at the staircase, then down at the floor. "It must have skidded under there when Peters fell. I bet he was using it to search for something."

Suddenly it hit Amy — *the object!* "He was looking for an object. Something hidden in the house by his uncle."

"What?" asked Emily.

"Why didn't it occur to me before?" said Amy. "I remember now."

"What?" asked Nick.

"It's a painting of some kind. Back in the '90s your father told me that Peters had asked about it. He was convinced it was somewhere in this house. He'd asked Vince about it after we moved in. I'd forgotten all about it. That was the mysterious object Mr. Onock had mentioned on the phone. When I brought up the subject with Peters yesterday, he dismissed it. I could tell he was lying."

As Amy was talking, Nick fiddled with the device. It booted up. The screen flashed, and a moment later a grid of green lines appeared against a black background.

"This is cool," said Nick. "These only came out a year or so ago. I read about them on a blog I follow."

He began going around the room, looking at the walls. Watching him, Emily suddenly remembered the child with the green smudge of paint on his face. *You see the shape. You see The Lady.*

"Hold it up over there," said Emily, indicating the place where she had seen the pear-shaped spot on the wall.

"That's right!" said Amy.

Nick went over to the wall and held up the device. The others got up and stood behind him. The screen showed solid objects as light gray areas, denser objects, like metals, were white. They could see the horizontal beam and on it, they saw a rectangular object, the size of a large book. "This is it!" shouted Nick. "This is it!

"We need to bust open the wall, Mom."

"Yes we do!" said Amy.

Nick handed the device to his mother. "Here. I'm going to go find a hammer."

Amy stared at the object behind the wall. It was almost white in color.

A moment later, Nick came back into the room with a sledge hammer. "OK, everybody, get out of the way."

"Be careful, Dear," said Amy, as she set the scanner down on a chair. "Whatever it is, we don't' want to damage it."

Nick began tapping around where the radar showed the object to be. He pounded a little harder and finally the wall began to dent in. Once he had a sizable enough hole, he reached through with his hand and pulled at the old sheet rock. A big chunk fell away to reveal the icon — still wrapped in plastic, standing upright behind the two partially driven nails.

Nick took it out and unwrapped it. He handed it to his mother, who stood with Emily so they both could hold it.

"It's the girl. It's the same girl who came to me when I was pregnant with Nicky," said Amy.

"The Lost Icon of St. John the Divine," Emily whispered.

There it was. And there, looking out from the last star on the right, was her friend Cassiel. Looking down on The Lady, but also looking at Emily — smiling at her. She began to tear up. She didn't know why, but she couldn't stop. She left the icon to Amy, then sat down. Amy then handed it to Heather and sat down as well.

Heather looked into the face of Mary and thought of Sarah. It occurred to her how painful it must have been to offer her child to another, even if it was her own sister. "She's beautiful," she said.

"There's a letter," said Nick.

He took the envelope from the place inside the wall behind where the icon had been. He opened it, unfolded it, and began to read.

When he got to the end of the letter, he said, "and then there's something written in pen at the bottom: '*The woman with the red hair will know what to do.*'"

All eyes immediately went to Emily who sat there weak and unable to speak. She opened her mouth, but there were no words. She simply shook her head from side to side.

This is all crazy, thought Emily. *The icon, the book, the angels ... and here we sit ... two middle-aged women, a high school girl, and a college kid ... God's rag-tag chosen bunch ... but chosen for what?*

"The letter said the red-haired woman would know what to do," repeated Nick.

"You're the only one with red hair, Mom," added Heather.

"Well I *don't* know," said Emily. "The letter's wrong. This all feels like Don Quixote flailing at windmills."

The image of windmills made Emily think of wings, and then of the angels ... "The Habits of Angels."

> *When faith returns, the signs will reverse: The Mother of God will then show herself, the angels will become visible again, miracles will follow, and mankind will love and believe.*

"I think," said Emily, "she is supposed to be seen by everyone. There's something about the icon that has power. We all agree on that, yes?"

"Yes," added Amy. "She should be seen by the world."

"Any ideas? We can't tell the media. They will treat it like a farce," said Emily.

"Maybe the church," suggested Heather.

"I don't think so," said Emily. "They'll only take her and hide her behind plate glass. There's a reason it was hidden in the wall. There's a reason we were the ones to find it. And there's a reason for why we found it now."

The four sat for a long while. Suddenly, Amy's expression changed. She looked down at the manila envelope on the table next to her. She picked it up, walked to the fire, and threw it in. She watched as the fire consumed the last of her pain over the matter of her late husband and Peters' secretary.

She then turned to the rest and said, "There may be a way."

All heads in the room looked toward her.

Amy let out a long sigh and studied the faces around her. "Nick already knows what I'm about to tell you, but I don't think anyone else ever did.

"Back in the early '90s, Vince and I were working on a project for media transfer protocols across networks. That's how we met. Up until then everything was text. No images, no sound. Vince was credited with developing a breakthrough technology that improved the transfer of binary media files. That's how we got rich. That's how we bought this house.

"What no one ever knew was that Vince didn't develop a thing. He barely knew enough to be able to explain it to people." Amy smiled at Emily.

"You were the one responsible," said Emily.

Amy nodded.

"But why? Why didn't you take credit for your own work?"

Amy shrugged. "I loved him. I wanted to see him succeed. He was egotistical and unfaithful, but he was also handsome and charming, and I was young and insecure. He also made a better front man."

There was pause. Finally, Heather asked, "So how does this help us?"

"Well, as I said, Vince was a bit of a player. In one of my fits of anger, I wrote a subroutine that would swap out every image on the net with whatever I decided to show. I could have shown him on the toilet, him puking drunk, whatever I wanted. Just to embarrass him in front of his colleagues. Keep in mind that the Internet wasn't anything like it is today. It was just in the process of becoming public. It would have been something that would have only been seen by a small community of mostly programmers and engineers.

"But, when we sold the technology, I never removed the subroutine. It could have been discovered and deleted, but it could still be there."

"You think you can still access it?" asked Emily.

"I can try."

In the basement of the house Amy and her son had what looked like a small command center, with servers, printers, workstations and a few large monitors.

"Wow, what is it you do down here?" asked Heather.

"This is where Mother runs her empire." Nick looked at his mother and shook his head, "Web hosting and development.

Most of the websites are for human rights charities ... battered women, abused children, human trafficking, that sort of thing."

"Nicky, please," said Amy softly.

"And while I'm in the mood for divulging secrets, I should tell you that the little poverty story my mother told you was nonsense. Mom's actually quite the financial wiz."

"Nick!" protested Amy.

"They might as well know, mother," said Nick.

"I eavesdropped on your conversation in the kitchen," he continued. "She doesn't run the center because she's down on her luck. She runs it because she wants to help disadvantaged families. About half the clients don't even pay.

"If you ask me, I that's why Mrs. Pettiford and her group went after mom in the first place. They found out she was charging on a sliding scale."

"That's enough, Nick," said Amy.

Emily stared at Amy. "This place has made you a saint."

"Hardly," said Amy, shaking her head. "I'm just trying to help people."

"That's what saints do, Amy," said Emily. "They help people."

"Looks like you could run a war from down here," observed Heather.

"I think that's what we're about to do," said Emily. "Wage a war for the heart of humanity."

"We'll see," added Amy as she sat down at one of the workstations. "First we need a scan. Heather, let Nick have the icon."

Heather looked at the icon in her hand. The face of The Lady seemed to be encouraging her — almost like she was excited. Heather handed the icon to Nick, who carefully laid it face down on the scanner. Meanwhile, Amy clicked away, looking for the obscure bit of code she had created decades ago.

After scanning the icon, the image appeared on the monitor in front of Nick.

There were coos of excitement throughout the room. In the darkness of the basement, the backlit colors showed brilliantly.

After about fifteen minutes of hacking away, Amy exclaimed, "I found it! Damn! I can't believe the idiots didn't even clean this up."

After a few more minutes, Amy said, "OK, here we go." She then cautioned, "Chances are very slim that this will even work."

Amy clicked *enter*. The screen then filled with characters. When the bottom was reached, the screen began scrolling, filling up with more and more characters. The scrolling became faster and faster, until finally, the screen suddenly went dark.

The four of them sat there waiting.

"Did it crash?" asked Heather.

"I don't know," answered Amy. "This is a first-time thing. I've never done this before."

Finally, the screen flickered.

The picture of *The Lady* then shone brightly on Amy's screen, her face so perfect and real that they expected her to start speaking.

"Oh my God," cried Amy. "There she is."

Nick took his phone from his pocket and touched the screen a few times. *The Lady* was there.

"It worked. IT WORKED!" He laughed. "Let's check the Internet."

Nick brought up a web browser and went to cnn.com. Many of the images on the page were of *The Lady*. He went to Google and did an image search. Almost every search result was *The Lady*.

"Everything that uses the backbone of the Internet has been affected. Everything!"

And, indeed, everything had. At that moment the picture of *The Lady* was showing on every computer, on every tablet, on every smart phone, on every TV, throughout the world. The effect would only last a short time before back-up systems would kick in and networks would be powered down and rebooted. But it had happened and it could not be undone.

* * * * *

Emily took her daughter and went out on the street in front of the house. West 74th Street was practically empty, so they walked down to Columbus Avenue.

Looking down the avenue, Emily saw people looking into their phones. She expected to see upset faces wondering what had happened to their messages and apps, but they were all looking into their small screens with calm smiles on their faces. No one was tapping, or powering off and on. They were just looking. Those who had no phones were crowded near those who did, yet no one was nudging anyone away. People seemed eager to share what was going on. As she watched, a light snow began to fall.

Emily and Heather smiled at each other.

"Merry Christmas, Mom."

"Merry Christmas, Heather."

As Emily continued to watch the crowd, she began to notice several tall figures walking in its midst — young men all of the same height. She let out a small laugh.

The angels had returned.

— Epilog —

The image of The Lady stayed up on the Internet for a full eighteen minutes before the programmers, hackers, and hi-tech cubicle goons managed to locate and unravel Amy's subroutine. But eighteen minutes was long enough.

For those who believed, their faith was strengthened.

Those who doubted began to consider the possibilities.

Even those who didn't believe had their waters troubled, moving a step from disbelief to uncertainty.

As for the icon itself, it was discretely returned to Athos. Amy and Nick made a trip to Greece. As only males are allowed on Athos, Nick made the trip to St. Pantelemon by himself. He stayed for two days, during which he visited an almost deaf, 102-year-old, Brother Jerome, who wept when he saw The Lady.

After Kevin's death, his sister Greta came from California and oversaw the disbursement of her uncle's remaining collection of lost art. Interestingly, none of the pieces could be identified as stolen. They were all from public museums in Germany. All had been legitimately purchased from the German government by the other Bronner. Nevertheless, Greta saw that they were placed in appropriate collections in the United States and Europe. Since there was no historical record of title for Van Gogh's Angel, there was no way to determine its legitimate owner. Greta cancelled the auction and gifted it to Rachel Balsam-Bennett.

Also found in the warehouse with the paintings were Klaus Bronner's personal diaries. These, too, were given to Mrs. Balsam-Bennett.

The copy of "*Habitibus Angelos*" remained in Emily's possession for quite some time. There was no entry for it in the Thomas J. Watson Library catalog. Emily shared its contents with her daughter and her sister and finally decided that the safest place for it was St. Hilda of Whitby Abbey, under the care of its librarian, Sister Lizzie.

After Martin Ellis's surgery, he was told to stay in bed and rest for two weeks. After that, he was to restrict his activity for the next three months. In light of his condition, he asked Emily to complete the book and delegated all final editorial decisions to her.

Emily decided to include Amy's story in the book. She also decided to rewrite the general introduction, as well as amending many of its chapters. Rather than focusing on similarities in the psychological profiles of the witnesses and crediting everything to some sort of genetic wiring, she focused on their sincerity. And, while not giving outright credence to any particular story, she did give them the benefit of the doubt, posing the question, *why else would anyone want to subject themselves to such public exposure?*

Not long after they had discovered the icon of The Lady, Emily sat down at her dining room table, in front of her laptop and began by writing a new introduction. It began: *Faith is like snow...*

HISTORICAL NOTES

Miracle-working icons

Except for the icon that is the subject of this story, the list given by Sister Lizzie in chapter 20 provides a good representation of miracle-working icons throughout history. The two historical icons that most influenced "Our Lady of Faith" were "Our Lady of Kazan" and "Our Lady of Czestochowa." "Our Lady of Kazan" for its sketchy popping in and out of history, and "Our Lady of Czestochowa" for the story of its having its origins with St. Luke.

Many miracle-working icons are reported to manifest myrrh-scented oil on their surfaces. Myrrh was one of the three gifts given by the wise men at the birth of Jesus. In Judaism of first century Palestine, it was used for burial preparation, the symbolism being that the Christ was born to die. Throughout the centuries, the Church has used myrrh-scented oil in its anointing rituals to symbolize death to the things of this world and consecration to God.

On Mt. Athos

The trip Klaus recounts at the beginning of the book did happen. In 1941 a team was assembled to go to monasteries on the Athos peninsula in Greece to survey and catalog works of art for the purpose of bringing them back to Germany. And there was a professor Franz Dögler who headed the expedition. The character of Klaus Bronner is entirely fictional.

Among the places Klaus visits on Athos are the basement levels of St. Pantelemon monastery. This is an actual monastery on Athos, and one which the Nazis did visit. I got the idea for the scene in the basement from a story told about St. John of Kronstadt, a 19th-century charismatic Russian preacher who, while visiting the monastery, had occasion to wander through its basement tunnels. It was there he encountered the great ascetic, St Silouan the Athonite.

In April of 2011, the news show "60 Minutes" filmed a segment on Mt. Athos in which the visit by the Nazis was recounted. For background on the history of Athos, I highly recommend watching it.

On the looting of art by the Nazis

The plunder of fine art by the Nazis that is mentioned in "The Voyage of *A Estrela do Mar*," tragically, is true. For background information, I recommend the 2006 documentary film, "The Rape of Europa," based on the book of the same name by Lynn H. Nicholas.

The two Van Gogh paintings listed as part of Klaus Bronner's collection are "Head of a Peasant Woman with White Cap" and "Half Figure of an Angel (after Rembrandt)." According to the Van Gogh Gallery website (vangoghgallery.com), they are simply listed as missing. Including them in Dr. Bronner's collection of Nazi plunder was something I did by way of artistic license. However, there were other Van Goghs known to have been taken by the Nazis.

On the nature of angels

I suppose when it comes to describing angels, any person is as qualified as the next. That being said, my ideas for Cassiel and his kind come from research and from certain artistic depictions.

In the Bible, angels are generally described as men. When angels appeared to Lot, Abraham, and Gideon, they were first mistaken to be men. The idea for angels not being able to grow beards comes from various artworks. In Byzantine iconography, as well as in most European medieval and renaissance art, angels are always shown as young men without facial hair. The idea for angels being the same height came directly from the Byzantine icon mentioned in Chapter 20: "Christ Enthroned," found in the Basilica of Sant'Apollinare in Ravenna, Italy. In the icon, the four angels surrounding Christ are all exactly the same height.

In the conversation between Eliaz and Klaus on the deck of *A Estrela do Mar*, Eliaz refers to the Kabbalah. The Kabbalah is a collection of mystical Jewish teachings, ancillary to the Talmud. My understanding (as a Gentile) is that these teachings are met with skepticism (or even distain) by some and embraced by others, similar to how Christianity regards its "apocryphal" writings and the traditions from whence they came.

In my research on angelic lore, I discovered that the Kabbalah is rich with information on angels, the organization of celestial hierarchical beings, and the powers they possess. My primary source for this information came from the book "The Kabbalah and the Magic of Angels" by Migene Gonzales Wippler.

The Bethesda Fountain Angel (The Angel of the Waters)

The Angel of the Waters (pictured on the cover) was created by New York sculptor Emma Stebbins in 1873. Its inspiration comes from the Gospel of Saint John which describes an angel blessing the Pool of Bethesda with healing powers.

For an angel went down at a certain time into the pool and stirred up the water; then whoever stepped in first, after the stirring of the water, was made well of whatever disease he had.

Harry Steven Ackley

Now a certain man was there who had an infirmity thirty-eight years. When Jesus saw him lying there, and knew that he already had been in that condition a long time, He said to him, "Do you want to be made well?"

The sick man answered Him, "Sir, I have no man to put me into the pool when the water is stirred up; but while I am coming, another steps down before me."

Jesus said to him, "Rise, take up your bed and walk." And immediately the man was made well, took up his bed, and walked.

ACKNOWLEDGMENTS

For her support and encouragement throughout the process: my dear Natasha.

For reading my early drafts and providing feedback: Peggy Ackley, Gloria DeLuca, Gilbert Padilla, and Cathy Duckham.

For his editing, for guidance on the self-publication process, and for leading the way: John Orr (a.k.a. Dr. Gone) — author of "Someone Dark Has Found Me."

For their help with information about merchant steamers, cruise lines, and the port of New York City: Bill Bourke — Sydney Heritage Fleet; Ted Miles — San Francisco Maritime National Park Library; Gloria DeLuca — Arrangements Abroad; Malachy Murray — Circle Line Sightseeing Cruises.

For graciously letting me use his beautiful photo of "The Angel of the Waters": Emilio Guerra.

For their feedback on the cover design: Natasha Cardenas, Peggy Ackley, Gloria DeLuca, Myron Maciejewski, and all those who voted on the color.

Made in the USA
San Bernardino, CA
24 February 2018